Keep
Forever

A Novel

Alexa Kingaard

ISBN: 978-1-54391-697-3 (print)
ISBN: 978-1-54391-698-0 (ebook)

For Jeff

For every veteran

For every serviceman and woman on active duty

For every family member touched by the heroics of their loved one
who has defended and continues to defend our country

Thank you

Acknowledgements

I would like to give a special thank you to The Veteran's Writing Group in Oceanside, California, who in February 2012, gave me shelter from the storm, literally and figuratively. As I fictionalized my experiences of living with and tragically losing a Vietnam Veteran, I realized I had but one story to share. They cheered me, consoled me, advised, and encouraged me until my manuscript was done. They will never be done, and continue to reveal their countless stories of combat and conflict on foreign soil and at home. Thank you, one and all, for being there for me.

This is a story of a young marine returning from war and the burden he brings home. It was inspired by the Vietnam Veterans I have known and loved, and their lifelong struggles with PTSD.

Prologue

PAUL O'BRIEN NERVOUSLY WAITED FOR HIS NAME TO be called with a mixture of anticipation and dread. His classmates sat in desks arranged in tidy rows, and listened with hands folded and feet planted on the floor, their books tucked neatly underneath their seats. Mrs. Turner warned her students, "Anyone who interrupts the speaker will have to stay after school and write 'I will not misbehave in class' on the blackboard fifty times."

The night before, Paul's mother had tried to help him pick out his clothes. He grimaced when he saw the brand new, never-been-washed pair of Sear's Toughskins she had chosen, and a T-shirt with narrow blue, gray, and white stripes.

"This color blue makes your eyes stand out."

"Oh Mom, I'm not a baby."

"No, you're not a baby, but you're my baby. You'll always be my baby."

Paul rolled his eyes. "I don't want to wear these jeans, Mom. They're not cool. I want the ones you put in the giveaway box."

"Those are too short, Paul. You've already outgrown them."

1

"I know. That's why I want them, so I can roll up the cuffs and everyone can see my new high tops. That's what the really boss guys are wearing."

"Where are you picking up these words?"

"In school. That's how everybody talks if you want to be with it. I don't want everyone looking at me like I'm weird."

Paul's mother let out a sigh at the notion of her third grader, her only child, growing up so quickly. She leaned over and gave her boy a hug and a quick peck on the cheek before leaving his room. *Don't get ahead of yourself, Paul. You'll be a teenager soon enough*, she thought as she shut the door behind her.

<hr />

Paul didn't hear a word, continuing to fidget as his friends showed off their new dolls, trucks, and pictures. *Something's missing! I forgot my belt! The black leather one with the big Roy Rogers buckle! How could I forget my belt?* His hands felt clammy, his ears grew red, and he fought the urge to tap his feet.

"Paul, you may come up. Class, let's be quiet. It's Paul's turn."

He rose from his seat and walked to the front of the room, feeling his classmates' eyes follow him as he made his way down the narrow aisle. In one hand he clutched a tan and brown portable phonograph, cardboard corners beginning to fray, and in his other hand a slick, black forty-five record obscured by a plain parchment cover.

Paul's stomach churned. He was sure everyone could hear the gurgles as he inched closer to the corner he spied as his target. Struggling for composure, he focused on his treasure.

"Mrs. Turner," he asked, "is it okay if I move the stool so I can plug in my record player?"

Smiling, she nodded.

Paul slipped the forty-five out of its protective sleeve, careful to hold its center and outer edges between his thumb and index finger. Positioning the record on the turntable, he twisted the knob to the "on" position, and with a trembling finger, lowered the needle onto the spinning piece of vinyl. He winced at the scratching noise it made, but was thankful the hardest part was over at last. Paul took a deep breath and waited for the reaction of the class, hoping they would love his record as much as he did. A chorus of thunderous applause filled the air when the first few notes of Elvis Presley's "Heartbreak Hotel" pierced the silence. A wave of relief washed over Paul as his shoulders relaxed and the tension in his face dissolved into a shy and reserved grin.

"Paul! Go to the principal's office right this minute, and take this smut with you!" Mrs. Turner's voice was agitated and loud. She lurched towards the record player and ripped the cord from the wall.

The harsh words from his teacher interrupted his silent triumph, and Paul's eyes stung as he removed the needle from the spinning record, slipped it back into the sleeve, and self-consciously closed the lid, making sure it was locked tight. His ears were ringing, and he could feel the heat of his flushing cheeks—a moment of adulation and joy disintegrated to one of humiliation and embarrassment. Head down, he avoided the scrutiny of his classmates as he ran through the classroom to make a quick exit. He wedged the forty-five under his arm, yanked the door, and burst through to the empty hallway.

It was 1956, and for Paul O'Brien, that was when it all began.

Chapter 1

"PAUL, YOU OKAY?"

Before responding, he thought what a stupid question that was, coming from his best friend. Since kindergarten, they had been inseparable. They surfed in Santa Monica as they grew into their teen years, taking taunts from the locals in stride. It was no secret they drove from the Valley every Saturday and once in a while came across a few territorial surfers who thought the beach was strictly reserved for locals. But still, it was worth the hassle. Over time they became weekend regulars, sprawled on their towels after they muscled through heavy surf, they'd turn up the portable radio as loud as possible and watch girls stroll by in their tiny bikinis, glistening from too much baby oil or tanning lotion.

It was a wonderful life—three months ago. Three months ago Paul was looking forward to starting his senior year in high school, surfing until the sun went down, and planning what he would do after he graduated from high school.

"Okay? Yeah, sure, if okay is watching your mother die four weeks after being diagnosed with cancer. I suppose I'm okay. I suppose I should feel better knowing she didn't suffer very long and I got to be with her every day till the end. I suppose those things should make me feel just bitchin."

"All I wanted to say is, I'm sorry, Paul. I really am."

All Paul heard was, "I'm so glad it's you and not me."

Paul's jaw clenched as he turned to walk into the small living room inside the tidy home, nestled in the suburbs of Los Angeles. Today it overflowed with people: well-wishers, clergy, and old friends. So many Paul had never met. The kitchen, with its brand-new coat of paint and yellow gingham wallpaper his mother insisted upon, was filled with fresh bowls of fruit, hot casseroles, cookies, cakes, salads—every inch on every available counter was brimming with food. The thirsty were helping themselves to Cokes, Dr. Peppers, and Orange Nesbitt's from the cooler on the porch, and a fresh pot of coffee was brewing on a side table, tended by his mother's best friend. Paul noticed she had created a job for herself so she wouldn't have to mingle or speak. He wished he could do the same.

The somber voices intensified as their words of condolences filled the air, and Paul could hear every word spoken by every person in a strange, melancholy chorus. He scanned the room and fought hard to keep his composure. He noticed the dining room table, where he and his parents ate dinner every night, where meatloaf, corned beef, or roasted chicken was always accompanied by Wonder Bread, a tall glass of milk, and easy conversation. Now it was covered with sympathy cards and a large floral arrangement that took up almost the entire surface. Paul closed his eyes in an attempt to douse the flood of memories.

The air inside the house was uncomfortable—warm, humid, and smelled of food, perfume, aftershave, and freshly brewed coffee. Paul felt nauseous. He struggled to make sense of the scene, loosened his tie, removed his sports coat, and wandered from one room to the next.

So many people stopped by to pay their last respects. His parents led a simple, almost solitary life. They had a few good friends in the neighborhood, and hosted small dinner parties and summer barbecues, but nothing of this magnitude.

Where were all these people when Mom was alive? Paul was angry at everyone: relatives, church people, old friends, new friends, PTA mothers, his father's work buddies. *Why didn't they stop by when Mom was so sick? Where were they when she was healthy?* Paul's mind raced. *Maybe Mom and Dad didn't like a lot of people around. Maybe they were happiest when it was just us. Our family. Maybe there is no "us" anymore, only me and Dad and quiet and sorrow. And maybe I don't know how to do this... I don't want to do this. I can't do this.*

Interrupting Paul's thoughts, his mother's best friend appeared beside him and wrapped her arms around his tense shoulders. "Your mother would be so proud, Paul. Lily loved you so much. Our sweet Lily. She raised a good, sensitive boy, and everything's going to be all right. Give it time. It will get better over time, I promise."

Paul knew she meant well and returned the hug. He wished it were his mother's gentle hand resting on his shoulder, not someone else's. He would have to etch in his mind the last time they hugged, the last time they laughed, the last time they spoke. He needed to anchor one lasting memory if he were to get through this and find a way to let time heal.

An awkward procession of people left, none convinced they could say anything that would make the situation any better. Paul clutched at the words he heard murmured throughout the day... "Lily was such a fabulous cook." "I remember when Lily and I were in fifth grade and we got caught in the rain outside the dime store and didn't have any money to call our mothers." "Lily raised such a kind, sensitive boy. This next year is going to be difficult for him." "I know we'll still see Paul and his father at the football games." "Paul Senior looked devastated, in shock. Time will heal." Paul couldn't wait for everyone to leave.

He stood in the shelter of the front porch, waved goodbye to the last guest, and turned to his father, "Dad, you okay?"

"Fine, son, fine. You okay?"

"Yeah, I'm okay."

They were not.

Chapter 2

"That's enough, Elizabeth. We've discussed this before," Mr. Sutton interrupted his daughter's familiar plea.

At the dinner table, when the conversation was peppered with debate on appropriate behavior for teenage girls, Elizabeth had brought up the subject of wearing tank tops and shorts, but the discussion stalled with a stern look from her father and a silent shrug from her mother. Sam escaped their father's nightly outburst against the moral decline of society and the evolving role of women. He was, after all, a boy, an Ivy League-college boy at that, home only for the summer and granted freedoms not given to Elizabeth.

Elizabeth persisted and hoped she could squeeze out a winning argument before the conversation ended. If it hadn't been so damn uncomfortable, she would have been in a much better mood. She dreaded the intolerable summers, with sunrises predicting the arrival of another day of stifling heat, and sunsets offering little relief. Her cut-off blue jeans were beginning to ride up the insides of her thighs, which were damp and sticky from the humidity.

"That's not fair. Laura and Tina wear sunsuits all summer. And there's no more fabric on them than a bathing suit."

"That's different. Your sisters are nine years old. You're fifteen and startin' tenth grade in the fall. You need to know these things and follow our rules. And no more dungies or long pants in school.

You're growin' up, becomin' a young lady. Your mother will take you school-clothes shopping for skirts and dresses when we get home from our vacation."

"Daddy…"

"This conversation is closed, Elizabeth. Help your mother with the dishes."

Mr. Sutton turned his attention away from his eldest daughter to the twins. "So, what did you do today, girls?" He directed his question to Laura and Tina simultaneously, knowing they would respond in unison. They were still too young to do more than set the table and loved to chatter with their father about riding their bikes in the driveway or reading books under the large red oak tree in the front yard. He loved the simplicity of their needs and their obedient natures. When his wife reminded him they weren't going to be little forever and that it wouldn't be long before he had two fifteen-year-old girls under one roof at the same time, he remained unconvinced they would ever change.

Identical except for the color of their eyes—Tina's a luminous blue and Laura's a translucent gray—the twins shared the same taste in clothes, food, and friends. Their natural blond curls had been trimmed to a short pixie for the summer, and Mrs. Sutton had to convince her husband it would grow back. "It's only hair, and they need to be comfortable. It's one of the hottest summers on record, in case you haven't noticed."

"I guess I'm lucky to work in an air-conditioned office—*that's one advance in a modern society that I approve of*—but I wish you left their hair long." Mr. Sutton's eyes rested wistfully on the twins' cropped, short hair. "Go play, girls. I'm goin' to get the evening paper and put my feet up for a while."

Annoyed at the unfair restrictions doled out by her father—how he still babied the twins and treated Sam like a prince—Elizabeth followed her mother to the kitchen. "Mama, can't you say something to him? Please? There's nothing wrong with wearing shorts and tank tops when it's this hot. It's like we're stuck in the dark ages. It's the Sixties, for Pete's sake!" her voice rose in exasperation. "Women and teenagers can wear dungies and sleeveless tops. All my girlfriend's parents let 'em wear whatever they want. I'll be the only one in my grade who looks like a nerd. Can't you talk to Daddy?"

"Don't use slang, Elizabeth. And don't talk back. You know your father doesn't allow it."

"Nerd isn't a bad word. And I'm not 'talking back.' I'm just explaining," Elizabeth sighed. "It's not the dark ages."

"Yes, you already told me that, and I'm telling you not to raise your voice or use slang... in the house. I'll talk with your father on the trip. Maybe he'll calm down once he has time to relax and unwind. It's been a year since we've been away and I know he's lookin' forward to our long weekend." Mrs. Sutton's eyes softened as she handed her eldest daughter a clean dish towel. She was well aware of the responsibilities placed on her first-born girl, and the unfair rules and expectations of a father firmly attached to a different generation. "We'll be leavin' first thing in the morning, and remember, you promised to help while we're gone. With your sisters. And the housework."

"Yeah, I know. I promise. What about Sam? Does he have anything he's supposed to do?

"He'll hold down the fort."

So all he has to do is hang around the house?! "I wish I was born a boy. That way I'd have my sisters, and then my wife waiting on me hand and foot, making sure dinner was on the table every night at six o'clock sharp. You've spoiled him, Mom. I'm never getting married." Elizabeth dried the last dish, and a mixture of dismay and disgust washed across her face as she hurried past her mother and upstairs to her room.

Even though Mrs. Sutton was nervous about leaving the four children alone, Mr. Sutton reassured his wife that their house would still be standing when they returned. "Sam's old enough to keep an eye on the girls. Don't worry so much," was all Mr. Sutton had to say as he carried the bags to the car.

"Elizabeth, we're leaving now." Her mother called from the bottom of the stairs. "Kids, can you please come down so I can say goodbye?" It sounded more like a plea than a question as her children reluctantly tore themselves away from their activities. Waiting for them one by one to reach the bottom of the stairs, she gave each a final kiss and hug before joining their father, who waited behind the wheel, engine running. He was anxious to put some miles on the new family car—a 1964 Bel Air Chevy wagon, with its elongated, flat lines and unblemished Daytona-blue paint reflecting the already-hot sun.

"Mama, don't worry. We'll be fine." All Elizabeth could think of was getting some relief from the heat in the new air-conditioned mall. The sooner her parents departed, the sooner she could jump on the bus. "You guys have a good time."

Mr. Sutton put the car in reverse, but before they got past the mailbox, Elizabeth frantically waved her arms, shouting for her father to stop. "Wait! One more thing!" She ran to the passenger side and motioned to her mother to roll down the window. She thrust her head inside the opening and surprised her with a quick kiss on the cheek. "Had to give you one more. Love you."

All four waved, smiled, and blew kisses while they watched their parents back out of the driveway and disappear into the landscape.

Elizabeth made sure that the laundry was folded and put away and the kitchen was clean, as her mother asked. Sam was glad she was handling the household chores he felt were beneath a college boy. He waited for her to finish her job in the kitchen before he poked his head through the door. "I'm going out for a few hours tonight, okay? There's a summer kegger in the quad, and I don't want to miss it."

"I thought you were supposed to hold down the fort."

"I won't be out all night. Only a few hours. You can do whatever you want with the rest of your day."

Elizabeth didn't feel like arguing and knew if there was any trouble at home this weekend, her parents would never leave them alone again.

"Okay. I had plans to go to the mall. I can catch the bus on the corner, take it downtown, and be back by four o'clock. Can you watch the twins?" She paused deliberately for dramatic effect. "Or is that asking too much?"

"Oh come on, sophomore." He could play her game, and his tone was just smug enough to show he still had the upper hand. "I'll let them play in the sprinklers. They'll be worn out by the time you get home."

Within an hour, Elizabeth caught the crowded bus to the mall, leaving Laura and Tina squealing, hot, wet, and happy in the backyard with Sam. The day was hers, and she felt free.

The sounds of downtown drew closer as the bus continued its winding route to the center of the hustle and bustle, towards the new indoor shopping center, an impressive array of sixty retail stores, ten restaurants, and a movie theatre. Elizabeth could feel the excitement as she thought about shopping with the twenty dollars saved from babysitting tucked into her new pink and white pocketbook. She had never seen crowds like this before. The noise level rose as children responded to the profusion of sights, sounds, and colors; parents seemed to shout names from every corner of the mall. Elizabeth luxuriated in the instant relief offered by the air conditioning. Piped music drifted from every store and invited shoppers to come inside, browse, and spend their hard-earned money.

Elizabeth visited three department stores, tried on shorts, T-shirts, and sundresses in each, and wandered in and out of a dozen boutiques scattered up and down the long corridors. She wondered what her parents might say if she came home with a tank top. Everywhere she looked teenage girls, college co-eds, and even young mothers escaped the heat dressed in the immodest fashion that made her father cringe.

She glanced at her watch and saw with dismay that it was almost three o'clock. She quickened her pace, wishing she could stay longer, but conscious of the clock counting down to her three-thirty bus ride home. She dashed back to the first department store, feeling bold and a bit rebellious. She wanted the pink tank top with spaghetti straps, and a white, eyelet-ruffled neckline. *Innocent enough*, she thought and mentally prepared a rebuttal to her father's objections as she scrutinized herself in the fitting room mirrors.

The sales girl, who didn't look much older than Elizabeth, gushed, "This looks so cute on you. Don't worry. Your parents will love it."

Elizabeth smiled. She was eager to get home, and out of the hot, drab clothes, her parents saw her wearing when they left, and into the cool, contemporary look of a modern teenager. She took her place in a long line of shoppers, wishing it would move faster and worried she would be late.

She made it to the bus stop with minutes to spare.

◇

Elizabeth stepped off the bus and noticed two police cars passing in the direction of home. She caught her breath as the cars pulled into her driveway.

From a distance, she could see her brother in the doorway, the twins still in their bathing suits, wet from the sprinklers, small puddles of water pooling at their feet. They clung to Sam's legs as he spoke with the officers.

Elizabeth ran the final one hundred feet like a seasoned sprinter, in time to see the policeman touch Sam's shoulder and lower his head as he spoke. "Son, I hate to have to tell you this… There was an accident on the interstate, just south of Boston, about an hour ago. A five-car pileup. There were four fatalities. Your parents were both killed. I'm so sorry. So very sorry for your loss."

It was July 1964, and for Elizabeth Sutton, that was when it all began.

Chapter 3

For months relatives, neighbors, and well-meaning friends filled the Sutton home, while Sam and Elizabeth combed through stacks of mail, condolence cards, and file folders. Offers poured in to help sort through the accumulation of paperwork and Mr. and Mrs. Sutton's personal belongings, but they were politely refused—one of the few things Sam and Elizabeth could agree on. Funeral arrangements were difficult enough, the thought of anyone touching these precious possessions was distasteful and offensive to Elizabeth.

Laura and Tina slept restlessly and had nightmares almost every night. They often woke in a fit of panic and screamed for Elizabeth, or quietly cried themselves back to sleep.

Sam found comfort behind his father's oversized, solid mahogany work desk in the corner of the formal living room, the perfect spot to ponder, reflect, and contemplate without interruption from his sisters. This room had stood the test of time and, as far as Sam could recall, had never changed, was never modernized from the previous owner's formal tastes, and was never "fooled with" as his mother used to say. It was the only room in the house left uncluttered by children's toys, jackets, or odds-and-ends that seemed to litter the remainder of their home. *Now I know why Dad spent so much time in here. I can finally think and get something done.*

Double-hung windows extended from floor to ceiling. They looked out onto the street, symmetrically flanking either side of the red oak in the front yard. Bright white wainscot paneling encircled the bottom half of each wall, and the original mid-century wallpaper—a sweetbriar pattern of vines and magnolias in moss green and sapphire blue—stretched to meet the glorious crown molding at the uppermost portion of the wall. It was a jewel of a bygone era that perfectly suited Mr. Sutton's unyielding desire to stay rooted in the past.

The formality of this space was meant for a piano and little else, but since the Suttons didn't own a piano, and none of the children showed any interest in learning to play, Mr. Sutton convinced his wife to allow him the luxury of keeping a desk at home. "We have the space for it, Lord knows." Mrs. Sutton seldom countered her husband's requests or wishes, and on this matter, a space reserved for grownups only, she quietly deferred to his judgment.

Elizabeth interrupted Sam as he sifted through paperwork. "Laura and Tina crawled into bed with me again last night." She hoped he might look up and say something, anything, but the quarreling over how to run the household and accomplish daily tasks continued. They avoided each other's company and resorted to brief comments. Summer was drawing to a close, the start of the new school year was merely weeks away, and Elizabeth felt a mounting urgency to formalize a plan.

Sam didn't look up or acknowledge his sister's presence. Out of the corner of his eye, he saw her standing in the doorway, but was lost in his thoughts. All those talks at the dinner table—he had felt like such a man, acting in concert with his father. Now, even at twenty-one, he felt like a boy, ill-equipped to take on the obligation of raising his sisters, caring for the house, and managing the unwanted life that had been thrust upon him. But he had found the solution. Elizabeth shrugged and left him to brood in silence.

Once the twins were asleep, Elizabeth eyed her brother, who still sat in the lone chair, behind the over-sized office desk in the sanctuary of his father's favorite room. When she beckoned him again to take a seat at the dining room table, Sam finally agreed and pulled up a chair. Elizabeth couldn't help but notice the air of confidence he once pulled off so effortlessly had been replaced with a grim, pallid look of defeat. He made himself as comfortable as he could under the circumstances.

Elizabeth had brewed a fresh pot of coffee for Sam and put the kettle on the flame to make a cup of tea for herself. She had never liked tea, but it seemed appropriate now, and she heard the caffeine would keep her awake and her mind sharp. Sam had become a frequent customer at campus coffee shops as soon as he left for college, and demanded a strong cup every morning before starting his day, drinking cup after cup well into the evening.

Sitting at the dining room table, forced to remember a family in happier times, unnerved him. He was prepared to get this conversation started—and ended—as quickly as possible. "What is it Elizabeth?" He'd had already made his plans for the future, and they did not include his younger sisters. *I need to get this over with once and for all*, Sam thought.

She sat opposite from him and began, "I thought we might all be able to stay in the house and try to be as normal as possible." She rushed on before Sam could interrupt. "You could get a job, sign up for night classes, I could take care of the twins and do the housework. I couldn't stand the thought of leaving home or splitting up the family."

Sam squirmed in his seat and studied his coffee cup, unable to hold Elizabeth's gaze. He knew he couldn't postpone this conversation any longer.

"Elizabeth, I can't be responsible for a family. I'm only twenty-one. There's gotta be a better solution." He put his hands on the table as if to leave, but she wasn't through.

"You're just going to go back to school as soon as summer is over? So you'll pick up where you left off as if nothing's happened? Go back to your dorm? Your political rallies—and your keggers? Who will take care of us?" Elizabeth's voice rose to a crescendo as she stared at her brother, and without words, dared him to reveal his plan.

"Ever heard of Vietnam?" he blurted and then dragged his eyes up from his coffee cup to meet Elizabeth's.

"Of course. I watch the news. But what's that got to do with anything?"

"It's only a matter of time before I get my draft notice. I could object, could claim I was responsible for raising a family…" Elizabeth's eyes narrowed, and her mouth dropped open with sudden comprehension. "But I want to go," Sam continued. "I joined the Marines. I enlisted. I went for my physical the other day, and I'll be leaving for boot camp in three weeks."

Of all the things Elizabeth expected to hear and hoped to talk about with Sam, this was not one of them. The air felt like it was being sucked out of the room, turning icy and cold, and all that came out of her mouth were intermittent sobs. As the tears flowed, she knew she had nothing clever, angry, or shocking to say to her brother in response.

"Do you want to die?" she spat out the words but choked at the thought.

Sam ignored her comment. "I spoke with Uncle Bill and Nana right after I signed the enlistment papers."

"And what did they have to say about this stupid, selfish thing you decided to do without discussing with anyone? With me!"

"Not much they could do. Once you sign something on the dotted line with Uncle Sam, there's no turning back."

Elizabeth wanted to throw things at Sam, smash his coffee cup against the wall, and turn the dining table and chairs over in one deafening crash, even if it meant waking up Laura and Tina. Instead, she slowly got up from the table, walked to the living room, nestled into her father's recliner, and fell asleep.

Elizabeth woke the next morning, stiff and sore from a fitful sleep on her father's lounger. She recollected her conversation with Sam and felt the anger rising to the surface once again. She resented her brother for abandoning her, and her little sisters, and wanted to talk with Uncle Bill right away. Without leaving the chair, she grabbed the telephone from the end table beside her and dialed.

"Hello Uncle Bill…" Elizabeth began.

Bill interrupted. "Hey, kiddo. Was just thinking about you. How's everyone doing at the house?"

"Not good, not good at all. Can we meet somewhere for lunch or something? Soon?"

"Sure, honey. Today's Friday, so we can all meet for lunch tomorrow. Somewhere in between. Would you like that?"

"Yes! Thank you, Uncle Bill. Sam told me last night he was going to join the Marines. What's happening? Who'll take care of us? Where will we live?" Elizabeth was crying again and anxiously waited for her Uncle's response.

"Sam called me the other day, Elizabeth. I know about his decision. Aunt Deborah and I have already had a chance to talk. Calm down; it's going to be okay. No one expects you to raise your sisters… you're not much more than a little girl yourself. We're here to help, and we'll talk about it on tomorrow when we see you at lunch."

Elizabeth let out a deep breath and hung up, feeling much better than she had in weeks. *Maybe, just maybe we'll all live with Uncle Bill and his family, and everything will be all right.* She ran to tell Sam and the twins about meeting her Aunt and Uncle and decided this might be a good day to stop worrying, at least for the moment.

◦◈◦

The sun was shining and that always made Elizabeth feel better. The two-hour drive was pleasant, and Elizabeth and Sam joked with Laura and Tina, pulling out a new book of Mad Libs to lighten the mood. Only Sam and Elizabeth knew what the outing was about, and by the time they reached the small cafe right off the interstate, they were drained from too much forced laughter meant to lift their sisters' spirits. The twins were jumping up and down in the back seat, and Elizabeth felt good listening to her little sisters' endless chatter.

They pulled into the parking lot and saw their Uncle Bill, Aunt Deborah, and their nine-year-old cousin, Ricky, walking towards the entrance. Elizabeth rolled down the window and waved her arms to get their attention. "We'll meet you inside."

"You all look wonderful," gushed Aunt Deborah. Even though she showered praise that would have sounded insincere from someone else, her words were genuine and her compliments were plentiful. A true lady, she wore dresses to the supermarket, gloves to church, and high heels even in the coldest of weather if the occasion called for it. Her shoulder-length blonde hair was pulled back in a neat bun. Elizabeth couldn't recall ever seeing it loose or disheveled. Her heart settled and the knots in her stomach relaxed. She felt safe with her aunt and uncle in charge.

They had not seen each other since the funeral and Elizabeth was hopeful they had good news to share. She was certain they had a plan, and even if it meant moving to another town, at least she and her sisters would be together.

The one available booth was meant for six, but everyone made room for one another. Aunt Deborah brought coloring books and crayons for Ricky and the twins, hoping they would be distracted while the adults talked. After the orders had been placed, Uncle Bill opened the difficult conversation. "Well, it looks like we have some planning to do here. We've had time to discuss everything like I told you on the phone."

His face showed concern, and Elizabeth's temporary relief reverted to worry and apprehension. She was beginning to feel queasy, like she was on a roller coaster that was about to go off the rails and send her flying into midair. She waited for her uncle to speak, as she noticed her aunt avert her gaze, and braced for bad news. She could feel her heart start to flutter, and after a long silence, looked up from the French fries she had desecrated in a pool of ketchup, pushed her hair away from her face to look her uncle squarely in the eyes, and asked "So, what's the verdict? Where will we be this time next year?"

Aunt Deborah spoke in a sweet, genuine tone. "Elizabeth, Sam, no one ever wants to make these kinds of decisions, but the plan is to do what we can to ease this burden and the impossible situation you've found yourselves in. Tina and Laura are the same age as Ricky, will be going to the same school, and they can share the one extra room in the cottage." Fumbling with her napkin and avoiding eye contact with Elizabeth, she continued, "But we only have room for the twins, and it wouldn't be the best situation to crowd us all into one little house, trying to keep everyone under one roof."

Stunned, Elizabeth sank back into the faded orange Naugahyde booth. She noticed the small slashes and scribbled initials, aware of all the sights, smells, and sounds in the restaurant; everything seemed magnified. Cigarette smoke curled through the air, exhaled by rude patrons from the smoking section. Crying babies could be heard from the farthest corner booth. The waitress's voice grated on her nerves and the aroma of the fried food on the table made her feel sick. She waited, certain what was coming next was more news she didn't want to hear. Her long auburn curls covered her face as she hung her head, wishing she could disappear. Aunt Deborah reached over to push her hair back. Elizabeth pulled away.

Uncle Bill, seeing the dismay sweep across the teenager's face, tried to ease into the rest of the conversation. Elizabeth could tell he was trying too hard to make it sound okay, but nothing he could say would make it so. She let her mind wander, no longer hearing or caring about what was to come out of his mouth next.

"Elizabeth, we thought it would be best if you went to stay with Nana in Boston. We would make sure the whole family got together at least once a month, and the high school in the city will offer you a much better education than the small high school on Nantucket. Nana agrees.

Elizabeth remained silent, hoping she could make everyone else as miserable as she felt. Instead, she looked at Sam, then to Uncle Bill, to Aunt Deborah. "I can't wait to get letters from Sam in Vietnam and see my sisters for a couple of hours a month. I'm sure Nana would love the company, and it doesn't matter what I think anyway, does it? When should I start packing?"

Nana was reading the newspaper when the phone rang. She kept it by her side so she would never have to rush to answer. At her age, standing up before she steadied herself made her light headed. She was proud to still be fit and alert in her advancing years, even though she was cautious with every step she took.

The death of her daughter and son-in-law brought her agony she never knew existed, but her pain began to ebb with the decision to have her eldest granddaughter share her home in Boston. At first, Bill, Deborah, and Sam were dead-set against it, preferring Elizabeth stay with one of her father's sisters, but in the end, everyone, especially Nana, felt living with her grandmother was the best solution.

"Nana, this is Sam. How are you? Is now a good time?"

The twins watched cartoons in the living room while Elizabeth sat expressionless in her father's chair, eavesdropping on the conversation between Sam and their grandmother. Elizabeth could hear Sam pacing in the kitchen as he spoke. She couldn't see that he was nervously twisting the phone cord in his hands and had no idea what Nana was saying, but was intent on getting as much information as she could by listening to her brother's side of the conversation.

"Well, the twins are pretty happy to be going to the island... with Ricky."

Popeye cartoons were making a racket on the TV, "I yam what I yam and that's all that I yam." The twins giggled, but the booming voice of Brutus and the shrill voice of Olive Oil was making it even more challenging to hear Sam's hushed responses. Elizabeth leaped from her chair to lower the volume. "Sorry, guys. It's a little loud." She settled back into the comfort of her father's chair. She wanted to hear every word Sam was saying.

"No, they probably don't understand where Elizabeth and I will be. Aunt Deborah and Uncle Bill think a move two weeks from today would be best for everyone. School will start for the twins the following week, and it will get them settled before I have to leave for boot camp and Elizabeth comes to live with you." Sam was not comfortable with this conversation and wanted to get it out of the way quickly.

He lowered his voice almost to a whisper and Elizabeth strained to hear. "I feel like a traitor, Nana... a traitor to my family."

Elizabeth overheard his confession and she nodded in agreement. She craned her neck to make out more of the conversation over the distracting laughter from Tina and Laura. "I know you don't blame me for... But now I wish I hadn't reacted so quickly. At the time, I thought it was a good idea. I didn't want to be responsible for taking care of my little sisters."

Sam paused again. "I had such big plans... Finish school, get my masters in history, become a college professor. It's all gone... wasted... Feels like everyone is talking behind my back, calling me a coward for joining the Marines... Running away to a foreign war instead of facing this struggle at home."

There was a long silence as Sam took in whatever his grandmother was imparting. Elizabeth felt left out, unable to hear the entire conversation, but she couldn't disagree with Sam's opinion of himself. At least he was having doubts and second thoughts about his hasty decision. Sam hung up the phone and rushed past his sisters, head down, hands in the deep pockets of his navy blue Bermuda shorts. "'Night you guys. I'm going to bed."

Chapter 4

A TAN, CHISELED SOLDIER, BEACH READY IN SWIM trunks, flip flops, and sunglasses that hid the intensity of his piercing blue eyes, approached Sam. He had wrapped his AM/FM radio in his beach towel and rolled it into a neat package that fit under one arm. Recruits were taking advantage of the rising temperatures and big waves, two days off for most, and a long-awaited opportunity to surf and mingle with the locals. Most hoped to meet a girl, maybe take her to dinner and a movie at the end of the sun-soaked day. Some hoped for more, but had been forewarned by their commanding officer not to get involved with the opposite sex. They would ship out in a month.

Paul extended his hand, drawing closer to Sam along with a trio of fellow marines, anxious to leave the barracks behind for the day. "Paul O'Brien."

The two young men shook firmly. "Sam Sutton. Looks like you're heading to the beach."

"Get your swimsuit and a towel. We'll wait. I'm gonna teach these guys to surf." The three stood behind Paul and waited patiently. "None of them are from around here." Paul turned to each one, nodding, "Right, Texas? Right, Montana? Right, Oklahoma?" They nodded in unison.

"You sure? I've never been in the ocean before."

"Well, that's where I learned to swim and I've been surfing since I was thirteen. To be stationed in Camp Pendleton, less than a mile from the beach is the only thing I'm grateful for since enlisting… come on… let's go check it out."

"Okay. Why Not? Count me in." Sam dashed back to his room, grabbed a pair of military-issue swim trunks, towel, and although he felt woefully out of place, was ready to take on the next physical challenge. *Better not be as tough as boot camp, but I better get used to risking my life.*

Though barely 10:00 AM, the beach already teemed with families, surfers, and the ever-present beautiful young women, who giggled and flirted with the marines stretched out on the sand. The unseasonable heat had driven most from their houses, and the easy access to the water along a ribbon of small beach towns up and down the coast became a popular destination when temperatures soared. The Oceanside Pier, with some of the best waves on the California Coast, beckoned seasoned surfers as well as beginners, and Paul was only too happy to help his buddies master the art in a day. *At least,* he thought, *they'll know how to dive under a wave by the end of the weekend.*

The five men spread their towels and Paul propped the radio so everyone could hear it. Youngsters dashed by, kicking sand onto the once-pristine towels, covering them in soft granules of beach gravel and salt water. Paul laughed as he readied his friends to enter the water with their rented surfboards. "You'll get used to it. And I promise—you'll never be the same once you catch your first wave." Like schoolboys, not the tough marines they had been molded to be, the foursome followed Paul, mimicking his entrance into the big, blue Pacific Ocean, and shuddering as they felt the first cold rush of waves crashing down upon them.

Elizabeth was excited to receive her first letter from her brother. The well-worn and familiar Adirondack chair on the front porch was the perfect vantage point from which to view the leaves on the oaks and sycamores beginning to turn red, gold, and orange, signaling the approach of the fall season. The crisp winds that were scattering falling leaves across the lawns and driveways up and down the street prompted the memory of an autumn afternoon spent in carefree play with her sisters, jumping into the piles of just-raked leaves and then being reprimanded by her father's booming voice. "I told you girls, if you're not going to help with the yard work, then go inside and help your mother with dinner." That and one stern look were all that was needed to keep everyone on task.

Daddy, I'm so sorry for all the times I argued with you for thinking you were too strict—I miss you! Elizabeth wiped away the tears blurring her vision and began to read.

October 5, 1965

Dear Elizabeth,

I'm glad we had a chance to patch things up before I left home. I meant it when I told you how sorry I am about making such a sudden decision and leaving you and Tina and Laura right after Mom and Dad died, but there's no way I can get out of this now.

So I finally made it through boot camp. Our platoon will be shipping out to Vietnam next month. I try not to think about it, about what's waiting for us on the other side of the Pacific.

Southern California is bitchin' (that's not a bad word, honest. It means super cool. I'm picking up on the local slang). The only place I've been outside base is the beach, and it's really different from Boston. It's dry and hot, and we're in the middle of something they call a Santa Ana. That's what the locals call this blistering, dry wind blowing in from the deserts and mountain passes. It makes our eyes itch, and our hair stands on end. Everyone is damned uncomfortable and cranky. I hear that the weather in Vietnam will be much worse. At least the Santa Anas blow through in about a week, but they say the jungle is hot and sticky all year round. Sounds like hell.

There are guys here from all parts of the country, and I hang out with them on our days off. Usually, we get weekends to ourselves, and I have to admit, being stationed in Oceanside is not bad duty. It could have been so much worse, ending up somewhere in the Carolinas or Arizona. Yeah… Southern California… a pretty lucky draw I'd say!

One guy named Paul is a surfer, raised in Southern California. He's from Reseda, right outside Los Angeles. He keeps calling it "The Valley" and makes it sound not quite as cool as some other areas of the city. He says they get some pretty hostile looks from guys his age when they go to the beach every weekend. Some territorial Los Angeles thing, I guess. He's probably about my age and he also enlisted, but I'm not sure why. At least he's not fresh out of high school as far as I can tell. Maybe about 19 or 20. So many of the draftees don't look more than 17 or 18, just babies. I know I'm not too much older, but at least I have a couple years of college under my belt.

Paul took me and three friends surfing the other day. The Oceanside Pier is only about a mile from base.

We rented boards from a little shack on the sand for a dollar an hour, and that was plenty for me. After we turned in our boards Paul went back out for another hour to body surf. He cuts through the water like a seal. It'll take me years to get up the nerve to do half the things he does!

Anyway, Paul is a regular surfing fool—surfed almost every weekend as soon as one of his buddies got his driver's license and they could drive the twenty miles to the beach. He mentioned his parents had a little beach house somewhere around here when he was about 14, and they'd come down every once in a while.

He also listens to rock and roll every second of his free time. He cranks the volume all the way up. He says he has over 400 LPs and 45s back home. That's a lot of vinyl! Not sure if I believe him… it's a different world on the west coast. I'm getting used to it, and you would probably love it.

Well, dinner around here is early so I should go. Give my love to Nana and the twins, and remember, don't believe everything you see on the news, read in the newspaper, or hear on the radio. Be good, sophomore!

Always Your Older Brother,

Sam

Every afternoon Elizabeth dragged herself home from school. She missed her old friends who she knew would soon forget her, and tried not to think about her sixteenth birthday, just weeks away. Her mother had said it would be her day to shine and Elizabeth looked forward, if only for a day, to pushing Sam out of the limelight and basking in the attention. If her parents doted on her older brother because he was the first one in the Sutton family to go to college, surely they must have been proud of Elizabeth for her sense of responsibility and supportive, caring nature. In her mind, that had to count for something, but it no longer mattered what they might have thought. There would be no celebration, no party, and she told herself that she didn't care.

Elizabeth shoved her thoughts aside when Nana appeared from the kitchen, carrying a plate of warm cookies and a tall glass of milk. "I don't need cookies every day after school. You know that, Nana."

"I know, dear. It makes me feel useful, though, and it passes the time. Besides, you're getting too thin."

Nana's grief was evident in those few words and her smile faded. "Elizabeth was caught off-guard. "Just one then, thank you. I have to do my homework, then I'll write Sam." She stared at the growing fire as the flames consumed the last log, and she felt the heat spread throughout the room. "Thanks for the fire, Nana. It's getting colder like it always does in October. I think I'll just curl up on the couch and do my homework in the living room. And thank you for the snack." Elizabeth took a cookie from Nana's outstretched hand and kissed her lightly on the cheek.

"You're welcome, dear. I'll be in the kitchen if you need me, getting dinner started, and we'll be eating at six."

"Sharp?"

Smiling in response, Nana nodded, "Sharp."

Elizabeth drew a few blank pieces of paper and a fountain pen with a fresh cartridge from her school bag. The hardback cover of her bulky history book, cradled atop her crossed legs, created the perfect impromptu table, an infinitely better use of the textbook than the assignment she was putting off.

Whatever did Sam see in history? Just a bunch of useless information about dead people and the old days. Why would anyone want to read this stuff, let alone teach it? She lifted the folded afghan from the back of the couch, lovingly crocheted by Nana for her mother's sixteenth birthday, and wrapped herself in the sweet memories of her parents, wishing it were ten years into the future—the only way she could think of to diminish the pain of the present.

Comfortable and snug, she wrote:

October 13, 1965

Dear Sam,

I'm also glad we had a chance to sit and talk before you left. I do understand and I'm sorry I was so mean to you.

I'm glad you're finding time to relax and have a little fun. Oceanside sounds fantastic! And I can't believe how warm it is! It's only the beginning of October and we've already had one early snow here. Nana built a fire for me and made cookies. I'm sitting in the living room, wrapped up in Mom's old afghan. It's a comfortable spot to write, but the sunshine in Southern California sounds even better.

I'm so glad you're making friends. Paul seems like a good guy. How cool that he knows how to surf and that you're only a mile away from the waves! Maybe he can teach you a thing or two. I'm sure you still have a few things to learn, even though you think you know everything already—ha, ha. Maybe one day I'll get a chance to see and experience places outside of Boston. I sure hope so!

I'm working hard in school to keep my grades up and I call Laura and Tina on the phone every night before bed. I try to keep it short, it's so expensive, but Nana keeps telling me not to worry about that part.

It still makes me nervous, so much money for a long-distance phone call! I'll be glad when I can see them in person at Thanksgiving next month. I haven't made any friends yet. I'm sure I will soon, but not in time for my birthday. Boo-hoo for me. I guess I shouldn't complain.

I know your situation is much worse than mine, and it's practically all I think about. You're a real hero, Sam. You all are. And even though so many people are against the war and act like they don't understand, I do. I know you'll be home soon and I'm sure Nana will make your favorite cookies. What were they again? Peanut butter? Snickerdoodle? Gingersnaps? Chocolate chip? Oh yeah, that's right, you love them all, especially Nana's! Please... I wish you were here to help me eat these cookies—she's going to make me fat! I miss you and can't wait for you to come home!

I have a few more pictures to take on my last roll of film before I can get them developed. I wish I hadn't bought the 36 exposure. There's not much to photograph around here with everyone gone, but I'll think of something. Maybe I'll have Nana take a snapshot of me under one of the sycamore trees. The leaves are turning, and I'm sure you remember how beautiful fall can be. I'll send a picture in my next letter. Maybe you could send me one of you and Paul.

Well, I have to get back to my homework. Stupid history assignment! Remind me why you wanted to teach it? Stay safe!

Love, Your Little Sister,

Elizabeth

"Nana, do you have a stamp?" Elizabeth called out and then jumped when she noticed Nana standing behind the couch, watching her while she was engrossed in her letter to Sam. Nana held a package in her hands, carefully wrapped in pink tissue paper and a white satin bow. "I didn't see you standing there—sorry."

"I haven't been here long. I noticed you wrapped in your mother's afghan, and even though it is a little early for your birthday present, I thought this would be the perfect time to give it to you." Nana sat beside her granddaughter and continued, "You're so young, it shouldn't have been this way, but I think your mother would approve."

Elizabeth choked as she saw a small tear fall from her Nana's cheek. She wasn't sure she wanted to know what was inside the beautifully wrapped gift Nana placed in her hands. "Nana? Are you okay? Should I open it now or wait till later?"

"No, this is a perfect time." Handing the present to Elizabeth, Nana struggled to get the words out, "Your mother and I planned this last year, for your sixteenth birthday. We finished it together right before your parents left on vacation last summer. I know this is the right time."

Accepting her grandmother's offering, she couldn't help but notice her clear, animated eyes and her soft, delicate skin, hardly a wrinkle even though she was almost eighty. *My Nana. I used to think you were just so old... Now I think you're just so beautiful.*

Elizabeth trembled and blinked back tears as she undid the bow and set the bundle down on the couch beside her. She deftly removed the scotch tape so as not to damage the delicate paper and unfolded the tissue to reveal an afghan quilt, so exquisite it took her breath away. Hues of pink and cream and white and a scalloped edge of gold metallic thread weaved through the delicate pattern. It must have taken her mother and grandmother months to make. It was not only a work of art, but a labor of love, so complete it made up for any party she would never have.

"Oh, Nana!" gasped Elizabeth, trying not to cry. "Thank you, thank you, thank you, for making my sixteenth birthday better than anything I could have ever wished for." Elizabeth gently folded and set aside her mother's old blanket and silently thought how well her mama—and Nana—knew her. They couldn't have given her a better gift.

"I'm glad you like it, Elizabeth. You're going to be just fine. Now, let me get you that stamp."

Elizabeth couldn't wait to tell Sam. Thankful she had not yet licked the envelope closed, she unfolded the letter and laid it flat on her makeshift lap table and wrote:

> *P.S. You should see the present Nana just gave me for my birthday! It's so gorgeous! A pink afghan she and Mama made for me last summer. My 16th birthday. I'll never forget it! xoxoxo*

❦

The last letter Sam wrote from the States was short and to the point.

> *November 1, 1965*
>
> *Dear Elizabeth,*
>
> *I hope everyone is well and you're starting to enjoy your new school. I know you feel robbed of a normal childhood, but it's important you still make friends, go to school dances, learn to drive, and be a teenager. I'm glad you got a special gift for your 16th birthday. That's a big one and I don't think you'll ever forget it.*
>
> *My battalion is shipping out in a week, and I'll write as soon as I get to Vietnam.*

Remember, don't believe everything you see on the news, read in the newspaper, or hear on the radio.
I love you all very much. Pass it on.

Always Your Older Brother,

Sam

Chapter 5

SAM AND THE REST OF HIS BATTALION STOOD AT attention on the hard, unforgiving asphalt of the tarmac at Oakland International Airport, anxious to board the Pan American Boeing 707 jetliner that would carry them, most of them teenagers, to the front lines. With a wingspan of over 130 feet and a length of more than 150 feet, the silver underbelly of the narrow-bodied aircraft glistened in the setting sun, and he watched intently as the narrow opening between day and night finally closed.

The commanding officer boarded his men. He wanted his troops as relaxed as possible, so he kept his thoughts to himself and, despite the approaching darkness, kept his gaze concealed behind a pair of government-issued aviator sunglasses.

"It's going to be a long, uncomfortable trip, men. Our first stop is Hawaii." Then before allowing everyone to break rank, the officer barked his final command, "No one is to leave the airport when we get there. Do you understand?"

A booming response of "Yes, sir!" followed his order.

The men marched up the stairs in an orderly fashion until reaching the cabin, where they elbowed and crowded each other in an attempt to get the coveted window seats. Flight attendants with broad smiles, crisp blue uniforms, and long legs assisted each young man as if he were their only passenger. Experienced, charming, and sophisticated, the women presented a stark contrast to the boys they escorted to war. Sam filed to the back of the aircraft that was filled with an unsuspecting band of young soldiers ready to endure the long flight to Saigon. He wasn't sure he wanted to speak with anyone aboard this trip, not even with Paul who was seated near the front with six paperback novels to keep him company and occupy his time.

As the last one to board, Sam drew a sigh of relief when he found one of the two window seats at the rear of the cabin was still empty. He settled in and removed a small stack of writing paper and a new ballpoint pen from his duffle bag before shoving it under the seat. What better way to spend the next twenty-four, maybe as many as thirty-six, hours on a pent-up, testosterone-filled voyage to hell. He hadn't planned on writing Elizabeth, wasn't even sure when she might get the letter, but writing would help pass the hours and maybe help calm his nerves.

"Prepare for takeoff," came the voice from the cockpit.

With one final shove, Sam used the tip of his boot to wedge his bag securely into the small space provided for personal belongings. *There, motherfucker—try getting out of that one,* he thought, as he blocked out the deafening noise from the revved-up engines and felt the aircraft slowly gliding onto the runway.

November 8, 1965

Dear Elizabeth,

> *I wasn't going to write until I got to Vietnam, but it looks like it's going to be a long flight, probably 36 hours. Good a time as any to get started, sophomore! Might be the last free time I have.*
>
> *All the guys are hooting at the stewardesses and singing and playing cards—almost like a party. Under different circumstances, I'd probably join in. What I wouldn't do to be back on the quad for another kegger.*

You'd think we were in a fraternity, by listening to some of these conversations. I suppose, in some way, we are. I'm glad I got the window seat at the back of the plane, because I really don't feel like talking. Our first stop is Hawaii. I'll send you pictures if I can, although it looks like we're landing at night…wish I could just disembark and disappear, but can't even if I wanted to. I'm struggling even more with my stupid decision to enlist. I was on my way to a degree in history – so damn stupid! The airport will probably be filled with happy tourists while we wait to get back on a plane that will take us to our destination - war. It's surreal.

Have to deplane for a bit. Hello, Hawaii!

<hr />

"Should've brought your surfboard." Sam caught up with Paul at the farthest end of the terminal, bustling with tourists, skycaps, and grinning stewardesses, excited their duties included two days off on an island paradise. The two stood in awe, gazing out the massive windows stretching from floor to ceiling, at a view that beckoned them to a dream vacation just outside their reach.

"Don't think it didn't cross my mind. Can't see too much in the dark, but I can make out just enough to know I'll be back one day," Paul said as he moved closer to the exit to peer at the wonderland beyond. He drew one deep breath of the sweet island air—pungent with the smell of plumeria and orchids—before joining the rest of his troop in the procession to reboard the aircraft. *See you in my dreams.* Paul settled into the front-row seat, waving to Sam as he muscled past the throng of men to his seat in the back of the plane.

❖

Okay, I'm back on board. Sure wish we could've landed before dark. There's not much to see at night but distant lights of hotels and glowing cabin lights from arriving airliners. Ran into Paul and it's not hard to tell the guy misses his beach and surfing days back home. We all miss something.

The guys are still too rowdy for my taste. They're all swearing. You'd probably blush if you heard them. Took a little getting used to myself. Mom and Dad would have been horrified, but Marines swear a lot.

Next stop, Guam. It's an island somewhere in the Pacific. I know there's a couple military bases there, but not much else. They won't let us off the plane. Damn, it's getting stuffy in here! My back aches and my head hurts, but at least I feel safe for now. I've heard stories about getting shot down from the sky while landing in Vietnam. Don't know if it's true, but hoping for the best on this flight.

Changing topics for a moment... Please write to let me know how you're doing in school. How many new friends are you making? And the boys—I'm sure there are a lot of them who'd like to date you. Not too close, Elizabeth. I was once one myself, so I can tell you boys are pretty rotten when we're that age. Have fun, but be careful. That's all I'm going to say on that subject.

We're making our descent. I think we're only here long enough to refuel, but I'll be stretching my legs a bit in the cabin... take a break for a bit... Maybe strike up a conversation with one of the guys, even though I'm still not too interested in talking with anyone.

Airborne again. I'm starting to feel the humidity. Even inside the airplane, I can feel the jungle. I think everyone else feels it too because no one's talking. Could be they're just tired, or thinking about what we're going to face once we land. Until now, it was just something we saw on TV, but every minute we move closer, the war becomes more and more real. I wish we could just turn this plane around and go home, but that's not going to happen… I wish I'd never enlisted. I'm just so damn sorry I made that choice instead of taking care of my sisters!

Our last stop before Saigon is the Philippines. The stewardess just walked by and told us to be prepared for heavy rains. Monsoons she called them. I guess they're pretty common this time of year. Vietnam has similar weather… looks like I'll be getting wet! They're letting us disembark when we land this time, so at least I'll get to walk around on land for a bit. Over and out, for now.

I'm back. Where the hell did all this water come from? The rain's coming in sheets, sideways and we all got soaked running across the tarmac! Our boots got waterlogged sloshing through ankle deep puddles and now we're sitting in this airplane, dripping wet. Maybe it's a test, and we'll have to get used to it sooner

or later. Everyone's getting more and more grouchy and agitated.

Whoa! I can feel the plane getting shoved around by the high crosswinds, and the pilot hasn't even started the engines. I don't even know how he's going to get this thing off the ground safely.

There's a stench on the plane, with most of us still wet. It reeks like a high school boys' locker room after a football game in 80° heat. Be glad you'll never know that smell, but that's exactly what it's like.

Some of the guys found a couple of shady drug dealers in the terminal. I'm guessing no one pays that much attention here. I saw a few pocket some joints, but I'm not going to criticize. Well, what do you know: not judgmental for a change. But don't you touch the stuff, Elizabeth! Ever!

We're approaching Vietnam now... so close I can see the jungle below. I've never seen a landscape like this before, even on TV. The vegetation is so thick I can't even see the ground. I'm imagining hundreds of the enemy hiding under that stuff and I sure hope it provides us some cover as well. I'm not liking this, Elizabeth.

The cabin has gotten quiet during our approach. Some guys have their eyes closed like they're praying. I can see the landing strip, won't be long. I'm glad I'll be last off the plane. I've barely talked to anyone during this entire flight, except for bumping into Paul in Hawaii, but I'm sure we'll catch up as soon as we get to the base.

This really is the end of the letter and I expect it'll be hectic and crazy for the next few days. I'll try to write again when I have a free moment. Just so you and Nana know, I'll be in Chu Lai. I'm sure we'll get more information once we've arrived. Be sure to jot down the military FPO address that you'll see on this envelope so that your letters find their way to me.

Remember, don't believe everything you see on the news, read in the newspaper, or hear on the radio. I love you all very much. Pass it on.

Always Your Older Brother,

Sam

Chapter 6

It was Saturday and Elizabeth was relieved she didn't have a weekend homework assignment. The day looked perfect, slightly cool, her favorite type of weather. It was a shame when these idyllic days were wasted on a Monday or Tuesday, stuck in a classroom or trapped in the school library waiting for the last bell of the day to ring. Her spirits usually lifted with the crisp breeze of a flawless autumn day.

This year would be different. Elizabeth knew it and tried not to think about it. The scent of winter. The musty smell of abandoned piles of raked leaves in the front yards mingled with the unmistakable aroma of smoke spiraling from every chimney on the block. The memories created a knot in her stomach and a longing for just one more dinner at the Sutton table, six o'clock sharp. She waited for Sam's first letter to arrive from Vietnam like he promised, and every day she anticipated an envelope with a foreign postmark, the proof that her brother had made it safely to Saigon.

She got her winter jacket, left untouched for the last few months. Shoving one arm and then the other into the cumbersome down-filled sleeves, Elizabeth bounded down the stairs and headed for the front door. *If I only get one present for Christmas this year, I would ask for a new winter jacket. This old brown thing is so ugly, but it keeps me warm.*

"Nana, I'm going to pick up my pictures at the camera shop. Do you need anything while I'm out?" Turning the knob, Elizabeth spoke loudly enough for her grandmother to hear.

Nana looked forward to the weekends as much as Elizabeth did. She hadn't noticed how lonely she had been, living by herself in the aging family home that was once the hub of activity, the holiday destination for her children—even when they moved away, got married, and had children of their own. Widowed after a long and contented marriage, Nana still grieved for her husband who never had the joy of watching their grandchildren play on the old tire swing, which still hung by the barest of threads from the majestic red oak that dwarfed the other trees in the yard. She tingled at the distant memory of him, throwing a two-inch thick rope over the strongest branch, tying the knot with the expertise of a seasoned sailor and proclaiming, "We don't want any accidents here. Best way to avoid a broken arm is to do it right the first time."

Composing herself, Nana responded from the kitchen, "No, dear. You have fun. Are you going by yourself?"

"Yeah. I'll be okay. I'll only be gone about an hour."

Nana moved towards the living room while drying her hands on the kitchen towel she kept tucked inside her pristine red-gingham apron. It was a well-known fact that Nana liked aprons with deep pockets so she would have the convenience of keeping a fresh dish towel at her disposal at all times. She preached the importance of time management and how extra steps were a wasted effort. Sometimes she had two or three towels folded in reserve, depending on the size of the pocket and the size of the meal.

She smiled as she gave Elizabeth a hug. "I know you'll be okay. But I had hoped you might have a few friends by now. Someone to spend the weekends with, go to the movies, shopping. It would be good for you to socialize."

Elizabeth wasn't upset she hadn't made new friends. She was concentrating on her schoolwork and looked forward to letters from her brother. Somehow that had become more normal to her than slumber parties and movie dates. "I'm fine, Nana." She called over her shoulder as she headed out the door, "Keep an eye out for the mail. I'm expecting another letter from Sam."

The short walk to the camera store filled her lungs with fresh air and she slowed her pace to observe the wondrous transition of the seasons. Her eyes transfixed on the stark branches of the oak trees, she noticed how the smattering of evergreens prevented the landscape from looking like a barren wasteland.

The concrete sidewalk felt cold through her thinning canvas tennies, the last pair her mother had purchased from the local A&P at the onset of summer. Elizabeth would never forget the day her mother returned from her final shopping trip. Brown paper bags perched on the kitchen table, filled to the brim with dry goods, fresh meat, and family treats, along with an array of household supplies. Sitting atop a canister of Quaker Oats and a gallon of milk were three new pairs of unblemished, white tennis shoes: one for Elizabeth, one for Tina, and one for Laura. *Cheap, and perfect for one season with three growing girls*, she remembered her mother saying. She reminded herself that she was long overdue for a warmer pair of shoes or boots and that it was time to comb through her drawers in search of her woolen socks, mittens, and scarves, even though she knew she would probably keep the tattered, well-worn pair of supermarket tennies forever.

Elizabeth was eager to look through her roll of developed pictures so she could include one in her next letter to Sam. Ripping the sticky back from the envelope, she was startled when she sorted through the photos. She barely remembered posing for pictures just before Sam left for boot camp. The surviving family had gathered one last time and spread a picnic feast in a nearby park as if it were some kind of celebration. To her, it was the beginning of life in ruins, and she quickly fanned past those snapshots, trying not to notice how unhappy most of them looked—Sam especially, flanked by his sisters, Nana, Uncle Bill, and Ricky. Only the twins were grinning, each sheltered under one of Sam's arms. Still summer, Laura, and Tina beamed in their bright orange sunsuits, while Elizabeth stood to one side, unsmiling, looking miserable in her tank top and shorts. She shuddered and pushed the memory aside.

Her mood shifted when she uncovered the more recent birthday photos. Wrapped in her new pink afghan, her head in an upward tilt, and an innocent smile captured at the right moment, she appeared not to have a care in the world. The light dancing off her scattered, auburn curls cast a glow of contentment, and she could have passed for any carefree, lighthearted teenager. *This is the one. This is Sam's.*

She carefully placed the photos back into the protective envelope as the clerk rang up her purchase at the cash register. Dashing back out into the winter chill, she didn't even notice how cold it was. A slight smile, almost beyond detection, remained as she hurried home to her Nana.

The mailman was just closing the box when Elizabeth rounded the corner. "Have anything for me, Mr. Holmes?" Elizabeth half-shouted, a little breathless.

"Looks like it. Noticed the FPO address. Your brother in Vietnam now?"

"He must be. He left Camp Pendleton last week. Thank you!" The envelope seemed thicker than the other letters Sam had written and the return address was the military-generated postmark—a sure sign it was sent from Vietnam.

Instead of running inside to the protective warmth of the living room or giving into the temptation of her Nana's fresh-baked home-made brownies that she could smell half a block away, Elizabeth settled into the most comfortable seat on the porch, a weathered rocking chair that had been there for as long as she could remember. She tucked her chin into the upturned collar of her coat, tugged off her mittens, and then ripped the corners of the envelope, careful not to harm the edges of the letter.

There, alone on the porch, she read each word over and over again. The gritty, detailed pages Sam wrote during the flight from California to Saigon were hers alone to read. She didn't think it was a good idea to share with Nana. Sam always wrote separate letters, mostly notes to the twins and his grandmother. The real war, the real struggles, he shared only with Elizabeth.

✧

"My hands are freezing," Elizabeth thought as she hurried to collect her mittens and Sam's letter before rushing inside. "Got the pictures, Nana!" She kicked off her damp, shabby tennis shoes and abandoned her offensive brown winter jacket in a heap at the bottom of the staircase.

Nana cautioned Elizabeth as she noticed her bounding up the steps. "Don't forget to hang up your coat, dear, before you go upstairs. Someone could trip."

Elizabeth heeded Nana's gentle command and doubled back, scooping up shoes and jacket as requested. She rushed to her room, tossed her belongings on the floor just inside the door, took a few pieces of lined notebook paper from her binder, and flopped down on the bed, stomach first. She settled into a spot that was uncluttered with stuffed animals and over-sized pillows. With elbows propped up and feet crossed in midair, she wrote:

November 20, 1965

Dear Sam,

I got your letter. I wasn't even expecting to get anything so soon. It sounds terrible and I can't even imagine what you must be thinking. We're getting ready to celebrate Thanksgiving and Christmas, and you have to know we all miss you so much. I just keep telling myself we'll be together next year and you need to tell yourself the same thing. It shouldn't come as a surprise that we're putting together a package for you. We'll ship it in plenty of time for the holidays. You probably won't be able to eat all the cookies, but I'm sure your friends won't mind helping you. You boys are always hungry!

I'm enclosing a picture of me that Nana took on my 16th birthday with the afghan that Mom made around my shoulders. It's so pretty—wish you could see it in person. It was the best birthday present ever!

I'm doing well in school, but I still haven't made any friends. Don't worry—it doesn't bother me. I think it matters more to Nana more than it does me. There are a few girls I eat lunch with now and then, but most of them have known each other since kindergarten, and I feel pretty much like an outsider. A few of them have brothers in Vietnam, but they don't seem to write them like I write to you. It's also pretty uncomfortable when I overhear conversations about dodging the draft, going to Canada, how much they hate our military. I'm allright, honest, probably better that I keep mostly to myself, and I'm actually having a good time with Nana. She's a special lady and I never even noticed until now. Mama's mom... A comforting thought.

I know this isn't a very long letter, but I want to get it to the mailbox before the last pick up. You probably won't get it until after Thanksgiving, so I hope you had a happy one with lots of turkey and stuffing. Try to stay dry and write me back. I'll tell everyone you said hello.

Love Your Little Sister,

Elizabeth

P.S. I hope you like the picture!

⊰◈⊱

Elizabeth never knew how long it would take Sam to receive her letters. She hated the fact that he was so far away, out of reach and out of touch. Almost every day she went to the school library, studying the large map that took up half the wall. She strained to find Chu Lai, Saigon, Mee Cong Delta, Hanoi, Nha Trang—any town or village that Sam had mentioned or that she recognized from the nightly news. They were a cluster of names she couldn't pronounce, and she had no real sense of where in the world they were. But one thing was certain: Sam was far-removed from his country, his family, and his home.

It was a relief when she didn't hear any stories about fighting in Chu Lai or the surrounding villages, and so far nothing much had been reported about that part of Vietnam, no broadcasts or reports of bombings nearby. Some evenings she and Nana ate dinner in front of the TV, on small trays created for convenience and solitary meals, so that they wouldn't miss Walter Cronkite and his stoic nightly accounts of the battles. Nana loved Walter.

"What's this world coming to?" Nana complained every time Elizabeth asked if they could eat in the living room. "It's a deplorable corruption of the traditional sit-down family dinner. Don't get used to this, my dear."

Elizabeth wasn't so sure she disapproved of this new dinner hour ritual as much as she claimed. She guessed Nana secretly looked forward to the time they spent together, even if it was to watch the news and little else. "I know you don't like it, Nana, but it's hardly corrupt. It's the only way we can eat dinner at six o'clock sharp and watch the six o'clock news at the same time. Sounds like a good compromise. Just you, me, and Walter."

"If I didn't think you were attempting humor, I would say you were starting to sound a little sassy," but Nana knew Elizabeth was right and chuckled as she responded. Since Sam left for Vietnam, traditions took a back seat to everything, while regular updates on the war became the most important part of their day. "Don't forget, Aunt Deborah, Uncle Bill, your sisters, and Ricky will be here day after tomorrow for Thanksgiving. And we're eating at the dining table together."

"Okay, Nana. That'll be nice. I'm looking forward to it," she said aloud and then added silently: *But I can't help but wonder what Sam will be doing.*

Chapter 7

"HAVE TO GET THIS LETTER TO THE SUPPLY SERGEANT after breakfast. I want to make sure Elizabeth gets it before Christmas, and that's in three weeks. Can't wait to dive into those powdered eggs and burnt toast." Sam nodded towards Paul and couldn't help but notice the growing number of men, almost overnight, that stretched the length of the mess hall tent.

"Anything seem strange to you? Just last week this base looked empty. Now it's filling up with new men, artillery piles, extra supplies. We'll have to rely on the grapevine if we want to know what's going on." Sam tucked the letter into his pocket as they took up the end of the line.

"Saddle up men; it's time to rock and roll!" The commanding officer burst into the tent shouting orders, disrupting conversation, and expecting every man to take action. "Drop your trays, don't take that next bite, and don't even chew that last bite of food. If it's in your mouth swallow it—now! Move it!"

All personnel came to attention. The calm was about to turn into a storm. "Keep packs light; we're moving out at zero eight hundred. We're motoring south to Thang Binh, and being heli-lifted to a landing zone. Expect heavy fire and casualties. God be with you." Men scattered to their hooches and did as they were told, hearts pounding, eyes on fire, and ready to dive into battle.

Ferocious winds and pelting rain pounded the camp, and fear tightened its grip on the men as they rushed to obey orders. Paul and Sam managed to scramble aboard the same helicopter, wondering if the pilot would be able to land in these conditions. One marine after another struggled aboard and it was questionable if they could make it off the ground. They were not prepared to fight in this kind of weather, in the soft soil of jungle mud, and didn't know if they were capable of the bloody fight they knew was imminent.

Dropped in the middle of a firefight, the men scattered for safety. The atmosphere was thick with humidity and the smell of rocket fire permeated the air. Huey gunships and jet fighters pounded the enemy with rockets and bombs, and soldiers on the ground were using every conceivable method of destruction in an effort to stay alive.

Still fighting after the sun went down, Paul and Sam found themselves closest to the hill crawling with the enemy. They followed their commander who was shouting, "Move up the hill! We're takin' the hill. I said move it!" No one hesitated to obey, and as the wounded and dying fell over one another, yelling, screaming, rifles firing, charging forward, Paul heard one distinct voice not far behind him. "I've been hit! My hand, my goddamned hand!" He knew it was Sam, and sliding back down on his belly to reach him, trying to be as inconspicuous as possible, he felt a searing pain on the side of his face. He didn't hear the explosion, only saw one blinding flash that illuminated the pitch-black night. In an instant, his world went dark.

North Vietnamese Army mortar shells continued to wreak havoc in the middle of the violent confrontation. No one was safe from the bullets and explosions that rained down on them. Sam called out in agony, "Oh my God, My sweet God, what the hell is happening?" He tried to stand, get his bearings, and come to his senses, but he fell backward into the mud-soaked hill. He bled profusely from his right hand, which was connected to his wrist with a few exposed muscles and tendons. Instinctively, he tore at his shirt with what little strength he had left, and managed to peel it off his body and wrap it around his wound in a futile attempt to stop the flow. He watched his blood blend with the rain water streaming past, mixed with a pool of mud and sludge already tainted red from the carnage at the top of the hill. Blood and life lost on both sides.

What seemed like hours was only minutes before he heard the familiar noise of the Huey medevac helicopter. The chopper hovered at a safe distance and waited. A group of four young marines were chosen by the commanding officer to set a perimeter to evacuate the wounded. One of them bent over Sam. "Hold on, man. Sit tight. We'll get you out of here."

Distracted by this boy's resolve and calm demeanor, all Sam could think was, *Kids. They're just kids! We should be home watching the fucking Ed Sullivan Show, not watching our friends die and killing someone else's son. How in the goddamned hell did we get here!*

Another young soldier joined the first and together they bundled Sam on a litter, made it to the landing zone, and loaded him in the copter for dust-off.

"That all we got?" radioed the pilot to the crewman in the belly of the copter.

"No. One more, just behind us. Is there room?"

The pilot turned his head and surveyed the approaching wounded marine before he answered. He wasn't sure if one more litter would fit in the already-crowded copter. He shouted into his mouthpiece above the noise, trying to be heard over the din of the persistent artillery fire. "Yeah, get him on board—hurry!"

With strength that nothing else but adrenaline can provide, two more men emerged from the bushes with the wounded marine. They crammed his litter inside, pushed and shoved to make room, and jumped back to give the pilot clearance to take off.

Sam was conscious and in searing pain. He wondered if he would bleed to death before he made it to the field hospital. He had just enough room to turn his head to one side and come face-to-face with the young man who made it aboard with moments to spare. Sam saw he was unconscious. He also saw it was Paul. His head was wrapped in bandages, his face covered with open wounds and small pieces of shrapnel protruded from his skin. His body was limp and he looked more dead than alive.

Paul groaned, and for a brief moment, opened his eyes. He rolled over on his side and managed to utter, "That you, Sam? Where are we? What's happening? My head, my goddamned head… feels like it's going to explode."

Paul drifted back into unconsciousness and Sam's eyes fixated on the ceiling above him. Ears trained on the whirling noise of the chopper blades, he hoped this helicopter ride would take them to safety. He looked at his friend, and murmured, "Don't worry, buddy. We're gonna make it out alive."

Chapter 8

THE OVERLOADED HUEY STRUGGLED TO LAND AT THE field hospital in Da Nang. The capacity in this tent city for the wounded had tripled, and operating rooms expanded to treat those who could be saved with emergency life-saving procedures. Corpsmen hurried from one litter to the next, sorting out the worst of the injuries within minutes, and making split-second decisions.

"Let's go! This guy's about to bleed to death! Already unconscious!" A capable corpsman yelled at the stretcher-bearers. Nurses were already prepping the incoming. The wounded were being unloaded like cargo and as soon as orders were shouted, they were carried out. The rush to get Sam inside to the pre-op room was urgent, and already unconscious, he was put under and prepared for surgery.

Dr. Leonard Shapiro cut away Sam's blood-soaked shirt. He shook his head and spoke to the two nurses and the assisting surgeon. "He already has signs of gangrene." He had seen wounds like this, and worse, too many times before. He took a deep breath while he examined the extent of Sam's injuries. "I don't think there's any way we can save this kid's hand. Too much blood loss. There's no way I can re-attach it. I can save his life—I can't save his hand."

"We need another room. Where's an empty room?" A nurse held Paul's hand. He opened his eyes and blinked fast, as if that would make this scene go away and he would wake up. He was dreaming. He was sure he was dreaming.

"You're okay, son. Just lay still. The doctor will be here as soon as he's out of surgery."

Paul touched his face and felt the dried blood and little shards of metal just below the surface of his skin. "Am I bleeding?"

"No, you're going to be just fine." The nurse stood up and reached for a clean towel just as the doctor approached Paul's bedside.

"Hello, young man. Dr. Shapiro."

Paul managed a nod. "Hi, Doc. Lance Corporal Paul O'Brien."

"We're going to run some tests on you, but I'm pretty sure there are no open wounds on your body. Looks like shrapnel pieces in your face and some are close enough to the surface that they can be extracted. Depending on what the X-rays show, we may or may not have to perform surgery to remove any rogue pieces we find next to a vital organ." Paul wordlessly nodded his head again.

He lay still on his cot while he waited for Dr. Shapiro to return with his test results. Hours seemed like days. Paul tried to lift his head and get a glimpse of the ward full of wounded marines. He couldn't recall how he got there, but thought Sam might have been with him in the chopper. He craned his neck to search out every corner of the room, but couldn't find his friend's familiar face. He gave up, feeling like there was a jackhammer ripping apart his brain inside his head, and one simple movement was more than he could bear.

"Good news, young man." Dr. Shapiro was back at Paul's bedside. "Besides the shrapnel we'll remove from your face, two larger pieces have lodged in your skull."

"That's good news?" Paul was being facetious even though his head continued to pound.

"It's good news since it would be more dangerous for us to remove those bigger shards, so we're going to leave them right where they are, and there will be no surgery. There is a possibility they could work themselves loose over time, but in most cases, they'll remain where they are for the rest of your life."

"I guess I'll have to be content with most cases. Anything you can give me for this headache?" Paul clenched his teeth, hoping to reduce the lightning bolts behind his eyes. He tried to remember how delicious it felt to be pain-free.

"We'll get you something." Dr. Shapiro turned to his nurse. "I'm ordering a mild sedative for Paul so we can remove the shrapnel. When we're done, find him a spot in the ward and—"

Paul interrupted. "I have a friend who was wounded. I think he was on the chopper with me. Do you know if Sam Sutton is here?" He looked at the doctor for reassurance.

Dr. Shapiro knew who Paul was talking about. He laid a hand on Paul's arm. "He just got out of surgery. I'll see if I can get him a bed next to you once the anesthesia has worn off."

"Will he be okay? Was it his hand? I heard him scream about his hand when we were hit."

"Yes, it's his hand." That's all Doctor Shapiro would share with Paul. He stood up and moved to the next patient in line. Paul struggled to prop himself against the wall, comforted only by a small pillow for his head and a thin blanket to minimize the shaking he couldn't repress. He surveyed the scene that unfolded before him and waited for Sam to join him. The room was filled with muffled groans from dozens of young men, many in critical condition with life-threatening injuries, mutilated limbs, and grotesque facial wounds that replaced the once handsome, strong, vigorous appearance of youth. Some screamed in agony as young nurses did their best to scrub lacerations and change dressings, while others lay silent with nothing more than a fixated stare and a vacant, faraway look.

Paul watched a trim and confident nurse, her chestnut hair pulled back in a ponytail that showed off her high cheek bones and almond-shaped eyes—rich, like the color of chocolate. She wrapped the final piece of clean gauze around the head of a distressed young soldier and whispered something in his ear. Whatever she had said appeared to relieve his agitation as a slight smile crossed his face and he surrendered his broken body to sleep, at least for the moment.

The nurse walked over to Paul, pulled up a chair, and introduced herself. "Hello. My name's Diane. Feeling okay? Any pain? It's almost time for another dose of medication." Amidst all the suffering, she smiled and waited for Paul's response.

"Hey, hi, I mean hello, Diane. My name's Paul. Waiting for my friend, Sam Sutton. Doc said they would bring him out soon. Ya know if his hand's okay?" He hoped Diane might have more information about Sam's condition, but she politely excused herself as she rushed to meet two medics entering with Sam, still groggy on a stretcher. They inched closer to Paul and the empty cot next to his. Diane's gentle hand guided the men as they lifted Sam from the stretcher to make his transition to his bed as comfortable as possible.

Paul gasped aloud. He couldn't help it. There was no way to silence the sound that rose from his throat when he saw his friend beside him, his right hand thick with bandages, wrapped as if to protect something that was no longer there. Paul slowly brought his hands to his face and felt the layers of soft bandages, only his eyes, nose, and mouth exposed. His head pulsated and his face felt tight and swollen. With crystal clarity, his mind flashed back to the instant when his life, when Sam's life, were forever changed. His body tensed with the memory—the sounds, the heat, the explosions, the cries for help, and the smell of death all around them. He choked back tears and resolved to remain stoic and grateful that his wounds would soon be invisible. Unlike Sam, he had escaped a lifetime of disfigurement and the constant reminder of his brush with death.

Diane hovered over Sam as he stirred. She had played this part too many times. She knew he would need a voice of reassurance when he realized where he was and the severity of his injuries. Sam's eyelids fluttered. He tried to focus on his surroundings and take in the stench and musty smell of the tent, lined from one end to the other with broken bodies. The odor of blood, humidity, and soiled linens stuck to the canvas walls of the makeshift hospital like glue, and he swallowed hard to prevent the nausea from taking hold of his body. Sam rolled his head to one side and looked at Paul, who was composed, determined, and calm.

"You made it, buddy. We made it," whispered Paul.

Sam hardly recognized his friend, his head and face almost totally covered, but his blue eyes were unmistakable. He knew it was Paul. He glanced back at his own bandaged hand and knew. He had felt his hand being ripped from his body on the battlefield. His last memory in the helicopter was blood spilling from the catastrophic wound that had already severed his limb, though he had prayed it could be miraculously saved.

"Yeah, we did. Lucky us." Sam turned to Diane and drew a deep breath. He was stunned, visibly upset. "What now?"

"You've done your job, now it's time for me to do mine. I'm not going to sugarcoat this. It'll be hard. You'll be fitted with a temporary prosthetic hook before you land stateside, and it'll take months of rehabilitation to learn how to use it properly."

Sam closed his eyes and continued to speak. "I'm alive. I know that's all that matters. If you say it'll get better, I have no choice but to believe you."

Diane patted his shoulder, little comfort compared to the cruelty of Sam's injury and the emotional blow he had just been dealt. "I'll be back tomorrow, and the next day, and the day after that. I'll be close by until you get your orders to leave this place. You boys rest."

Sam opened his eyes just long enough to watch her melt into the sea of wounded men, a new group of damaged soldiers in need of her attention. "Hey Paul, you know her name?"

"Yeah… Diane. Her name's Diane."

Fourteen days in the field hospital was almost more than Sam and Paul could endure. Along with everyone else in the ward, they received Purple Hearts from a stony-faced commander as he moved from bed to bed, followed by a military photographer, who captured the unsmiling face of every man in one snap of a shutter and flash of light. It made little difference if a head was wrapped in bandages, an arm was in a cast, or a limb was missing. He strolled by each soldier, one at a time, propped the black leather box on his chest to show the medal, shook each hand, and moved on to the next in line. Paul and Sam buried the six-by-three-inch black leather boxes with the snap hinge at the top and the words "Purple Heart" emblazoned in gold letters, deep inside their duffle bags.

"I think it's time for you boys to go home. You've earned your Purple Hearts; you can leave Vietnam forever. We've done everything we can for you here. Get the hell out of this horrible place and go back to your families." Dr. Shapiro stood up and saluted the men, then added, "And it's a little out of protocol, but I'm going to see if I can get you on the same plane back home, which will make the trip a little longer for you, Paul, but I think it would be good medicine for you to fly back to the States together."

Paul and Sam liked Dr. Shapiro. He was a straight shooter and sincere. He had no glossy diagnoses, treated everyone the same, and worked into the night to see that every man brought into the field hospital had the best possible chance of survival. Everyone he encountered was treated with respect and dignity, and he never left the bedside of an ailing marine without a kind word and a salute.

I think this will be my only fond memory of this shitty hellhole, thought Sam, extending his left hand to Dr. Shapiro for one last handshake. As the men watched him file past the rows of wounded comrades, Sam turned to Paul to ask, "How long those Christmas lights been up?"

"I hadn't noticed until you said something."

Strings of red and green lights flickered around the perimeter of the ward. In between choppers young nurses, determined to celebrate under the worst of circumstances, attempted to bring a little comfort and joy to the wounded and dying, even though it might go unnoticed by the men in their care. It was still Christmas, an unforgettable Christmas. Paul and Sam rolled over in their cots, too weary to think about it or care.

Chapter 9

NOVEMBER TURNED THE CORNER TO DECEMBER AND the long-anticipated letter from Sam was waiting for Elizabeth when she got home from school. Nana placed the envelope on the front entrance table for Elizabeth to see the moment she walked through the door. She didn't need to look twice at the letter propped up against the candy dish Nana always kept filled with Good 'n Plentys, Sugar Babies, or Boston Beans.

"Finally!" Elizabeth exclaimed as she got a fresh cookie from the kitchen that she knew would be waiting, whether she wanted it or not, and sat next to the Christmas tree Nana insisted on decorating the night before. The last thing she wanted to do was celebrate Christmas without her parents, but she was glad there was a semblance of holiday cheer in Nana's house.

Elizabeth read the postal date stamp: November 18, 1965. Sam must have written after he got to his base camp, just as he promised. She also noted the day it had been written and knew he hadn't seen the picture she sent before Thanksgiving. She would have to get used to long delays and letters crossing in the mail. For now, she savored the moment.

November 16, 1965

Dear Elizabeth,

How are you doing now that winter is almost here? Remember how angry you used to get in the summer when your skin would stick to the chairs, and you'd have to wait for the sun to go down for a little relief? What I wouldn't do now for those warm, sticky summers in Boston! Even though it's November, the weather never seems to change, as humid as it is hot. It doesn't cool down, even at night, and the monsoons are the worst. It rains sideways with such force, it takes a lot of effort to stay dry, and you know you'll get soaked in the middle of the night if you need to go outside to use the bathroom.

All the guys sleep in their shorts and in the mornings we have to struggle to get on our wet fatigues. Nothing ever has time to dry. Boots don't last very long, rotting off our feet, especially if we have to trudge through the swamps, trying to avoid getting those blood sucking leeches from attaching themselves to our skin. They're huge reddish black, slimy bastards, and even the toughest of us get creeped out as soon as we see or feel one climbing up our pant leg. They have no shame, they pick any spot on your body, and God help you if you have more than one clinging to your flesh. If the water is high, we have to hold our rifles over our heads, so they don't get wet, and that means there's more body parts to choose from. No one in my battalion has gone untouched, and we can either burn them off with a cigarette or spray them with insect repellant. Watching them curl up and die is our only satisfaction.

We're also issued a couple 4 ounce plastic bottles of something we call bug juice, for the mosquitoes, and we get more on every resupply chopper. Can't live without it in the jungle. What I'm trying to say is, appreciate home, sticky summers and all. They keep telling us that's what we're fighting for.

It's been quiet around here the past few days, but I'm sure I'll have more to write about next time. I'll miss you all this Thanksgiving and Christmas, but I'm told we'll get something different than the boiled meat and powdered eggs we've become accustomed to. No one's sure where the meat comes from around here, but if I get a piece of pumpkin pie and a little stuffing this holiday season, it will be the highlight of my tour. No sugar for coffee either. Had to learn to drink it black. I miss the sugar and milk, and what I wouldn't do for a 6-pack of ice-cold beer!

Well, gotta go for now. I'll write before Christmas, and I can't wait to start getting letters from you and everyone back home. Remember, don't believe everything you see on TV, read in the newspapers, or hear on the radio. Give my love to Nana, and the twins. Over and out.

Always your Older Brother,

Sam

Chapter 10

"Do you think Sam's all right? I mean, I keep seeing news about fighting right where Sam is, and I haven't gotten a letter from him since that one before Thanksgiving. Why won't he write?"

Nana laid a reassuring hand on her granddaughter's shoulder. "I'm sure he's just fine, dear. Remember, he always tells you at the end of every letter, don't believe everything you hear on the radio, read in the paper, or see on TV. Good advice."

The family nestled into the comfortable surroundings of Nana's home, every corner decorated with tender memories of holidays past. Christmas morning was a whirlwind of commotion. Laura, Tina, and Ricky dashed down the stairs before dawn in a foot race to be the first one to find the heap of presents waiting beneath the tree, and the racket made it hard for the rest of the household to sleep much past five o'clock.

Nana brewed a large pot of coffee for the grownups, asking Elizabeth if she would like a cup. Elizabeth willingly obliged, using one of the festive holiday mugs Nana kept on the kitchen counter the entire month of December. Her favorite, a bulbous likeness of Santa Claus, held just the right amount with ample room for cream and sugar. She didn't think she was quite ready to take her coffee black. Even Sam didn't like his coffee black, but she supposed he was getting used to it. *Cream and sugar are probably the least of his worries;* she thought as she settled in with the rest of the family to enjoy the best part of Christmas morning—opening presents.

Although this year was leaner than years past, there were still plenty of gifts to unwrap. No one was forgotten.

"Tina, would you mind handing me that package by the console? The big one with the gold stripes and red bow? I think that might be one for Elizabeth." Nana knew that it was her gift to her eldest granddaughter. She watched as Elizabeth tore at the wrapping paper, every bit as eager as her younger sisters.

"How did you know? I never said anything!" Elizabeth almost knocked her coffee off the wobbly TV tray when she jumped up and ran straight to Nana, throwing the mangled wrapping paper to one side and clutching a brand-new navy-blue car coat under her arm. She managed to lean over and squeeze Nana tightly, amidst the new toys, discarded ribbons and gifts strewn throughout the living room, but her huge grin was all Nana needed to see. "This is perfect Nana. It's what everyone's wearing! Toggle buttons all the way up the front and look: the hood is removable! I can wear this coat in almost any weather."

"Are you happy?" Nana gazed at her whole family, directing her question to no one in particular.

Uncle Bill looked at Nana. "Are you happy, Mom?"

"Yes. I believe I am. At this moment, I'm very happy. A little tired now that the hubbub has simmered down, but I'm happy."

Christmas day melted into Christmas night and Sam was on everyone's mind. Though it remained unspoken, they were aware that no one had received a Christmas card or a letter. It wasn't like Sam to not communicate on the holidays.

The TV was humming in the living room, news reports about an acceleration in combat were being repeated over and over, and pictures not meant for children to see were flashing across the screen.

"It's Christmas. It was a lovely day. Look, the snow is starting to fall." Aunt Deborah pulled the curtains apart in the living room so everyone could see the snowfall, awash with color from the Christmas lights illuminating the neighborhood.

"Think of how nice it is just to be together." Sweet Aunt Deborah, she was always trying to make everyone feel better, pretending the situation wasn't grave. But Elizabeth knew better, knew her Aunt, and had to thank her at least for trying.

After putting the three younger children to bed in the spare upstairs bedroom, Uncle Bill, Aunt Deborah, Elizabeth, and Nana sank into the overstuffed living room furniture and surveyed the emptiness. Snow accumulated on the cold ground, and ice crystals formed on the frozen window panes. Inside the family was toasty and warm, protected from the chill of night, but Elizabeth wanted it to be late enough for her to fall asleep. She wanted this day behind her. In spite of everyone's efforts to stay in good spirits, in particular for the twins and Ricky, the thought of her absent parents and the uncertainty of Sam's whereabouts still consumed her every thought.

A knock on the door, out of place for the neighborhood this late on Christmas night, startled them all. Uncle Bill approached the door and peered out the window. His heart sank when he saw an official military car parked at the curb. Two men in uniform stood on the front porch and knocked again. He trembled as he opened the door, unable to say a word. Nana, Elizabeth, and Aunt Deborah rushed to his side.

The older officer asked if he could come in and speak with them. Escorting them inside, Uncle Bill took them to the living room, offered them a seat, and started the conversation. "May we please ask what this visit is about?"

Unflinching and without expression, the officer gave no hint as to the message he had been directed to convey. He looked at Elizabeth and Nana, and asked, "Are you the sister and grandmother of Sam Sutton?"

Motionless, holding hands, they whispered, "Yes." His broad chest was resplendent with perfectly aligned ribbons, patches, and medals. Elizabeth's eyes were fixated on this array of power as she prepared for the awful words she knew would follow.

Nana cleared her voice and spoke. "Is Sam okay? " Her voice was strong and composed. She didn't want to ask if he had died—too horrible a thought to consider, even though every article she had read explained how a military car, dispatched with two officers, would come to your door if your son, father, or husband had been killed in action. She was waiting for an answer from these two very polite gentlemen who stood before her with devastating news, she was sure.

"Ma'am, I want you to know Sam has not died in action. He is the only son of Mr. and Mrs. Sutton, who we understand are deceased. When this is the case, it is military policy to inform the family in person of severe injury or wounds. Sam was in combat just outside of Chu Lai, and was injured in a firefight. From there he was helicoptered to a field hospital in Da Nang where he underwent emergency surgery." The officer paced himself and took a deep breath. He hated the duty he had been assigned, especially during this time of year. "The doctors had to remove his right hand due to the severity of the wound, and because gangrene had set in almost immediately. I am so sorry to have to tell you this on Christmas night."

Elizabeth remained still as she silently processed the shocking words she had just heard. She feel light-headed, as though she might faint, but purposefully fixed her eyes on her grandmother, a tower of strength even in these tragic circumstances. Instead of tears, a broad smile swept across Elizabeth's face. Knowing that her big brother was alive and that she would see him again was all that mattered to her.

Nana's composed demeanor veiled her breaking heart, but she managed to stay brave in a situation that was about to send shockwaves through the family once again. She brushed past her son who was preparing to coax additional information from the men. With one arm wrapped around his tearful wife, Uncle Bill was surprised to see his mother step forward and shoulder the responsibility.

"I can handle this, Bill. I've had a lot of practice." Nana's tone was gentle, but Uncle Bill never knew his mother to back down or falter in an emergency. He stepped aside and accepted her determination to take charge in the wake of misfortune, just as she had done so many times before. Elizabeth shadowed her grandmother, and Nana cautiously proceeded with the questions that were most urgent in her mind.

In hushed voices, the officers discussed the protocol, the phone calls that would follow, and Sam's expected arrival from overseas. "I see, yes, I understand. That sounds fine," was all Uncle Bill and Aunt Deborah could overhear from the brief exchange. "Four weeks? We'll be ready. Yes, I understand he'll need a lot of rehabilitation stateside." Bill saw his mother nodding as she escorted the officers to the front door with Elizabeth close behind. "Thank you, officers. You've been very kind."

"No need to come outside, ma'am; it's too cold." Nana followed them outside, ignoring their cautious suggestion. She couldn't help but notice how incongruous the porch decorations of festive colored lights and oversized plastic angels were in light of the painful news they'd just received.

Nana directed her gaze from one officer to the other, bidding each a happy Christmas as she continued to absorb the impact of their conversation.

"Merry Christmas, ma'am." The officers returned the sentiment to Nana, followed by another "Merry Christmas," as they nodded their heads towards the open door and delivered a solemn salute to the family.

Chapter 11

ELIZABETH BALANCED ON THE LADDER AND TOOK THE last box of ornaments from Nana's hands. They had become quite a team over the past few months and they wanted the house to sparkle by the time Sam got home. "I'll get the rest of it, Nana. Don't worry. All I have left to do is sweep the fallen needles out of the carpet. Not sure if the sweeper will do the whole job, may have to take the whole rug outside for a good shake, but at least it's not snowing. I'll drag what's left of the tree to the incinerator too. Why don't you go lay down?"

"I could use a little nap. It has been a hectic week. Getting ready for Sam, cleaning the house, putting the Christmas decorations back in the attic. Thank you, dear. I'll be down in an hour or so."

Elizabeth was ready for a few moments to herself, and after finishing the remainder of her tasks, she eyed the overstuffed chair in the corner and the welcome warmth of the fire. *I see hot chocolate in my future,* she mused, but before she could retrieve the saucepan from the cupboard, she heard a slight tap on the door. She met the mailman as he was preparing to knock again.

"Hello, Elizabeth. A little bit bigger envelope than normal. I couldn't push it through the mail slot. Thought I'd hand it to you personally."

"Thanks a lot, Mr. Holmes. You have a nice afternoon."

"You too, young lady."

She clutched the larger manila envelope and scrutinized the return post. She neither recognized the sender or the handwriting. *Dr. Leonard Shapiro, Da Nang Field Hospital, Vietnam.* She got comfortable before she opened the package. Inside was a short note held by a rubber band around two more letters.

December 23, 1965

Dear Elizabeth,

I will be brief. My name is Dr. Leonard Shapiro, and I'm a doctor in the field hospital in Da Nang. By now you've probably been informed of your brother's injuries, but he's a strong young man and there's no reason why he can't live an entirely useful and normal life with the use of his prosthetic hand.

When he was brought into the hospital, this letter was in his breast pocket. With his permission, I have bundled it with another letter written after his surgery, dictated to a nurse who regularly assists the soldiers who have suffered this type of wound. Please know how sorry I am for this life-changing occurrence for Sam, as well as the rest of his family. Find joy in one another.

Best Regards,

Dr. Leonard Shapiro

Elizabeth shivered, even though the fire was blazing and the flames were burning dazzling shades of purple, red, and yellow. She reached for her pink afghan and wrapped up inside the silky threads before she opened Sam's first letter.

December 8, 1965

Dear Elizabeth,

Boy, have you changed! I leave you alone for a few months, and you grow up! That was a great picture, and it sure is nice to see a friendly face from home, even if it is a sister. No... just kidding, honest. I showed my friend Paul, and even though he's too quiet and polite to say anything out loud, he sure did have a big smile on his face! I don't think he's gotten any letters since we arrived. There were a few that came from his buddies in Los Angeles when we were at Pendleton, but nothing since then. He likes hearing about our family because I don't think he has much of his own. He sure is enjoying the Sunday radio broadcasts from Saigon though. He's the first one to the mess hall and stays until the sign-off. He's a nut for the Rolling Stones and the Beach Boys— says they remind him of surfing with his buddies. He knows the background of every singer that ever held a microphone. The guy likes his music, that's for sure. I think it helps all of us take our minds off being here.

I hope you and the family had a great Thanksgiving. The holidays have never been this hard for you and everyone else too, I know. I keep thinking of the white Christmases we shared, and shoveling snow is nothing compared to the continuous rain in Chu Lai. I guess if you're born here, you'd get used to it. I know I never will.

It's been pretty hard to sleep because of the heat and noise in the distance from mortar fire and bombings. Helicopters always seem to hover nearby, but they have to be prepared to take any wounded to the field hospitals as soon as they can. If they can get soldiers off the ground and into the capable hands of medics and nurses, there's a much better chance they'll survive. So many kids, Elizabeth. Sometimes—no all the time—I wonder why we're even here.

We take shifts when we go out on patrol, and the jungle is dark like you've never seen. I've heard of friendly fire casualties in the Valley. That's our guys, accidentally mistaking one of our troops for the enemy, and firing right into the midst of them, only to find out they killed or wounded one of their own. It hasn't happened with us, don't worry, and so far, the only fighting I've seen is some skirmishes in our hooches (they're like huge tents), after some of these boys have had too much to drink when they're off duty.

No matter what, have a great Christmas. I'll miss all of you, and promise to write again next week. It will probably be more of the same, not much to report, but writing keeps my mind sharp. If only my professors could see me now! It's too late tonight to take this letter to the supply sergeant, but I'll mail it right after breakfast. Be good, and remember, don't believe everything you see on TV, read in the newspapers, or hear on the radio. Give my love to Nana and the twins. Over, and out.

Always Your Older Brother,

Sam

Elizabeth took a deep breath and tried to imagine her brother writing this letter with his right hand, no inkling of what was lurking in his unscripted future. It made her sad to feel his mood of self-assurance and no sense of imminent doom. She returned the pages to the envelope and reached for the last one, bound to be equally as heartbreaking.

December 24, 1965

Dear Elizabeth,

It's Christmas Eve, and I don't have to tell you what you must already know. How pathetic am I? Can't hold a pen, have to rely on a nurse to write for me. Although I'm not good company for anyone, she is very kind to let me dictate this letter to her. I suppose I should try to say something heartwarming or festive, being that Christmas is tomorrow and everything, but I just wish I could fall asleep and never wake up. I'm in constant pain and I have no idea how I'm going to learn to live without my right hand. I am dreading my future, but maybe in a few weeks I'll feel differently and be a bit more positive. I'm told that's what will happen. We'll see.

My buddy, Paul, was also wounded, but the swelling in his face has already started to go down and his stitches will be out by the time we get home. Dr. Shapiro said he still has some pieces of shrapnel embedded in his skull, but they're too close to vital arteries to remove. We haven't talked much since they helicoptered us in, but his cot is right next to mine. I guess getting wounded is the only way to get a one-way ticket home and exit this dreadful place.

You might not get this letter until after the holidays, but tell everyone I'm thinking of them, and can't wait to be home. Don't believe everything you see on TV, read in the newspapers, or hear on the radio. Give my love to Nana and the twins. Over, and out.

Always Your Older Brother,

Sam

A postscript followed Sam's letter, and Elizabeth shifted in her chair to get comfortable as she continued reading.

> *P.S. My name is Diane Wilson, and I'm a member of the Military Nurse Corp on assignment in this field hospital. I know this is a very rough time for your brother and the rest of your family. There are lots of adjustments you will need to make, but he is coming home, and even he is aware of how fortunate he is. He seems like a nice guy with a very bright future. I wish you a peaceful New Year, and many warm memories throughout your lives. Take good care of each other.*

Elizabeth felt drained, but couldn't help feeling optimistic about her brother's homecoming. All she knew was he would be here in three weeks and she was prepared. She watched Nana navigate the stairs, looking more rested than when she retreated for her short nap. "Everything okay, child? You look toasty and warm."

Elizabeth tucked the letters back in the large envelope and clutched them to her chest. "Yes, Nana. I've had a good rest. I'll help you set the table."

Chapter 12

REMINDERS WENT OFF IN ELIZABETH'S HEAD EVERY hour like an alarm clock. The one she painstakingly set for 6:00 AM and placed on her bedside table inched slowly towards dawn. But still, her restless mind prevented her from sleeping through the night. She wanted to have plenty of time to shower, dress, help the twins, and prepare breakfast, even though Nana said no one would be hungry at such an early hour. "I've never seen a youngster worry quite as much as you do, dear. We'll bring snacks. Everyone will be fine."

Uncle Bill's family wagon only had enough seats for six, and it would be crowded once they picked up Sam from the airport. "Where are we supposed to sit?" Ricky complained. "There isn't going to be enough room. We'll be squished!"

His mother had convinced him there was plenty of extra space in the back behind the seats, and he and the twins would simply have to do the best they could. "It's not the most comfortable situation, I agree, but we'll do whatever we need to do to make it work." For all her ladylike demeanor under most circumstances, Aunt Deborah was firm and unyielding, and even Nana took notice. "I'll not put up with any whining or complaining on a day like today. Sam needs to come home to a happy family and we'll do our part to make sure that's exactly what happens." She winked at Nana, but she had never been more serious.

The knot in Elizabeth's stomach grew tighter as daylight approached and she finally gave in and slammed down the button on her Big Ben alarm clock. She rolled out of bed, and whether it was nerves or too little sleep, she was already agitated. Her hair was wild and in complete disarray, and she hardly recognized herself when she caught her reflection in the mirror. "Why today?" she grumbled aloud. "What am I going to do with this mess? Not the day to look like I haven't slept in weeks, even though it's true."

Elizabeth sat on the edge of her bed and gingerly drew a hairbrush through her tangled curls. As the spirals relaxed, she did the same. She drew two side tendrils of the shiny tresses away from her face and gathered them softly in the back of her head with a rubber band. She reached for the wide white-satin ribbon that had so lovingly secured her sixteenth birthday gift and tied it loosely around her pulled back hair. Cautiously, Elizabeth applied a hint of rose blush to her delicate, creamy cheekbones and a little cherry-colored lipstick to her full, innocent mouth. "You have no idea how beautiful you are, child," Nana once told her. Elizabeth heeded her advice that "less is more" when it came to wearing makeup.

"I think I see him!" Elizabeth teetered on tip-toes. "I'm not sure. So many guys in uniform." The whole family waited to get their first glimpse of Sam. As they watched dozens of passengers exit the gate and stream past them, Elizabeth chewed her lower lip, nervous and worried.

Laura and Tina struggled to position themselves in front of the crowd, scrambling to be the first to notice their brother. "I got here first! Don't push!" The twins shrieked.

"Settle down, you two. Sam's not going to walk off the plane any faster just because you guys are pushing and shoving." The twins continued to jostle Elizabeth as she struggled to maintain her balance. She had to remind herself this was not the time to get irritated with them. She bit down hard on her lip. The crowded airplane seemed to disembark at a snail's pace, but she was sure she spotted her brother bringing up the end of the line.

Gaunt and thin, but shoulders back and standing tall, Sam scanned the crowd for a familiar face. The end of his sleeve dangled empty just below his wrist where a two-pronged hook emerged, clearly visible. His thoughts raced... *Everyone's looking at me... I can feel it... they think I'm a freak.* He was sure every person he passed was staring at the cold, lifeless piece of hardware. A clumsy, repellant appendage that was a poor substitute for a hand, and a bitter reminder of the consequences of his decision to join the Marines. *I can't even shake hands like a man. I made the wrong choice... I should never have left the girls... Left Boston... Left school...* Sam looked straight ahead and, as he caught sight of his family coming into full view, his thoughts were unexpectedly disrupted, and he broke into a warm, grateful smile.

Elizabeth couldn't wait a moment longer and burst through the crowd of passengers. Sam saw her running towards him with open arms and braced for the bear hug to follow, as he didn't want to get knocked over by his sister's enthusiastic greeting. Neither spoke at first, but after Elizabeth had loosened her grip, she looked up and said, "I'm glad you're home, Sam. We missed you so much."

"Thanks, sophomore. I missed all of you too."

Paul watched as his friend embraced his family, cheering, laughing, crying, as they greeted him in the narrow hallway of the airport. He felt awkward and out of place. This was Sam's homecoming, not his, and he stepped aside to avoid the commotion. Ricky and the twins clamored for Sam's attention and Uncle Bill and Aunt Deborah waited patiently for their turn. Nana could hardly move, relieved, overjoyed, and thrilled to finally touch her grandson, but inwardly devastated as she averted her eyes from his right hand.

Sam embraced each one in turn before noticing Paul standing off to one side. He motioned to his friend to join them.

"You okay, buddy?"

Paul shifted nervously, feeling uncomfortable and out of place. "Always. It's good to be home."

"We'll stay in touch. Thanks for the surfing lesson." A slight smile crept across Sam's face at the recollection.

"Anytime, m—"

"Flight thirty-six forty-five to Los Angeles is now boarding at gate sixty-five." The announcement for Paul's connecting flight blared through the terminal.

"Gotta go. That's my flight." Paul slung his duffle bag over one shoulder and turned to leave.

"Wait, hold on. I want you to meet my family before you go, especially my little sister, Elizabeth." Sam noted that she didn't look so little anymore. At sixteen she was beginning to fill out, wear the slightest amount of makeup, and appear more grown up than she had when he left for boot camp. As cute as she looked in the picture, it didn't do her justice.

"I've heard nothing but good things about you, Elizabeth. Your brother talked about you and his family all the time. I feel like I know you already." Paul was trying to be polite and not say anything offensive. Inside his heart was melting. He had never seen a girl this beautiful—long auburn hair touching her shoulders with the slightest curl at the end, the greenest eyes he had ever seen, skin the color of fine porcelain, and, as he had to remind himself, only sixteen years old.

"I've heard so much about you too, Paul." Elizabeth leaned in to give him a hug, genuine, heartfelt, and happy that he was going home to his family who must be waiting for him in Los Angeles. "I hope you can make it back here some day, maybe in the spring when it's a little warmer. There's an awful lot to see and do around Boston, and I know Sam would love to give you the grand tour."

As wonderful as that sounded, Paul knew he might never return and perhaps he and Sam would never see each other again. He took one long look at Elizabeth so he would never forget the angelic face that greeted him, or the smile that warmed his heart his first moments back on American soil. Paul started for his gate and, unable to resist the temptation, stole one more backward glance. Elizabeth managed another smile and a shy wave in his direction. Once he disappeared from view, the reunited Sutton family gathered around Sam, and headed to the parking lot, ready to take him to the warm comfort of home.

After takeoff, Paul closed his eyes, etching the memory with Sam and his family in his mind forever. It would be so sweet, compared to the real homecoming that awaited him: a drunk for a father, melancholy memories of a mother taken too soon, no brothers or sisters, and emptiness all around. He would walk through the door like he had never even been gone, like he had merely stepped out for a drink with his buddies, a night of dancing, or a day at work. That would be his homecoming. No fanfare, no one rushing towards him with open arms. He would find his father passed out on the turquoise Naugahyde living-room couch, like always. He wasn't looking forward to any of it, but with a wave of relief, felt safe to be back in the USA, with the freedom to stroll down the boulevard, straight to the nearest hamburger stand and order a burger, Coke, and fries.

Paul waited for the rest of the passengers to disembark, the last one out of his seat. He swallowed two more aspirin without water, picked up his worn, tattered duffle bag, and sucked up the courage to walk the aisle into the large Los Angeles International Airport. Even though the hour was late, it was still alive with passengers, packed departure gates, bright lights, and crackling intercom announcements. *Maybe someone's looking for me.* He couldn't make out the muffled voice on the PA system, catching every other word, but still hoped he would hear his name being paged to the nearest telephone. Praying to see someone he recognized, Paul trained his eyes on every face and saw nothing but a sea of strangers. No one was rushing towards him with a warm hug or open smile, no one to shake his hand, no one to make his long journey home worth a damn. At least on this night there were no protestors, no one screaming at him, or spitting in his face. For that, he was grateful.

As he made his way down to the baggage claim and taxi area, he fought off the searing pain in his head, took deep breaths as he had been instructed, and stepped into the closest taxi lined up curbside. "Please take me to eight zero one Hoover Street, Reseda." It was all Paul had the strength to say, as he lay his head back on the old, smelly seat of the cab and fell asleep.

Chapter 13

SAM FELT LIKE A FREAK. HE KNEW HE WAS A FREAK. Everywhere he went, people stared and he was aware that they were uncomfortable. Children could be blunt, but at least they were honest. They would blurt out something like, "Where's your real hand," or "That must hurt." They tended to be curious or sensitive, but most grown-ups remained mute. After three months, instead of settling in and becoming comfortable in the family home, Sam still kept long hours into the night. The light in his room only dimmed as the rest of the household greeted a new day. Elizabeth let herself believe it was probably a matter of getting used to the time change and everything would return to normal soon.

Sam and Nana were talking at the kitchen table when Elizabeth came home from school. "Pour a glass of milk. I baked fresh cookies too, Sam's favorite." Nana was doing her best, but she had no idea how to deal with a severely injured grandson. All she knew was it would take time. It was far too soon to expect great change, so she let Sam set the pace.

Elizabeth put her books on the side counter and welcomed the invitation. She searched Sam's face for a clue of how he might be feeling and thought she discerned a little more color in his face, the tension beginning to release its grip.

"Learn anything today?" asked Nana.

"Well, probably my most valuable lesson was learning that even if the sun is shining, it doesn't mean it will be warm. And if it's March on the East Coast, you better be prepared with a heavy jacket and mittens. I'm so tired of this wicked cold."

Sam and Nana chuckled. "You wouldn't complain if you had just spent nine months in a jungle climate, ninety-five degrees, and ninety-five percent humidity almost every day. And the monsoons. I can't even put into words just how awful that experience was. I'll never complain about the weather again." Elizabeth knew there was a lesson in this and felt put in her place, but happy Sam had become part of the conversation, at last.

"I'm going to leave the two of you to carry on without me while I take a short nap. I haven't been feeling well lately, but I'll be back down in a couple of hours to cook dinner."

"Don't worry about dinner, Nana. Sam and I can take care of it. We'll come and get you when it's ready."

"That would be lovely, dear. I defrosted the hamburger and was going to make spaghetti and meatballs. Salad fixin's are in the refrigerator, and I picked up a fresh loaf of French bread at the bakery this morning. You two have fun."

"Oh, it's good to be home." Sam seemed pleased the responsibilities of war, the effort needed just to stay alive, was really in the past. He raised his long, thin body from the kitchen chair, as if he would be leaving, but instead got a glass of milk and another handful of peanut butter cookies to see him through until dinner.

"I love seeing you eat," Nana murmured as she got up from her chair. "You need to put some meat back on those bones."

"That won't be hard to do with your cooking, Nana. Elizabeth's cooking, not so sure, but I guess we'll find out tonight." A hint of a smile crept across Sam's face as he hugged his Nana. "Go rest. We have it under control."

Elizabeth stood too, hugging her Nana, squeezing her shoulders, and realized she was taller than her grandmother. She wasn't sure if Nana had shrunk, or if she had grown.

"You heard him, Nana. We have it under control. We'll make dinner and wake you at six o'clock, sharp." Glancing at the clock, she saw it was almost four. Plenty of time to prepare dinner and allow Nana a much-deserved afternoon nap.

"Do you need any help?" Elizabeth offered her hand, but Nana hugged them and went upstairs on her own.

"I don't have a lot of homework tonight. Feel like playing cards or something before we start dinner?"

Sam feigned amusement. "Really, one handed?"

"I don't see why not. You could probably play with one hand, but you won't know unless you try."

The card deck was slippery and they had to remind themselves how to play Gin Rummy. Elizabeth glanced down at her brother's right wrist where his hand should be, hoping he wouldn't think she was staring. "Does it hurt?"

"Not so much any more. Getting used to it and just a bit of phantom pain. Therapy in Da Nang and here is helping a lot.

Elizabeth changed the subject. "I'll deal."

"No, give me the deck. I'll deal." Sam took the fresh, shiny stack of cards from her and she eyed him with concern.

"You look determined. It's all yours."

"So, how many cards are dealt in this game? Remember?"

"I think ten, but you have to shuffle first."

Sam split the deck in half and, using his left thumb and the awkward hook that took the place of his right hand, held the cards by the edge. *This should be easy*, he thought, as he attempted to weave the cards together and bend the pack to create the uplifting effect of the first shuffle. He felt clumsy and childish. The cards got tangled between his hand and hook and flew from his hands, landing on the floor, chairs, and table in an unceremonious mess.

"Fuck!" Sam pushed his chair back in disgust, attempting to retrieve the fifty-two cards spread throughout the kitchen.

"What did you say? I've never heard you use that word before." No one in their family swore, at least not in her presence.

"Well, maybe it felt like the right time to say it. Fuck, fuck, fucking cards, fucking hand, fuck! There, that felt good. I'm done."

Elizabeth could feel the color rise to her face. "If I ever said that, I'd be grounded for a week."

"Then don't say it. Don't be such a prude, Elizabeth. That was common vocabulary in Vietnam. That, and worse. Damn, hell, shit, crap, motherfucker, asshole, son-of-a-bitch, bastard, slant eye, gook." Elizabeth turned a darker shade of red as she listened to her brother's sudden tirade.

"You get the picture. I'll try to be more careful from now on. Why don't you get those meatballs going while I practice shuffling cards? We should have time for a hand before we call Nana for dinner."

Even though she hated to admit it, Elizabeth was relieved. It was painful to watch her brother do the simplest of tasks, but watching his anger burst forth seemed far healthier than keeping it bottled up inside. *Better this way*, she thought, as she got the dinner ingredients from the fridge and started cooking. Once she put the spaghetti sauce on a low flame to simmer, Elizabeth sat down with Sam and marveled at his tenacity and his attempt to adapt to this difficult task. Eventually he mastered the challenge and shuffled like a pro—fluid, smooth, and effortless.

After they had cleared away the cards, Sam helped set the table, while Elizabeth tended to the last-minute dinner preparations. "You can still tell Nana it was a 'we' effort. I set the table."

"Damn, that looks good, Elizabeth. I'll go get Nana. Be right down."

Sam was gone a long time, and when he walked back into the kitchen without Nana, his face was ashen. "Sam, what's wrong?" She started to tremble.

"It's Nana. I couldn't wake her. She passed in her sleep." Sam's voice was so quiet, it was almost inaudible, but Elizabeth didn't need to ask again. She heard, she knew, and she felt sick to her stomach. Sam reached for the phone and dialed their uncle. Everything else could wait.

Chapter 14

"A CHANGE OF SCENERY. THAT'S WHAT I NEED."
Elizabeth talked to herself as she finished the last page of the essay
for her English Lit class. It was assigned weeks earlier, but school
felt meaningless to her. She was finding it harder and harder to
concentrate. Nana's sudden stroke stunned everyone, and even
though the doctor told them she had passed peacefully and there
was nothing they could have done, it didn't lessen the pain.

From down the hall, Sam interrupted her thoughts. "Elizabeth,
got a minute?"

Elizabeth called back from her room, cluttered with research
books and manuals, colored pencils, and ballpoint pens. She was
oversensitive lately and didn't feel like talking. "Can it wait until
tomorrow? I just want to get this darn paper written, which I am
sure is only 'C' work, but at this point, I could care less."

"Just want to ask your opinion on something. It'll only take
a minute."

"Then you come into my room. I don't want to get up."

Back and forth, they shouted responses. Sam appeared at her
door, poked his head in, and without invitation, sat down on the edge
of her bed, pushing back a stack of clean laundry. He planted his feet
on the ground. "Elizabeth, I have to get out of here. I'm suffocating."

"So, go take a walk... I'm not stopping you."

Elizabeth noticed a slight smile emerge from her brother's usually stern countenance. "No. That's not what I'm talking about. I mean I have to get out of this city, out of Boston. Anywhere but here. I've been thinking about California."

Elizabeth put her pen down and turned to Sam.

"Remember Paul? He was the one on the plane with me the day I returned from Vietnam. I wrote him a letter after Nana died and he suggested I move to California. What I was wondering though, is if you would like to go with me?" He was silent, hoping to see Elizabeth smile, an expression he had only seen a few times in the last year.

"Well, funny you should mention it because I'm not looking forward to another hot Boston summer. And with Aunt Deborah and Uncle Bill outgrowing the cottage on Nantucket, it could be perfect timing for them to pick up and move to this house. They always said they wanted Ricky and the twins to go to Boston schools. I can't believe you're asking me to go with you! I don't even care where we end up, but who wouldn't want to move to California?"

Sam tried to dampen her enthusiasm just a bit. "You still have one more year of high school and I'm not even sure where we'd live." He knew Paul would help him navigate the city and act as a tour guide as well as a friend, but there were plans and adjustments that would need to be made. Calmly, he looked at his sister. "Pace yourself… slow down a bit. We need to get you through your junior year first. Not sure yet where we're gonna live. Paul has offered, maybe somewhere else. Still a lot to do."

Elizabeth jumped from her seat, rushed to her brother, and hugged him for the first time since his homecoming from Vietnam. "I'm just so happy. I'll live anywhere; I'll go to any school. I don't care. I'm done here!" She continued to prattle, animated and energized, but stopped to take a breath as reality cast a shadow over her excitement. She blurted, "But what about Laura and Tina?" She hoped Sam would give her a reason to feel better about moving away from their little sisters.

"We know it'll be a much longer stretch between visits. Won't be like it is now: a two-hour drive to the island and every holiday under the same roof. Flights aren't cheap and it'll take a week to drive coast-to-coast. I've already thought about it and I'm goin'. You can finish high school here, Uncle Bill and Aunt Deborah will move into the house with the little kids. It'll be like a regular family. Or…" Sam drew out his last sentence, but Elizabeth knew what was coming. "You can join me in California. You don't have to decide right now."

Elizabeth processed her thoughts quickly and her mind skipped past everything that could happen, might happen, probably would happen if she joined her brother. She took a step back, cocked her head to one side with an air of confidence, looked at Sam and planted her hands on her hips. "Get two plane tickets."

Chapter 15

THE SUN KISSED THEIR FACES AS SOON AS THEY STEPPED outside Los Angeles International Airport. Autumn in LA, so they had been told, was more like summer on the East Coast, and so far "they" had been right. Elizabeth had read about the unrelenting smog in the city, the way it sucked the breath from your lungs, and the smog alerts that kept everyone inside on the hottest of days, but today was not one of those days. It was gorgeous, mild, and beautiful. Not quite sunset, the air was still warm, and it was a far cry from the chill in the air they were so accustomed to right after Labor Day back home.

As Paul had instructed, they waited for him curbside, just outside baggage claim, and watched for his black VW Beetle to approach. "I think I see it," chimed Elizabeth, as it seemed to pass them by and vanish into traffic.

"Well, maybe that wasn't him. There is probably more than one black Beetle in this city."

"Here he comes." Sam reached down to pick up his luggage. Again, the black Beetle drove right past, the driver seemingly not looking in their direction.

"Gee whiz, does everyone drive a black VW Beetle in this town?" With that, Elizabeth giggled, then broke into a full-blown laugh at the thought of so many identical cars in this vast city.

"Welcome to LA!" They were caught off guard as they saw Paul racing towards them on foot. Out of breath, but all smiles, he panted, "I couldn't get close enough to you… hurry… run… my car's parked in a red zone and I'm afraid it'll get towed. Here, let me help with those bags. By the way, I'm so glad you made it. Run!"

The threesome barely made it back to the car, with an airport traffic officer only one car behind Paul's, and ready to approach his VW, idling and waiting. Wasting no time, they tossed as many suitcases as would fit in the trunk. They forced the rest of them in the back seat with Elizabeth wedged between Sam's duffle bag and the old, brown case with the snap locks, and small leather handle she had taken from her parent's closet when sorting through their possessions. Lurching forward, Paul put the car in first gear and pulled out into the flow of traffic towards his home in Reseda. The Valley, not quite Los Angeles, not quite the West Side, not quite affluent Pasadena. Paul explained it was a good option with cheaper rents, and still made the vast possibility of things to do in LA readily available. "You'll probably get teased, though." He merged easily. "Enjoy the ride."

Paul effortlessly maneuvered between lanes and cars rushed past at a high rate of speed. It made Elizabeth wonder if she would ever get her driver's license. One freeway merged into another, long arcs of concrete overlapped another and pointed in all directions. Back home, traveling by surface streets was normal, but freeway travel in LA seemed to be the preferred method of navigation throughout the city.

Finally able to relax, Paul broke the silence. "So bitchin' you're here! I know finding a place to live, a job, getting Elizabeth enrolled for her senior year isn't gonna be easy, but I'm glad you're staying with me for now. I found a small apartment right after I returned from Vietnam, only one bedroom, but it can work." Looking in his rear-view mirror, Paul marveled at how gorgeous Elizabeth had become. He tried not to be too obvious, but he was glad the picture he had kept in his head wasn't tainted. She was even more beautiful than he remembered. "Elizabeth, you can have the one bedroom. I don't think your brother will mind sleeping on an air mattress. I won't. God knows we've seen worse."

Elizabeth blushed, but quietly thanked Paul for his offer. She could only think about the new life awaiting her, not where she would sleep. Out of the corner of her eye, she saw Paul, handsome, strong, kind, and eager to help his old friend Sam and his little sister blend into this new city and start over. "Whatever you say, Paul. Thanks for going out of your way to make us feel comfortable."

As promised, Elizabeth had the bedroom, but she had never shared a bathroom with two grown men. *Guys are so messy,* she thought, as she wiped the shaving cream from the sink. *Hopefully Sam and I can find another apartment close by as soon as he finds a job.* Grateful for the small inheritance Nana left each of the children, she had no doubt she and Sam would be just fine.

"Hey, Paul. Can you join Elizabeth and me for lunch after we're finished registering her at school?"

"Maybe you know some bitchin' little place nearby," Elizabeth added.

Paul and Sam looked at each other and shook their heads.

"Somehow that word doesn't sound quite right coming out of your mouth, Elizabeth… cute, really cute. Guess I better get used to it. And no—got classes, then work. Maybe next time."

"It's not a swear word, right? You told me it wasn't a swear word." She turned to Sam. "You told me in one of your letters it meant something that was cool, right?"

"Yes, sophomore. That is correct. Paul's right though. It does sound strange coming from you."

"And how about this coming out my mouth… quit calling me sophomore. I'll be a senior next week." Elizabeth tried her best to look pouty as she put her hands on her hips and squared off with her brother.

"Sorry—don't care how old you get. You'll always be sophomore to me."

"See how juvenile he can be?" Elizabeth faced Paul for reassurance.

"Hey, leave me out of this. I have no idea what this sibling rivalry is about, an only child, remember?" Paul gathered his books, dashed out the door, and took the steps, two at a time, to the street below, leaving Sam and Elizabeth to finish their skirmish without him.

"The next two hours belong to us. Where would you like to eat?" Sam got to the door first so he could open it for Elizabeth, and she noticed he was not as painfully shy about his missing limb as he once had been. Being a total "righty," it had taken Sam months to relearn skills with his left hand. Except for an occasional moment of frustration and a few curious comments from strangers, his level of acceptance became more and more apparent as time progressed.

Sam continued, "I saw a hamburger stand about a block from the high school. Can we try it out? Didn't look like there were too many seats inside, but plenty of benches on the outside. Apparently, you can eat outside year round in Southern California… bitchin." Elizabeth rolled her eyes and finally had the appearance of the young girl she was supposed to be, not the ever-responsible grown-up she had been forced to become. She sighed deeply and exhaled all the burdens of the last few years.

Sam could see the change in his sister occurring before his eyes. *Best decision I ever made.*

Chapter 16

ELIZABETH *WAS* EXCITED ABOUT HER FIRST DAY OF
senior year at Reseda Valley High School. She was feeling stronger,
happier, and more lighthearted than she had in years. She relished the
clear September air of Southern California as she leisurely strolled
the two blocks to school.

Already the streets and parking lot were filled with teenagers
of all shapes and sizes, some on bikes, others in cars, and many on
skateboards. It was as though she had stepped into a movie, the
whole atmosphere, the constant drench of sunshine, the dress code,
were so different from Boston. Elizabeth would never have been
allowed to wear jeans to school, much less paired with a tank top
and a peace sign strategically placed over ample breasts. Some of
the jeans had clearly been torn off to well above the knee, exposing
flesh on campus she had never seen. Others were covered in patches,
ranging from daisy chains to anti-war sentiments, which brazenly
said, "Hell no, I won't go." Wearing these sentiments so shamelessly
on your clothes bothered Elizabeth at first, knowing Sam and Paul
were plagued by the role they played in Vietnam and still felt a fair
amount of rage at the reception the veterans were receiving upon
their return. Eventually, she had to let it go and turned her thoughts
to making new friends and getting the grades she would need to
enter college as soon as she graduated.

"Could you tell me where I can find the classroom for Seniah English?" Elizabeth directed her question to a boy goofing around in the hall who was sporting a friendly, mischievous grin.

"What did you say?"

"Seniah English."

"You mean SENIOR English? Stumped me for a minute. Around here, you'll need to pronounce your R's."

"Ok, sure. I'll try to remem-BER that." Elizabeth felt a little smug about her witty comeback, and wasn't going to let anything dampen her enthusiasm. Her Boston accent would fade over time, she hoped.

"I'm going there now. Follow me, and you'll never be lost."

Tyler Hamilton was known as the class clown, full of energy, always smiling, and perpetually driving every teacher in the school crazy. They were glad this was his senior year and he would soon be graduating. "You must be new here. I know everyone, and I mean *everyone*. By the end of next week, I'll know all the incoming freshmen too, and now you know me. My name is Tyler Hamilton."

Startled at such friendliness and charm, Elizabeth nodded her head, followed him to Senior English class, found a seat in the back of the room, and sat quietly as Mr. Williams introduced himself to the classroom. During roll call, Tyler took one more glance towards Elizabeth, mentally noted her curly, auburn hair, deep green eyes, and adorable smile, and managed a quick wink, which she never noticed.

Elizabeth bounded home after the final bell, eager to see her brother, and hoping to catch Paul before he left for work. Sam sat and typed at the kitchen table, and Paul napped quietly on the couch, taking advantage of the last thirty minutes of free time before he had to leave. Sam looked up when he heard the door unlock. He put his index finger to his lips, motioned to Paul and mouthed, "Shhhh…

he has to get up in thirty minutes. I can tell you had a great day—nice smile."

Elizabeth gently lowered her books on the kitchen table and searched the refrigerator for a snack. She was interrupted when she saw Paul waving his arms. He shouted and yelled unintelligible orders and gasped as his booming voice turned to a whisper. "There... over there... quiet men... they're over there behind the bushes. Stay down." He sprung up, went to the middle of the room, and fell to the floor. Crawling on his belly, an imaginary rifle in hand, he looked furtively from side to side. Stunned, Elizabeth and Sam weren't sure how to react. Elizabeth made the first move. She leaned over Paul, laid her hand on his forehead, and said softly, "Paul, wake up. It's me, Elizabeth. Please, wake up. You're scaring me."

Paul opened his eyes and found his bearings. As he did so, a look of embarrassment and shame washed over his face. He jumped to his feet and retreated to the bathroom as though nothing had happened, put on his uniform for work, and rushed past them without saying goodbye. Sam and Elizabeth looked at each other, dumbfounded by what they had seen.

Sam spoke first, "I saw it in the trenches. Read a little bit about it. Damn! I thought losing a limb was the worst thing that could ever happen to a soldier, but now I'm not so sure."

Elizabeth quietly reached for a pen and piece of paper, deliberated for a moment, and wrote, "Dear Paul, it's OK." She folded it neatly and tucked it under his pillow where she hoped he would find it when he came home.

"Will this ever get better?" Elizabeth hoped Sam had some answers. "I've never seen you do this."

"I guess it's different for everyone. All I know is no one ever talks about it. Paul and I don't talk to each other about Vietnam. We talk about a lot of other things, but never about the war."

"Do you think he would talk to me?" Elizabeth sounded hopeful.

"Definitely not."

"What about a therapist, a shrink?" She knew she was grasping for a miraculous cure, but doubted one existed.

Sam's voice rose. "Absolutely, Definitely not. That would be cowardly and weak."

Elizabeth was shocked. "You think it's weak for someone to ask for help, Sam?" They were entering territory they had never explored, but Elizabeth felt her heart sink when she heard what her brother felt not only about himself, but for every other soldier who laid their lives on the line, without question, without reason.

"I know it sounds callous, but yes, I do. We were trained as warriors, combat soldiers, disposable, and replaceable. We did what we were told, and we knew better than to complain about anything, while we were there or when we returned."

Elizabeth started to fume and Sam could see her reaction to this conversation. "I don't understand why he can't go see a military doctor, or any doctor, or have some tests or something. Maybe get some medication."

"What medicine? What tests? Paul's going to have to see this through on his own, and the only thing we can do is be his friends."

Sam picked up Elizabeth's books and shoved them into her arms. "Go do your homework." These were not the answers Elizabeth was looking for from her brother, but she let the matter drop, if only for the time being. She took her schoolwork and closed the bedroom door behind her just loud enough so Sam would know she wasn't happy.

Chapter 17

WITH HIGH GRADES AND TOP SCORES ON COLLEGE entrance exams, Elizabeth had options of four-year universities across the country. Instead, she enrolled in the local community college to complete her first two years, a strategic move to not only save on tuition, but stay a little closer to Sam and Paul, whose recurring nightmares still troubled and concerned her. Settled in a little apartment at the end of freshman year, Elizabeth felt free, with no responsibility for the first time in her life.

Paul and Sam, though sad to see her go, assisted her one bright, sunny day in May with a move that took one borrowed-truck load and the space in the back seat of Elizabeth's own VW Beetle. She didn't want a black one, indistinguishable from all the others she had seen, so she bought an older, cream-color model, and paid twenty-nine dollars for an exterior paint job, and changed it to British racing green. She joked that what she really wanted was a British Leyland MGB GT, if for nothing else than the color. For a sports car, it was affordable, but far beyond the reach of a college student.

"That's cool, I guess. If you don't mind the interiah doesn't match the exteriah." Sam was teasing her, but Paul interjected.

"It's her car, leave her alone. I think it looks pretty groovy. I always thought that was a neat color. And when are you going to start pronouncing those R's? You'll never pick up a Southern California girl that way."

Elizabeth nodded in agreement. She had long ago gotten used to the Southern California slang and embraced it like a local. "Thank you, Paul. I appreciate your opinion, and it would have cost another twenty-nine dollars to paint the inside dashboard and trim, so I convinced myself that having the only two-toned Beetle in LA would be perfect."

By the end of moving day, everything was neatly tucked into drawers, closets, and storage spaces, and the one lonely dish, knife, fork, and spoon were prominently displayed on the Formica-covered breakfast bar. Elizabeth knew her little home was sparse, but furnishing it was on the short list of things to do. For now, her bed and dresser, plus a small sofa and dining set she had purchased from Goodwill, would have to be enough. She was grateful for the large picture window in the living room, which made the unit feel grander than it was and gave her the bonus of a view of the tree-lined street and the hustle and bustle below. It would take some time to fill the empty corners, a stark contrast to the jam-packed existence she had become accustomed to in Paul's small apartment.

Paul and Sam were anxious to get back home, glad to have Elizabeth settled after a long, hot day of moving, and only thought of the cold beer waiting in their refrigerator. As she waved from her front door that overlooked the courtyard, and watched Sam and Paul disappear down the street, Elizabeth was alone—really alone—and wondered how she would manage. Alone, all she ever wanted, but now that she was, she questioned if she had made the right decision to leave the safety of her familiar surroundings. *Don't overthink it, Elizabeth.* She gathered her sweater and keys, locked the apartment behind her, and headed to the supermarket. In the car, she turned up the radio as loudly as it would go, and sang along badly with Mick Jagger and the Rolling Stones. She felt grown up and ready as she made a mental inventory of what she would do when she returned to her apartment. First on the list, call Sam and Paul.

❖

At least twice a week Elizabeth spoke with her brother or Paul. She never told either of them that living on her own wasn't what she hoped it would be. She joined the requisite clubs on campus, made new friends, met for coffee and study groups, but was lonely for the little apartment they had shared. She didn't want to admit it to either of them. Most Saturday nights she was alone, but always told the boys she had gone dancing, to a movie with friends, or out for Sunday brunch—all the cool things she was supposed to be doing. They believed her, envied her, and told her how happy they were for her.

Elizabeth let the phone ring three times before she answered. "Hello."

"Hi. It's Sam. Say, I know you're always busy on the weekends, but I was wondering if you wanna go for hamburgers at the Hamlet in Westwood and out dancing. You haven't met my girlfriend, Linda, yet, and I don't think Paul has anything to do this weekend."

Elizabeth had wondered when she would meet the lovely Linda her brother always talked about. It seemed to her they had been dating for years, but in reality, it was only a couple months. "Let me check my calendar." She shuffled some papers loudly enough to make Sam think she was checking a full schedule. "Looks like I'm clear. That sounds like fun, Sam. Thanks for including me. Are you sure Paul won't mind having your baby sister tag along?"

"I would probably say just the opposite. We'll grab a burger first, and Westwood has some great bars, dance places, good cover bands."

"I'm not twenty-one."

"No problem. Girls only have to be eighteen, guys twenty-one. You'll get a wristband when we go in and no beer for you. Linda's only a year older than you. Paul and I will do all the drinking. See you Saturday at seven. We'll pick you up, and drive in one car. Gotta go."

Linda must not be from Southern California, thought Elizabeth, and smiled at the way her brother still insisted on speaking with his thick Boston accent.

"Bye, Sam. Thanks." Elizabeth slowly returned the phone to the cradle and was excited and nervous at the same time. *Is this a date? No, it's not a date. Quit thinking it's a date. Get ahold of yourself... Oh no, what am I going to wear?*

Westwood Village was always busy on the weekend, but that was part of the excitement. Even driving around for thirty minutes looking for a place to park was more fun than stressful.

Sam pulled over and double-parked, while cars honked in a long line behind them. Under his breath he muttered, "Calm down," and quickly turned to Paul and Elizabeth in the back seat. "Time to bail, guys. Put our names in for a table, and we'll keep looking for a place to park." Paul and Elizabeth jumped out and slammed the car door, as irritated drivers still blasted their horns in an effort to move forward a few more car lengths.

"Well, that was fun. So much excitement in the air." Elizabeth was breathless.

"Yeah, some people get upset. Doesn't bother me. I like the hubbub. Hope you don't mind waiting for a table... it could be awhile."

Paul took Elizabeth's hand and guided her through the crowd, finally making it to the front door behind a throng of people waiting to be seated. She liked how Paul took control, his strong hand wrapped protectively around her delicate fingers. She didn't know what was happening, and at this moment, didn't care. "Paul, party of four." He nodded to the hostess and she scribbled his name at the bottom of the list behind twenty others that were waiting patiently outside.

"It will be about a thirty-minute wait if that's okay."

"Not a problem."

"You've done this before," Elizabeth observed.

"Yeah, a few times." Paul squeezed Elizabeth's hand and she squeezed back. They took a place in line and leaned against the cold brick wall of the restaurant, a perfect vantage point to observe the hustle and bustle of a Saturday night in the village. There were four movie theatres in a four-block radius, and just as many bars and places to dance. The air smelled like youthful exuberance, time to let your hair down after a long week of classes, and tests—drink, get loud, have sex, and have fun.

"Oh, I see them." Linda pointed to Paul and Elizabeth, inching closer to the front of the line. "I hope Elizabeth likes me." Linda wasn't sure and looked for reassurance from Sam. "She didn't say a lot on the drive over."

"Don't worry. I'm sure Elizabeth's as nervous as you are. It'll be easier at dinner to talk and visit. Driving the LA freeways on a Saturday night makes everyone edgy. I'm sure she didn't want to distract the driver." They walked to the front of the line and joined Paul and Elizabeth.

Immediately they heard, "Paul, table for four." They almost missed their call. The noise level was so high, with diners' voices becoming louder as they struggled to talk over each other in the crowded room. When they followed the hostess past the myriad of tables and into the back room to an oversized, comfortable booth, a slight hush fell. The dimly lit room was for the overflow crowd, and was quieter than the main eating area. "This is so beautiful," Elizabeth gushed.

Most of the time dining out meant a sidewalk café or fast food restaurant, so her heart beat faster as she glided into the buttery soft leather seats. Paul slid in beside her. The seating arrangement was a large horse-shoe configuration with high, tufted backs and a rich mahogany table set with white cloth napkins and gleaming silverware. Elizabeth was glad she chose to wear her new bell-bottoms—dark navy denim—and a soft, white angora cardigan, the top two buttons left open to create a more attractive neckline. She had thought about a casual, cotton peasant top, but at the last minute, decided the sweater was the right touch. She liked the way it made her look with her auburn hair, now down to her waist, the perfect contrast to the cream color of the sweater, and her green eyes highlighted by a little eyeliner and mascara. She felt confident and joyful and ready for the evening to begin.

"Elizabeth, I think you and Linda have a lot in common. She has one rotten older brother and two annoying little sisters." Sam smiled, hoping to get the conversation started between the two of them.

"I don't have two annoying little sisters."

Sam shook his head, still smiling. "Good one, sophomore."

Without skipping a beat, Elizabeth turned to Linda. "I've heard so much about you. It's about time Sam introduced us. He tells me you're studying Computer Science at Pasadena City College. That's a new field. I'm still scared of word processors, and not ready to give up my Selectric II typewriter, but it gets the job done. Where did you say you were from?"

"I was raised in Rhode Island, but came out here for college. Don't know if I'll ever go back home."

"That's nice. Not too far from Boston. I didn't think you were from Southern California—no way you could put up with Sam's thick accent. He's a lucky man."

Paul and Sam sat quietly and pretended to be interested in the conversation, but neither one of them knew too much about the topic. By the time dinner was ordered, the girls were deep into a heart-to-heart exchange, learning, talking, and getting along well as far as Sam could see. With no parents, it was important Elizabeth approve of the girl who was becoming more significant to him with every passing day, and who he might even marry one day, although it was much too early to tell. Paul and Sam devoured their bacon burgers and French fries, listening to Linda and Elizabeth, silently glad they didn't have to talk.

"Are you ready for dessert?" The waitress broke in on their conversation. When everyone said they were too full for anything more, she tallied their check and left it on the table. One by one, they peeled themselves from the booth, strolled out of the restaurant, and stepped into the night air. Elizabeth felt more alive than she had in her entire life, tingling from head to toe as she absorbed the sight of people, cars, sounds, and excitement beginning to spill into the streets.

Paul stayed close to Elizabeth as they entered the bar, and though careful to remain a gentleman, couldn't keep his eyes off her. Somehow this evening she seemed magical to him, and he felt good just being around her. Although this was not a date, he was proud to show her off to all those college boys and no one needed to know any different. They managed to find an open table as the band started their second set and Paul immediately asked Elizabeth to dance. They easily sweat off their meals dancing well into the evening and closing down the bar.

Paul gently put his hand on the small of Elizabeth's back and guided her through the still-crowded room, down the stairs, and out to the sidewalk that was packed with people in no hurry for the night to end. Elizabeth felt something, not sure what, but mostly safe, warm, and happy.

When Paul walked Elizabeth to her door, he glanced at his watch and couldn't believe it was already 2:00 AM. Sam and Linda waited behind at the curb, car in neutral, waiting for Paul to say good night. With a charming smile, Paul said, "Thanks for a great evening, Elizabeth. I think that's the most fun I've had since I came home from Vietnam."

Still feeling a bit light-headed and tingly, she didn't let on to Paul, just nodded as she was turning the key in her door. "Me too, Paul. That was fun. Thanks for a perfect evening."

Paul, aware of the watchful gaze of Sam and Linda, leaned in for a kiss, tasting the sweetness of Elizabeth's lips—the long-awaited moment he had been thinking of since he first laid eyes on her. Elizabeth returned his advance and felt his gentle lips pressed against hers, careful not to linger. They stepped back, nervous and uncertain of what to do next. Elizabeth spoke first, "Well, 'night Paul."

"'Night Elizabeth. Thanks again," was all Paul could think to say as he turned and walked back to climb into the back seat of Sam's car.

Chapter 18

"WHERE DID THE TIME GO?" UNCLE BILL WAS ON THE
other end of the phone, glad to hear from Elizabeth and catch up
on her life in LA. "Seems like decades since we last saw you. I'm so
happy you and Sam decided to come to Boston for Thanksgiving.
Paul too. It'll be good to see him again. I'm just marveling at how
time has flown, and how quickly you finished college."

"I know. I can hardly believe it myself!"

"What's next for you, dear girl, now that you've graduated? I'm
sorry we couldn't make it to the ceremony, but it was just wasn't in our
budget to fly the family to California. Teenagers are expensive." Uncle
Bill had nothing but admiration for his niece that had overcome so
much in the last six years.

"I understand, Uncle Bill. The flowers you sent were gorgeous,
and I nursed them for at least three weeks. I got a paid internship at a
small private elementary school in Santa Monica. I'll put my teaching
degree to use right away. I'll have to move. It's more expensive, but
closer to the beach. I'll have a little less space, but I'm excited. I'm
tired of the heat and smog in the Valley anyway."

"And what about Sam? He called and told us he got engaged.
Will his fiancé be joining us for Thanksgiving? Linda, I believe her
name is."

"We're all planning on being there, and thanks so much, Uncle Bill, for inviting everyone. I can't wait to see my baby sisters, you and Aunt Deborah, and Ricky!"

Elizabeth heard a chorus of voices in the background, disrupting hers and Uncle Bill's conversation, "We miss you too!! Can't wait for you to get here!!!" In unison, unmistakable, Tina and Laura squealed into the mouthpiece.

"Oh, you guys! You sound great. Be there the day before Thanksgiving, and we'll be staying until Sunday. Let's get the tree decorated before I leave. Too much time between visits. Can't wait to see everyone!"

"You get here whenever you can. Bring your boots! We've had a lot of snow already."

Elizabeth felt a smile flash across her face as she hung up the phone. *Never thought I'd ever look forward to freezing temperatures and snow. I can't wait.*

Linda and Sam took their seats in the middle of the plane, while Paul and Elizabeth were fortunate enough to snag the bulkhead seats, making their trip much more comfortable. Though never uneasy in each other's company, it had been two years since they danced in Westwood Village, and they had never moved past the brief kiss they shared that night. Elizabeth felt a little twinge when Paul brushed up against her arm as he heaved his duffle bag into the overhead compartment of the plane.

"There. Done. Barely fit." Paul grinned at Elizabeth, then promptly plopped down beside her, gave her a bear hug, and pulled a paperback novel from the back pocket of his wide-whaled, tan cords.

Elizabeth noticed everything about Paul today, so handsome in his navy blue V-neck sweater with a plain white T-shirt underneath.

His hair was neatly combed and parted on one side, and his kind eyes sparkled when he spoke. Even the timbre of his voice was soothing, calm, and familiar. She thought how nice it was just to see him well and apparently getting over some of his anxieties, though she hadn't lived with him for some time and never asked Sam for updates on their friend. For now, she would believe he had conquered his demons, and that this would be the best Thanksgiving any of them had for a long time.

By the end of the weekend, everyone had caught up on the comings and goings of three seventeen-year-olds under one roof and had learned about Elizabeth's new job. A wedding date was set for Sam and Linda, and everyone agreed they would travel to LA in the spring to see the happy couple wed. Life was moving forward after all. Paul and Elizabeth were the talk of the family, who all sensed there was something between them, but they vehemently swore there was not. "We're just friends," they insisted.

Sam and Linda chose to stay a few more days in Boston, as Linda was warming up to the idea of finding her wedding gown on the East coast. The twins and Aunt Deborah were excited to accompany her, and Linda's mother, who lived in Rhode Island, made last-minute plans to join them for a few days.

"I wish I could stay longer and help you find your wedding dress," Elizabeth complained to Linda. "That's the best part of the planning the wedding. Darn, if only I didn't have to get back to work so soon."

Paul overheard the conversation and added, "Hey, I have to get back to work too. I've used up all my vacation time, but at least you'll have a traveling companion." He gave Elizabeth an unexpected squeeze around her waist, and she wondered why, a little annoyed that they would certainly be gossip fodder for the family once they left.

Arriving at the airport early, they checked their bags at the counter, got their boarding passes, and took their time walking to the departure gate. "I'm going to get a couple of magazines for the trip." Paul made sure Elizabeth was settled with their carry-on luggage before he returned to the newsstand they passed on their way to the gate. "Do you want anything?"

"No, I'm fine. I'll just wait here with our stuff till you get back."

Before Paul was ten feet down the corridor, an announcement blared. "Flight number thirty-four seventy-eight with service to Los Angeles has been delayed. Your new departure time is nine PM. We are sorry for any inconvenience this may cause our valued passengers."

Out loud, Elizabeth groaned, "Oh no. That's a three-hour delay. I was hoping to be home early enough to get ready for work tomorrow. Now it'll be one in the morning before I get to bed."

Paul heard her mumble as he returned to their seats. "Well, at least there's a three-hour time difference and we'll be back in LA before the sun comes up." He grabbed his duffle bag with one hand, offered Elizabeth his free arm, and started towards the long line of restaurants and bars, all good ways to pass the time for hungry, weary travelers. He turned to her.

"Would you like to go on a date with me? An official date?"

Elizabeth was confused, but hung on tight and kept pace. He obviously had a destination in mind. "Like when we get back to LA? I think so, yeah, that sounds nice."

"Nope, like right now. We have three hours to spend together, and I would like to treat you to the finest restaurant in Logan International Airport. Call it a date, call it whatever you want, but I'm seizing this opportunity to spend a few quiet hours alone with you." He smiled ever so slightly as he walked and waited for Elizabeth to respond.

"Well, in that case, I accept." She let Paul steer them into the comfort of a dimly lit airport steak house. As her heart began to flutter, she realized she wasn't even hungry. She reveled in Paul's invitation, but decided not to read much more into it and let fate take its course.

Dozing beside each other, Paul and Elizabeth awakened as they heard the flight attendant make the announcement to fasten their seat belts. The lights in the cabin began to glow and interrupted their slumber, and Elizabeth was caught off guard when she noticed she had fallen asleep with her head on Paul's shoulder. He didn't mind a bit, and gently nudged her. "We're home."

They strained to peer out the window and take in the view of the city. Resplendent with lights, it looked more like a fairy tale than an over-populated metropolis. As the plane approached the gate, Paul leaned over and gave her a quick peck on the cheek. Instead of startling Elizabeth, she took his hand while they waited for the doors to open. They were still a bit groggy as Paul pulled their carry-ons from the overhead compartment and Elizabeth followed closely behind. Holiday travelers packed the terminal even though it was almost midnight, and she groaned when she glanced at her watch.

"Ugh, it's three AM in Boston. I didn't think I would be this tired. I don't know how I'm going to make it to work in eight hours. I must look awful." Elizabeth was hoping she could sneak into the nearest ladies room before Paul noticed her weary eyes, disheveled hair, and dry lips.

"Actually, you're beautiful. I don't know how you manage it, but the older you get, the prettier you become."

"I never knew you were such a sweet talker, Paul." Elizabeth couldn't stop blushing. Paul let her wrap her arm inside his, linking elbows on the way to the baggage claim. Elizabeth hoped this moment would never end and savored every second.

Her thoughts were interrupted when Paul turned to her. "No disrespect intended, but would you consider spending the night with me tonight? Could you call in sick tomorrow?"

Elizabeth was bewildered, but only for a moment. "Yes, I will, if you will," and she gripped Paul's arm even tighter as her heart skipped a beat. They got their suitcases and hailed a cab as soon as they got curbside. Paul turned to her, "Your place, or mine?"

"Yours this time." Elizabeth caught her breath, as they curled up in the warm cab, ready to take them home.

⋞◇⋟

The morning crept up on them too soon, and Elizabeth jumped to her feet when she realized the time. Almost seven o'clock, she grabbed the phone and quickly dialed work. It was not like her to lie or bend the truth, but she decided her night with Paul was well worth any reprimand she might have to endure. As it turned out, the secretary accepted her excuse of the long delay at the airport and told her they would see her the next day. *Too easy,* she thought. *I better not make a habit of this.*

She snatched Paul's button-down shirt that had landed on the floor during the night, suddenly feeling shy and embarrassed. Covering her bare breasts, she handed the phone to Paul. "You better call work. I'll make coffee."

Chapter 19

Saturday mornings, particularly in the summer, were perfect for being lazy, listening to records, and doing a whole lot of nothing. After Sam and Linda rented a place of their own, it took some getting used to for Paul to feel comfortable living alone. But the past few months, weekends, and moments he shared with Elizabeth filled the empty spaces.

"You weren't lying." Elizabeth slowly let her fingers glide along the neatly alphabetized collection of Paul's albums. A cheap particleboard, floor-to-ceiling shelf unit was beginning to sag from the weight. Most of his furnishings were the same ones he had acquired upon return from Vietnam: thrift shop items, castoffs, they too old for anyone else to keep, but quite comfortable for Paul. Nothing had changed since she shared this apartment with him and her brother, and though she didn't quite feel at home like when she was younger, she didn't mind spending the weekends in the old apartment with Paul. The drive between them was too long on the congested LA freeways to see each other more often. Elizabeth loved her little space in Santa Monica. The rents were almost twice as high, but it felt good to be on the West Side, a working girl who could afford a small one bedroom just two miles from the beach. She pulled a Simon & Garfunkel album from the crammed record assortment and started to remove it from the paper sleeve. It looked as though it had never been played.

"Be careful, Elizabeth." Paul cringed as she tugged on the precious vinyl to free it from the protective cover.

"That's not how you handle a record." He was irritated.

"Don't put your fingers on the vinyl. It'll scratch the surface and ruin the sound. You have to hold it with both hands, on the edge." Not entirely trusting she would sense he was serious, he walked over to her.

"Like this." He removed the record from her grip, demonstrated the proper way to hold a record, and asked, "Lying about what?"

"Oh, I flashed back to one of the letters I got from Sam when you two were in Vietnam. He had just met you, and you told him you had a collection of four hundred albums and 45s. He wasn't sure if he believed it. That's a lot of records."

"Now why would I lie about something like that?" Paul looked hurt. "It's true."

"Well, I can see that. I noticed your collection as soon as Sam and I stepped foot into this apartment, but it made me think of his letter, that's all. We never knew anyone who had that many."

Elizabeth was trying to repair any damage she may have caused and hoped Paul didn't think she was calling him a liar. He seemed overly sensitive to certain subjects, but maybe it was because he was more protective of his values than his records, and wanted Elizabeth to know he always told the truth. She observed Paul's heartfelt instruction on how vinyl should be handled, and as she lowered the record on the turntable, looked to him for approval. "Paul, do you ever think about Vietnam?"

"All the time. All day, every day. I left Vietnam. It didn't leave me." His eyes watered and Elizabeth could tell he was getting nervous. She quickly changed the subject.

"Sam called me yesterday and wanted to know if we would like to join them for Fourth of July.

"Sounds okay to me. Sure, tell him we'll be there. Must be fun to play house, under the same roof." He winked at Elizabeth and she pretended she didn't hear what he said. Instead, she kept right on talking, turning the volume up slightly, filling the room with the warm harmony of Simon and Garfunkel.

"You know, they live a lot closer to me than you. Why don't you plan on staying over instead of getting back on the freeway so late at night? You can sleep on the floor." It was Elizabeth's turn to wink.

"Seen worse, and I accept your invitation. Whatever happened to boy asks a girl?"

"Please." Elizabeth feigned a shocked response. "It's the Seventies."

"I'm surprised you're so liberated. A sweet little girl from Boston, under the protective umbrella of her big brother."

"Maybe I've been in LA too long. And I told you, you're sleeping on the floor."

"Whatever you say. Although I don't believe you for a moment." Paul retreated to the kitchen to make breakfast, happy they were under one roof together again, even if it was only on the weekends.

Sam and Linda had rented a small, old house not far from Elizabeth's apartment and what it lacked in square footage, it made up for with the large back yard. Houses were decorated for the Fourth of July, little American flags on sticks piercing every lawn, and as many larger ones proudly waving in the breeze attached to pillars or posts.

As Paul and Elizabeth turned onto the street, there was no parking in sight. "Quite a party. Sam didn't tell me the whole neighborhood was invited." Elizabeth was excited, but Paul looked uncertain.

"Are you sure this is a good idea?" Paul continued to drive around, looking for a parking spot, but hoped Elizabeth would suggest they give up and go back home to celebrate by themselves.

"What are you so nervous about? There's probably going to be a lot of families, kids, and people our age. I think it's great everyone is taking the time to enjoy the long weekend." Elizabeth spied an opening. "There, Paul. Grab it."

Volkswagen Beetles were good for one thing. They could squeeze into small spaces and, as Paul was maneuvering into the opening barely large enough to fit even his small car, he added one last thought, hoping Elizabeth might change her mind. "There are a lot of people in our country who are not in favor of the war, and your brother and I certainly didn't come home heroes. There's still plenty of leftover rage, Elizabeth. What if someone gets drunk, finds out we were in Vietnam, and wants to start a fight. I just don't want any trouble."

"You're totally over thinking this. Did you forget Sam's hand? How do you think he explained it to his neighbors? I'm sure they're well aware he was wounded in Vietnam. It's a big neighborhood barbecue, that's all. Relax, Paul. It'll be fun." Elizabeth couldn't understand why Paul was so concerned, and Paul was having a hard time figuring out what Elizabeth didn't understand, but hand-in-hand, they approached Sam and Linda's house.

"Hey, Man. I'm glad you two could make it—and find a place to park." Sam handed each of them a beer and motioned to the back yard that was already filled with friends and neighbors.

"I don't think you had this many people at your wedding, Sam." Elizabeth was only half joking as she quickly surveyed the patriotic decorations in the yard and drew in the aroma of the barbecue, which was already laden with hamburgers and hot dogs. Linda joined them.

"We had no idea it was going to be a block party, but when we found out we were all planning the same thing, it just sort of grew. We didn't think you'd mind." Sam's new bride was beaming, as she excused herself to retrieve more food and drinks. Her new bob, just above her shoulders, and neatly trimmed bangs defined her child-like features, and the sunlight intensified the warm chocolate shade of her hair. Petite and full of energy, entertaining looked good on her and she clearly made Sam very happy. Elizabeth smiled as she followed her inside.

"Anything I can do to help?"

"Just hold the door open. I've been planning this for days and I think I have everything I need."

"I feel like an idiot. We didn't bring anything. We could have at least brought a six-pack. I feel pretty silly."

"Don't worry, Elizabeth. We have so much food already, and I know how busy both of you are with work. Besides, your turn will come. You and Paul look cute together. Getting serious?"

"I don't think about it. We have a great time together and that's all I care about. We go to lots of concerts, almost every Friday or Saturday. He lives for music and rock concerts. The distance between our houses keeps our visits to weekends only, but he's spending the night with me tonight. Too much to ask him to take me home in the opposite direction of where he lives, then drive home late at night. He'll be sleeping on the floor, of course."

"Whatever you say," Linda teased. She nodded at Elizabeth as she squeezed through the open door, arms full, with Elizabeth right behind.

"Big fireworks display tonight from the Santa Monica Pier." Sam said as he and Paul joined the girls, taking the precarious hot dog buns and chips from Linda. "The neighbors said you can see them from here, as long as it's a clear night."

"Looks like it will be." Elizabeth glanced at the bright sky just to be sure.

"How are you doing?" Elizabeth took Paul's hand and led him to one of the many comfortable chairs their hosts had provided. "I'm getting hungry. I've never seen so much food, and that aroma of charcoal and meat. My mouth's watering."

"I'm hungry too," said Paul. "I'll go get a couple burgers. I know how you like yours. Don't go anywhere. I'll be right back."

"I'll save your place." Elizabeth looked into the crowd while she waited for Paul to return, silently sizing up the mixture of guests. She wondered if each young adult male at the party had been in Vietnam, dodged the draft, or was a fortunate son, lucky enough to have wealthy parents who could pay their way into a four-year university, hoping the war would simmer down before their sons would have to serve. She turned her eyes to Sam, standing over the grill with a big smile on his face, no longer embarrassed by the hook that was now his right hand. He teased that if a marshmallow ever fell into a bonfire, he would be the only one who could fish it out and not feel a thing. "Funny," was all she could ever say in reply.

⬥

The sun set and darkness crept up quickly. The children squealed with pent up excitement, while they finished their ice cream sandwiches and watermelon, and the adults fished around the coolers for one last beer in the frigid water baths that had once been mountains of ice.

"Take your seats, ladies and gentlemen. The fireworks are about to begin." Sam urged everyone to get comfortable, as he dragged two chairs in the direction of Elizabeth and Paul.

"You don't seem to have any trouble with your new hand." Paul made an effort to assist.

"Not anymore. It was so hectic today, I barely had a chance to talk to you guys. How are you doing, friend?"

"Good, really good." Paul put his arm around Elizabeth as the first set of fireworks started their colorful dance in the sky. The children were awestruck. For most, it was a long-awaited spectacle. Elizabeth glanced at Sam, who seemed to be enjoying every new explosion, caught up in the celebration. The neighbors had been right. You could see everything from their back yard, and the clear night created a perfect backdrop for the show, each eruption more spectacular than the one before. Elizabeth wished she could relax and not worry so much about Paul. Loud noises and sudden movements made him jump, whether they were in a crowd or alone. Every episode was different. Some were fleeting, others lasted for hours.

With barely seconds in between each set of explosions, the anticipation of the celebrating crowd grew, and the ever-increasing display of light and echoing din in the distance beckoned the grand finale. Teeth clenched and hands balled into fists, it took every ounce of restraint Paul could muster not to jump out of his chair and run for cover. Elizabeth grounded him with a gentle stroke on his tense shoulders and whispered in his ear, "We can get out of here as soon as they're over. It's okay, Paul." She glanced once more at her brother, grinning from ear to ear. *They're so different*, she thought. *Not all wounds are visible.* At that moment, the National Anthem came to mind: *And the rockets' red glare, the bombs bursting in air... That must be what Paul is thinking.* It made her very sad for the man sitting next to her. The man she loved.

⌗

"Quite a party," Elizabeth said as she turned the key in the apartment door. She felt it would be best not to say anything to Paul about what she felt, what she saw, what she knew. At least not tonight, and maybe never.

"Were you serious about me sleeping on the floor? Should I get a blanket and pillow from the closet? Paul was too polite to assume spending the night was an invitation to something more and he was in no mood for cute conversation. What he wanted to do was jump in his car and go back to his own apartment alone, but he knew that would hurt Elizabeth's feelings, and at this moment, she was more important to him than his anxiety.

"Follow me." Elizabeth grabbed his hand and led him into the bedroom. Paul didn't resist.

Chapter 20

EXCEPT FOR WEEKENDS, THE DISTANCE BETWEEN them was making it too difficult to be together as LA's freeways were becoming ever more congested. Paul vacated his apartment in the Valley, found a job as an assistant warehouse manager in Santa Monica, and moved in with Elizabeth. She was getting used to the music that played all day, every day, even when they were both at work. "The radio keeps the four walls warm," Paul would tell her, and they were greeted with a low decibel of noise whenever they entered their apartment.

"What do you want to do tonight?" Paul asked Elizabeth for the second time. Dragging for most of the day, she didn't want to leave the house, fight the crowds, drive the dangerous, rain-slicked freeways at night, or listen to loud music. Paul, never one to push, knew exactly what he wanted to do, and had the tickets in hand. If he could only get some enthusiasm from Elizabeth.

"I have two tickets to a rock concert at the Rose Palace. It's a pillow concert—bring your own, open seating, first come first serve, free parking. I know you're tired, but please, please, forget that we'll get wet. Let's just go." The rain had been relentless for the last week, pounding the pavement, causing pile-ups, and flooding intersections around the city.

"Why would you want to go out on a night like this? It's horrible outside. Can't we just curl up with a cup of hot chocolate and watch TV?" Elizabeth sounded like a whiny teenager.

"Really, TV? Over a rock concert?" Paul laughed out loud, amused by the sincerity of Elizabeth's plea. "I just feel like going out." He smiled, but meant it when he said, "This could be historic and we'll be glad we went. Please, I promise I won't ask you to do anything like this again." Paul took Elizabeth in his arms and moved in for a kiss.

Elizabeth couldn't resist his advance, leaned in and savored the moment. The sensation of his warm mouth against hers and the familiar scent of Old Spice that lingered in the air reminded her how much she loved this man. She gently pulled away from his embrace. "Okay. I'll go. Maybe we can tell our children about the time we saw this amazing concert, sat on a pillow in the middle of a warehouse, and got a contact high from the marijuana smoke swirling around our heads and sticking to our clothes like superglue."

"They probably won't believe you," said Paul. "But sure, a contact high. Sounds like a good story." A look of contentment swept across his face as he imagined himself as a father. "Grab the umbrella, I'll get the pillows and a blanket. Let's get outa here."

Elizabeth never liked rain. It made her hair frizz and she was concerned that she didn't exactly fit into the nice, tight little package of what Southern California girls were supposed to be or look like. Her hair was red, for one thing, and even though everyone politely said it was auburn, she knew it was more like what you would get if you mixed a carrot and a beet together. It bounced and was impossible to control in humidity. Yet Paul always told her how beautiful she was, frizz or no frizz. He never could understand why she used gels and slept with beer cans in her hair so it would be straight and perfect, and look like every other girl's hair in the room. The curls that Elizabeth always hated suited Paul just fine, and the fact she was different is what drew him to her in the first place.

Arriving in the blustering downpour amidst hundreds of other concertgoers, Elizabeth was tense from fighting their way through the heavy traffic. Despite her unenthusiastic mood and the damp, chilly air, she was determined to keep her spirits high and gave Paul a peck on the cheek as he switched off the ignition. He raced around to the passenger side and helped Elizabeth from the car, opened the umbrella that was barely big enough for one person, and raised it over her head to shield her from the pelting rain. They ran through the crowd clutching their pillows and blankets, and hoped they would be dry by the time they reached the entrance. Paul stopped suddenly, pulled Elizabeth under the cover of a sagging awning, and gave her an unexpected, delicious kiss. "Stay with me forever," he said.

Elizabeth was startled, but managed, "I'm not going anywhere." She didn't feel cold anymore.

The line into the auditorium moved quickly and every entrance door was open to accommodate the growing number of ticket-holders. A throng of wet, disheveled people moved inside, and the icy blast of cold air that met their faces eventually gave way to a more temperate atmosphere as the collective body heat made it more comfortable. The noise level rose with each new person who entered, and the pungent aroma of marijuana began to fill the room.

I hate that smell, Elizabeth thought.

Simultaneously, Paul muttered under his breath so only Elizabeth could hear, "That smell makes me nauseous. Reminds me of the constant stench in Vietnam, everyone too stoned to shoot straight or care. Let's go find somewhere to sit."

With that, Elizabeth tightened her grip on Paul's hand and allowed him to drag her into the crowd that got bigger by the minute. They stepped over a dozen people, apologetic all the way, and exercised great care not to step on anyone's hands, bota bag, or overly full Styrofoam cup of cheap beer. They found a spot just big enough for the two of them and spread their blanket. Paul was excited and

Elizabeth was excited for him. She knew this was good medicine for his wounded heart.

Without warning, the lights dimmed, and even though no one had taken the stage, deafening applause erupted. Elizabeth couldn't help but be energized by the pulse of the room, the excitement of the crowd, and the sheer volume of the experience. In his quiet way, she could tell Paul was relishing the moment, and they jumped to their feet when the first band bounded onto the stage. She couldn't see past the crush of people or hear the emcee over the ear-piercing noise of the crowd, but Elizabeth screamed and clapped along with everyone else when the announcement boomed, "Ladies and gentlemen…!" In the midst of the commotion, she once more wrapped her arms tightly around Paul and felt a surge of happiness overtake her. His smile was all she needed. She was glad she came.

Home at last, grateful for the break in the storm, they threw down their dirty blanket and pillows, reeking of marijuana and spilled beer. What seemed like necessary items to bring along to a pillow concert had turned out to be more of a nuisance than a help. From the minute the first band took the stage to the last encore of the evening, no one sat. For two hours, hundreds of concert goers packed themselves into one giant, pulsating throng, like a single unit, hands waving, feet stomping, and cigarette lighters casting an amber glow above the crowd.

The sad heap of linens they brought home had been trampled by dirty feet, and soaked in spilled beer, cigarette ashes, and worse. Unable to bear the odor, and remembering laundry day wasn't until Wednesday, Paul stuffed everything in a trash bag and set it on the balcony of their tiny apartment.

"We'll get to it later. Right now, I wanna take a quick shower, have a piece of leftover meatloaf, and go to bed. With you."

Elizabeth set about removing her smelly clothes, equally as overpowering as the pillows and blanket. She added them to the sack after she had taken a quick rinse, and changed into a warm pair of flannel pajamas. Paul was eating the meatloaf right from the plate, using a knife to cut one slice at a time, making sure there would still be some left for dinner the next night.

"Ah, cold meatloaf. Nothing better for a late-night snack." He reminisced about coming home from basketball practice in his junior year of high school, his mother's meatloaf and mashed potatoes ready to take center stage at the dinner table. It was a memory tinged with comfort and sorrow, one that rarely visited his thoughts. He brought himself back to the present and turned to Elizabeth, "Want some?"

Elizabeth shook her head, "No, I'm going to bed. Hurry up, I'm freezing and I need your body heat to keep me warm."

With that, Paul carefully wrapped what was left of the meatloaf, returned it exactly to the same spot in the refrigerator from which he had taken it, and laid the knife in the empty sink. Before turning around, he removed a clean glass from the cupboard and, with no intention of using it, put the knife inside the glass and placed it in the sink. He sheepishly glanced at Elizabeth. "I didn't want the knife to be alone all night."

Is that odd or sweet? Elizabeth thought, but hesitated to utter it out loud. Paul gently led her into the bedroom, turned off the light, and curled up beside her.

Chapter 21

PAUL DREADED THE SIGHT THAT WAS ABOUT TO GREET him behind the sterile, unwelcoming door. He slowly shuffled through the hospital halls one more time, passing the vending machine for the third time, the restroom, the drinking fountain. He stopped at the nurse's station to ask the time, making sure his watch was accurate, pause, stop, start—anything to avoid pulling back the curtain to see his father, emaciated and weak, waiting for his only child to visit him for perhaps the last time. The O'Brien family name was the only thing Paul and his father had shared since his mother died.

Paul Senior's deterioration was rapid, but came as no surprise to Paul. He often wondered, with the brutal way he treated his body and soul, how his father lasted this long, well into his 60s. The death of his wife had rattled him to the core, and any semblance of the life they once shared as a happy, loving family had been shattered. As soon as the last guest said goodbye on the day of his mother's funeral, Paul's childhood became nothing but a memory, and his father accepted a life of solitary mourning. Neighbors tried to help by bringing warm meals and visiting, but no amount of attention and support could release the senior O'Brien from his depression. Paul felt helpless as he watched his father turn to a fifth of gin a day for solace.

Their house began a slow decline into disrepair, the lawn grew tall, turned brown, and died in the summer year after year, until there was no lawn left, and a front yard full of dirt took the place of the once-manicured, lovingly maintained property. Neighbors turned a blind eye to the debris that piled up in the side yard, the siding that rotted from termites, and the white paint, once pristine, that peeled from lack of care or interest.

After Paul graduated from high school, the draft was upon him. When all his friends waited in fear of their notice, Paul surprised everyone by joining the Marines and reporting to Camp Pendleton for basic training almost immediately. His father mumbled a cursory, "Goodbye... I'll miss you, Son," at the bus station, and seemed relieved that the burden of paying attention to his only child was lifted. He preferred to live as a recluse, and now there would be no one to question, complain, blame, or interrupt the life of pain he chose.

As Paul made his way closer to his father's room, he suddenly felt guilty he hadn't invited him to their wedding. It had been an intimate, minimal affair, made up mostly of Elizabeth's family. It was only Sam, Linda, and their two children, Elizabeth's twin sisters, Aunt Deborah, Uncle Bill, and their son, Ricky, who was now a father and husband. At the time, he wasn't feeling generous enough to disrupt the nuptials and celebration by having his father attend. Paul Senior had turned into an uncontrollable alcoholic, subject to blackouts and rage, and would have turned the wedding into a three-ring circus. Elizabeth's heart was a little larger and she urged Paul to reconsider, but on this topic, he could not be swayed.

The announcement to marry was sudden. "Please don't tell me you're only marrying me because I'm pregnant," Elizabeth had whispered in Paul's ear when she joined him in front of the minister.

As always, a smile and a wink from Paul were all she needed. "All right, I won't tell you I'm marrying you because we're pregnant. Baby or no baby, Elizabeth, I love you."

The impending birth of his first child and the thought that this little person would grow up without grandparents made Paul choke back tears. *I could have done better. He should have done better. It never would have been like this if Mom hadn't died.* Immense sorrow swept over him as he recollected the better times, the early times, the precious times, when it was the three of them—the wonder years before his mother was taken. He felt melancholy as he realized there was no more time. His father's life was running out, and he, in his stubbornness, had never extended the final olive branch or reached out to try and repair the damage that the estranged years magnified. For the first time, he saw his father was every bit as damaged as he was.

Paul took a deep breath, stood up straight, and took the first step into the room, aware of every little sound of the machines and the short, shallow breaths of his father. He felt compelled to speak to him one last time. Even if Paul Senior was too weak to respond, Paul would utter the words that were left unsaid for far too long.

Paul's whole body tingled as he realized this would be the last time he would see his father and his opportunity to be a better son would vanish. Approaching the bedside, he leaned in close to his father's face, being careful not to disturb the tubes hooked up to his nose and arms. His eyes were trained on the machine in the background, keeping a steady record of his heartbeat and pulse. The bed beside his father was empty and he felt fortunate he had total privacy to have this last conversation.

Taking his father's hand, no longer strong and full of life, but frail and weak, Paul spoke softly. "Dad, I know you were in pain after Mom died, and I'm more aware of that now than I have been in the last ten years. I was so consumed with my own grief, not only at losing Mom, but at the sights, sounds, and horrors I witnessed in the war. I was not equipped to pay attention to your sorrow, only to my own. I removed you from my life because I thought you removed me from yours. I didn't have the strength to battle both our demons, so

I concentrated, selfishly, on my own. I was not there for you and I should have been, even if you couldn't be there for me."

Paul hesitated and wished it wasn't one-way conversation. He wanted to know his father could hear him. "You're almost a grandfather and my child will be the one to lose, because he'll never know his father's father or his father's mother. I know I should be elated, but I'm feeling lost and regretful, and wish I could do these last few years over again. I wanted to tell you how much I love you, and how grateful I am for the memories we made a long time ago."

Paul took a deep breath and grasped his father's hand. He thought he felt a movement and a slight grip in return, but it was hard to be sure. Mostly he felt peaceful, content, and forgiven as the line on the screen became flatter and flatter, and his father silently slipped away.

Chapter 22

THOMAS FITZGERALD, ATTORNEY AT LAW, WAS notified soon after the passing of Paul O'Brien, Senior, and he dutifully gathered the necessary documents to meet with Paul and Elizabeth. While sorting through the years of clutter and debris in the home of his father, Paul had uncovered a last will and testament, which was quite visible and neatly packaged in comparison to the rest of the rubble. He immediately contacted the law agency whose name was attached to the folder and learned the name of the attorney in charge of his father's legal matters. Paul didn't recall any discussions of wills, assests, or inheritance. He was not expecting much when he placed the call to Mr. Fitzgerald.

Exactly on time, Mr. Fitzgerald approached the landing of the apartment building where Paul and Elizabeth were trying to bring order to the chaos that came along with a three-month-old child. Rex was a loud and robust baby who took up almost every waking and sleeping moment of Elizabeth's time. There never seemed to be enough hours in the day to clean, shop, cook, and dote on the precious little boy she and Paul adored. The small house that was crowded with two adults felt even tighter and more uncomfortable as Rex's toys, crib, bottles, and pacifiers swallowed up most of the once-vacant floor space. At some point the young parents knew they would need to move, but Elizabeth had quit her job right before Rex was born and Paul's small salary wasn't enough to accommodate a larger living space.

Paul was expecting the attorney and opened the door immediately after he knocked. Elizabeth was cradling a sleeping Rex in the rocker that was a baby gift from Sam and Linda, and wanted to make sure he was peaceful and asleep during the meeting. She made an effort to greet Mr. Fitzgerald, but instead nodded in his direction after being introduced, so as not to jostle the baby.

Mr. Fitzgerald sensed the need to speak quietly. "It's so nice to meet you, Paul. I knew your mother very well. We went to high school together. Your father and I became best of friends after your parents married. He kept in contact with me on a regular basis after your mother died, and made me promise to keep all his policies in force and not let anything lapse. He was a good, kind man."

Who's he talking about? Paul wondered. He could barely remember this "good man" that Mr. Fitzgerald spoke of. At the same time, it gave him solace in knowing his father had one good friend he kept and trusted for a lifetime, and throughout his sorrowful last years, had some joy and contentment.

"Please, sit down, Mr. Fitzgerald. I'm sorry for the clutter, but I think there's enough room over here for you to spread out and show us whatever you brought with you." Paul pulled out a chair at the small dining room table which moments before had been cleared of a stack of diapers and freshly laundered baby blankets. Mr. Fitzgerald graciously sat down and turned his seat towards Elizabeth so she could also hear what he had to say, while not expecting her to move from her comfortable spot with baby Rex.

"Water, coffee, iced tea? I'm sorry I didn't have time to bake cookies. It was the plan, but the day got away from me, as you can see."

Mr. Fitzgerald smiled, said water would be fine, and thought how pleased this scene would have made Paul's parents and his dear friends. He was happy for what he was about to reveal and graciously accepted the glass of ice water Paul brought him. "So let's begin."

Turning to Paul, he began, "You may or may not remember the beach house your parents bought when you were starting high school? Shortly after they purchased it, your mother got ill, and they were never able to enjoy it as they had hoped and planned. Your father worked very hard and saved for many years to purchase a second home for their retirement, but as we know that didn't happen. For the last fifteen years I've been managing the property, which has seen a variety of tenants, but is still basically in excellent condition. Your father had a fund for repairs and improvements and insisted maintenance was the top priority."

Again, Paul thought, *Who is this man he's talking about?* Given the condition of the place his father called home, Paul could hardly believe they were one and the same. He allowed Mr. Fitzgerald to continue without interruption, remembering the house he hadn't thought about in years.

He listened intently as Mr. Fitzgerald continued, "The beach cottage now belongs to you, Paul. There's no mortgage, I'll deliver a thirty-day notice to the current tenants, and the deed will be transferred to you."

Paul was stunned. "I thought that place would have been long gone." He turned to Mr. Fitzgerald. "Are you sure? The little house down by San Diego? In Carlsbad? My dad kept it after mom died?"

"I'm not sure how I can reassure you, but trust me, it was always your father's plan to pass it down to you upon his death. It's all here in this folder." Mr. Fitzgerald handed Paul a large stack of papers with paper clips holding little notes protruding from the pages that required his signature. "This is a lot to take in," he acknowledged, "and I'm sure you have a lot of questions to ask me and each other. Please call me in the next day or so and we can get down to the business of making this situation a reality."

As Paul fought back tears for his lack of compassion for his father, the missed opportunities to repair the past, and this sudden wave of good fortune, he felt a warm wind sweep past his face and knew his parents were smiling. Showing Mr. Fitzgerald to the door and grasping his hand to shake, he felt the urge to latch on to this man, and embraced him in a warm hug. "I'll call you tomorrow to set up our next appointment, Mr. Fitzgerald. Thank you so much for everything you've done for our family."

Closing the door behind him, eyes trained on Elizabeth and his sleeping baby, Paul sank into the last available spot on the sofa and let out a long sigh. The room was still as the full meaning of the gift he had received sank in. Rex stirred, and as Elizabeth tried to quiet him again, Paul interrupted, "I can't be quiet at a time like this! Let's wake up our baby, turn the radio up as high as it will go, and dance! I want to celebrate!" Rex was fully awake and Elizabeth didn't mind, not one little bit.

Chapter 23

TWO YEARS AFTER REX WAS BORN, PAUL AND Elizabeth welcomed their second child, a daughter they named Lily. It wasn't a difficult decision to name her after Paul's mother. Lily rounded out their lives and brought another dimension of joy to their growing family. They had long since settled into their cozy little bungalow by the beach, and when Paul played with Rex in their massive back yard, Elizabeth would scoop Lily up in a papoose-style wrap and hold her close to her chest, which freed her arms to do chores around the house. Sometimes she joined her boys on the back porch and rocked Lily into a peaceful slumber.

"This is all I ever wanted," she would think as she watched Paul and Rex chase each other in and out of the bushes, hide behind trees, and see who would win the race to the back fence. Elizabeth never doubted she was the luckiest girl in the world.

One afternoon Elizabeth noticed she hadn't heard a peep from Rex in a few minutes. After settling Lily into the baby swing in the living room, she called him, "Rex, where are you? Where's my little guy?"

Rex had managed to open the door to their bedroom and pull a cardboard shoe box off the dresser, scattering its contents on the floor. It was the box that was the unceremonious depository of Paul's daily treasures: watches, glasses, pens, receipts, checkbook, paper, receipts, loose change, and anything else that would fit. To him it was simply an easy way to keep everything in one spot, even though the box was overflowing. In the corner of the room, Rex tried to balance his father's glasses on his nose while he twisted them with his chubby little fingers. She saw one of the bows had broken off and, after being held together with white adhesive tape for years, held out little hope they could be repaired.

"Why don't you throw these old, useless things in the trash? They're from Vietnam, for crying out loud. The prescription can't be any good anymore." Elizabeth questioned Paul on more than one occasion, and his answer was always the same.

"You never know when I might need a second pair. Please, Elizabeth, leave them alone. Don't throw them out." The thing was, Paul refused to throw anything away, and the stacks of "keepsakes" were getting increasingly higher and more unmanageable. Elizabeth could only hope this accident would prompt Paul to throw out the old glasses, but knew that even if he did get a new pair, these would never be abandoned.

"No, no, Rex. I have to take those from you and your daddy's not going to be happy you broke his glasses." Rex looked over with his beautiful, big blue eyes that matched his father's, and handed them to his mother. Simple as that. No tantrums, no tears. Not much upset their little boy. She set them on a closet shelf, put everything back into the shoe box, returned it to its original spot on the dresser, and led Rex into the dining room. At the same time, Paul pulled into the driveway, and she allowed Rex to tug at the front door to open it for him. Without waiting for his father to set down his lunch box or jacket, Rex jumped up and down and begged to be picked up to welcome his daddy home. As always, Paul didn't hesitate to scoop up his son and let him slobber all over him with the well-practiced kiss of a two-year-old.

With the children down for the night, Elizabeth retrieved the fragmented glasses from the bedroom and handed them to Paul. "I think it's time to consider buying a new pair. I didn't realize how big Rex is getting. He opened the door to our bedroom when I was tending to Lily and pulled over your shoe box that was on the dresser. Nothing appeared to be harmed or out of place except your glasses. Maybe it's time to replace them."

She looked at Paul's crestfallen face and saw he was more hurt than upset with Rex, and probably wouldn't relinquish the now-unusable pair of glasses. Paul got up from his chair, turned down the TV, and took them from Elizabeth's hand. He walked into the bathroom and reached for the adhesive tape. Like a little boy trying to breathe new life into a dying pet turtle, he wrapped the fractured and inanimate friend one more time, a fragile cast of white tape that grew larger than the actual pair of glasses. Without a word, he walked into the bedroom, pulled out the shoe box from the safety of the closet shelf, and laid the glasses on top of the overflowing stack of paraphernalia.

Paul stepped back into the living room, turned up the volume on the TV, and motioned for Elizabeth to join him. "Time for Johnny."

Chapter 24

SCHOOL BREAKS AND SUMMERTIME WERE FAVORITE moments for Elizabeth and the children. While most mothers complained about needing more adult companionship and longed for school to start again, Elizabeth never understood. She loved spending time at home with Rex and Lily. They built cities out of cardboard boxes in the backyard or took the short walk to the beach to spend an hour or so in the sand. Whenever possible, Paul would join them, but more and more frequently he spent overtime hours at work, catching up on reports that were too time-consuming to complete during his regular hours. He never asked to or got paid for the additional time. When Elizabeth complained, he would tell her he couldn't leave the job until it was complete, even if it meant he missed dinner or worked a few extra hours. His moods shifted from easygoing and mellow to agitated and distressed. He was becoming more of a stranger with every passing day and resembled little of the man Elizabeth and the children knew. He'd often fall asleep in his lounge chair as the TV droned in the background, the radio set at an almost-inaudible volume in the kitchen. The scene was becoming too familiar, and the whole household was restless. Paul's frequent outbursts in the middle night, of which he had no recollection, concerned Elizabeth, and Rex and Lily knew that something wasn't right with their father.

"Why does Daddy get up in the middle of the night and crawl around on his belly?" A frightened Lily broke into tears as she told her mother what she saw her father do the night before.

Elizabeth scooped up her little girl and settled her on her hip. "You know how sometimes your arm falls asleep if you're lying on it the wrong way and you have to shake it around to wake it up? That's all it was, sweetie. Your daddy's feeling better. He's already gone to work. You and Rex need to get yourselves off to school."

An easy explanation for a six-year-old, but she knew the truth was not so simple. Paul was fighting demons she dared not imagine. They were recurring episodes. Almost nightly he would throw over a coffee table to hide from an invisible enemy, seek cover behind the couch, huddle in the corner with a watchful eye on the door, or flatten his body on the floor, slowly pulling himself along the baseboards. After she dried the final dish from that morning's breakfast and wiped the last crumb off the counter, Elizabeth sat down in the living room, the worn Yellow Pages in hand. She licked her right index finger to turn the fragile pages and stopped at "P" for "Psychiatrist." Hands shaking and not sure she was doing the right thing, she went by instinct and the sound of the doctor's name to determine her choice of professionals for her broken husband.

Elizabeth wasn't sure how Paul was going to react or even how she should approach the subject, but after settling Rex and Lily with a favorite bedtime story, she finally had a free moment for her husband. Paul was nowhere to be found. She searched the entire house, then scoured the pitch-black backyard. The whole street was dimly lit, and once the sun went down, it wasn't easy to see even the closest object. Paul once told her, "You don't know dark. Dark is a jungle, a long line of weary, battle-scarred comrades, stealthily trudging a breath away from one another, seeking out an enemy you can neither see nor hear. Dark is fear and uncertainty and knowing that death can grab you in an instant. Dark is hearing your heart beat like a giant kettle drum and feeling the blood rush through your veins because there is no sound, no light, and no sense of anything around you but your own terrified soul. That's all I'm going to say. This backyard is not dark."

Elizabeth heard those words in her head as she continued to search for Paul. What was a child's dream playground during daylight hours, with room for cardboard cities, Slip 'N Slides that stretched the length of the property, and temporary forts for lunchtime shelter, took on a different tone once the sun went down. One good rain could bring a densely, tangled web of tall grass, and although Paul worked every weekend to manage the growth, he could hardly keep up with it in the winter months. Coyotes roamed in the darkness, hid insidiously behind bushes, and waited for an opportunity to pounce. It was not unusual to hear the cries of the pack as they made their way through the yard and found a small animal that tried to escape their grasp, but that failed to break away.

Paul was quiet when he left the house. He had made up his mind, and he knew how to appear and disappear without making a sound, a stealth tactic perfected by his training in that bitter conflict that robbed him of his self-worth, value, and ability to provide the American dream to the family he cherished. *Elizabeth won't even realize I'm gone for another hour. Bath time, story—by then it will be over."*

There was almost a spring in his step as he considered the ultimate sacrifice he was about to make for his wife and children. He had checked the train schedule before closing the door behind him for the last time, and had been careful to hide it under his box of treasures in the bedroom he and Elizabeth would never share again. He looked at his watch. One hour. Paul made it to the park on the corner within minutes. He noticed every blade of grass, every tree, every piece of playground equipment, and every picnic table illuminated by the street lights. Once darkness cleared and the early morning cloud cover parted for the sun, the park would come alive with the happy sounds of children and young families. Delighted toddlers would hang on for dear life to the swings and merry-go-rounds, and older brothers would coax little sisters down the slide for the first time. Paul stopped briefly and gazed at the pitch-black, deserted playground.

I remember that day, the first time Lily went down the slide. Rex was behind her, legs around her waist, his arms tight around her shoulders so she wouldn't be scared. He drew an audible breath. *There was no stopping her after that.* And nothing could stop Paul. He took one final look behind him, positive that Elizabeth had not yet noticed his absence.

The sudden amplification of the freeway noise brought Paul back to the present. Sounds of the interstate, a constant drone in the background of nearby homes, interrupted the tranquility of this beautiful piece of paradise. Like a watermelon that falls gently to either side with one deft slice, the east portion of I-5 was punctuated by the serenity of older houses and quiet neighborhoods, while west of the freeway was a coastal ribbon, a thriving downtown village, and an open invitation to tourists year round. Elizabeth had no problem with the expansion and ongoing growth on either side of the freeway. It made walking to entertainment so much easier than packing everyone in the car, but Paul hated change. He couldn't remember anything but Coast Highway when his parents bought their summer home in the early '60s. He hardly heard the freeway sound anymore, though, except for tonight. Tonight he noticed everything.

He quickened his pace and felt himself drawn towards the main intersection. He sensed how close he was to the ending he had planned so carefully. Memories of his mother started a meddling monologue. *Mom, I'm almost there. I'll see you and Dad soon. If everything you taught me is true, I'll be there. I'm coming. Wait for me.*

By the time he found his way to Elm Avenue, he was short of breath. He glanced up at the street sign. He'd heard talk about changing the name of the main street to Carlsbad Village Drive, but the conversion stalled while the city worked with CalTrans, converted freeway signs, and reviewed the cost involved. Many locals hated the idea of a name change, but the city council felt it would increase revenue through additional tourism. He thought about the changes his family would see in years to come. *This is the only way I can show them how much I love them.* Paul's thoughts raced as he checked his watch. Forty minutes.

The noise and exhaust from the freeway off-ramp heightened his awareness. His heart beat faster and harder as he realized the tracks were blocks away, just within reach, his final destination. *This is a good thing. Everyone will be happier. Can't swallow one more pill. Nothing's helping. Can't sleep, can't protect my family, mission failed.*

Consumed with his thoughts and momentarily blinded by oncoming headlights, Paul stepped off the curb against a red light and startled when a car swung left to the on-ramp, directly in his path. With the quick reflexes of a soldier in battle, he jumped out of harm's way, missed by inches, and heard the blare of the angered driver's horn, along with, "Asshole! What the hell are you doing?"

⬭◈⬮

Every second that passed, Elizabeth became more frightened. Her mind raced with horrible thoughts and she hoped not to come into contact with anything or anyone but Paul. She trembled to think that she was feeling only a sliver of the fear Paul must have felt while he marched through the jungles of Vietnam. The dime-store flashlight she had grabbed from the kitchen drawer seemed like little protection, but she hoped it would be a warning light for animals and a beacon for Paul to see her searching for him in the black night. Elizabeth was frantic. Trying not to wake the children and almost at a whisper, she continued to call his name as she made her way farther and farther into the shadowy back yard, peering behind bushes, checking out every tree, and becoming more and more fearful of what she might find. *Oh, Paul, where are you?* Dread crept into her thoughts, and even though she wanted to find him, she hoped she would not.

⌎◈⌏

Paul could see the tracks, just past the supermarket, a couple of gas stations, banks, and fast-food restaurants lining Elm Avenue. *Not sure what side of the street. Should I cross first? How long should I stand there? I should jump when it's a few feet away. I don't want anyone to stop me or get hurt trying to save me.*

Paul waited for the green lights at every intersection. He learned his lesson at the on-ramp. He didn't want to get injured. He needed it to be done. He mentally checked off every block, noticing for the last time the presidents' names running north and south. Harding, Jefferson, Madison, Roosevelt, and finally State Street. He saw the railroad tracks with the train station to the north. He made sure his train wasn't scheduled to make a stop in the village. He needed the momentum of a fast-moving engine. He wanted quick and painless. *I still have time for one last look at the water.* He checked his watch again. Thirty minutes.

The winter sunsets came early, and even though it wasn't quite 7:00 o'clock, the streets were almost empty. The January night was unseasonably warm, and Paul realized the jacket he wore wasn't

142

necessary. He had considered leaving it behind, but grabbed it from the back of his lounge chair at the last moment. The zippered pocket would be the safest place for the note. He wasn't sure if anyone would find what he painfully penciled out if he tucked it into the pocket of his jeans. Even if he put it inside his shoes, he had read that sometimes an impact such as this could knock the shoes right off your feet. Paul wanted Elizabeth, Rex, and Lily to know how much he loved them.

Paul scanned Coast Highway in the distance, a few short blocks away. He could see the brilliant lights of the new hotel, a beautiful addition to the village and the coastline. The Carlsbad Inn was an homage to old-world architecture, and as far as change was concerned, it was positive. Paul walked briskly, not much time before his train would arrive. He wanted to take in the breathtaking sound of the ocean one more time, pleased it was a clear night so he'd be able to see the dancing lights from Oceanside pier bounce off the water in the distance. *I must say goodbye to this place I love. Five minutes, just five minutes.* As he lowered his body to sit on the edge of the cliff, a perfect spot to listen to the crashing waves below, he glanced again at his watch. Twenty minutes. He reached inside his pocket and retrieved the note, written in his darkest moment, but with a resolve to bring an end to the pain and suffering for everyone.

Perfectly folded in four quarters, he glanced at his uneven handwriting on the top right-hand corner, *For Elizabeth.* He imagined a police officer handing it to her after they retrieved his body, but dismissed the thought with a shiver as he slowly unfolded the piece of paper, one corner at a time.

Dear Elizabeth,

I never wanted to leave you this way, but was always afraid I might. Remember the line in our song, 'Maybe I'm Amazed?' You've loved me more than I ever thought possible, but my soul is rotted, hollow.

You can't fix that. I can't fix that. I'm not good for you. I'm not good for Rex or Lily. The music will never be loud enough. The memories will never be dim enough. You will eventually leave me and that would surely kill me. I'm sorry. I don't know what else to say. Please understand this is for the best. Take care of each other. I love you all—

"Go home, Paul. You haven't said goodbye. You can't leave without saying goodbye."

Surprised and panicked, Paul turned to see who had spoken. How could he not know someone was standing in his space? Too close. He looked in every direction. He saw no one and tried to ignore it. His palms began to sweat and the once-fresh, crisp note started to wilt from the ocean air and his sticky hands. He wadded it up in ball and, as he stuffed it into the pocket of his jeans, hoped no one had been close enough to read it or peer over his shoulder. He thought he recognized the voice, a woman's voice.

"Mom? Was that you?"

He knew he heard something, distinct and direct. Perhaps he was thinking out loud, but the seed was planted. He listened and, as he raised from his perch, stood motionless, until the final urge to glance at his watch one last time pulled him closer to the moment of truth: five minutes. In the clarity of the moment, he knew the voice was right. He hadn't said goodbye. Not to Elizabeth, not to Rex, not to Lily.

He retraced his steps through the village and advanced to State Street. The oncoming train blared its horn and the safety arms lowered in slow motion as Paul approached the tracks. There were a mere few feet between him and the monster machine that would determine his fate. He took a deep breath and took one giant step—backwards. The rush of air and the acrid smell of steel and smoke caught him by surprise, and within seconds the decision was no longer his to make. The moment had passed, the train raced southbound to the next station, and an unsuspecting engineer would finish an uneventful journey to the end of the line. Paul struggled to compose himself, unable to comprehend the last hour of his life. As he gathered his thoughts and crossed the tracks in the direction of home, he murmured, "There's always tomorrow."

⊰◇⊱

It was not the time to call the authorities, but Elizabeth knew she had to do something. Paul could have taken a walk around the block, and although he never left the house without saying goodbye, his recent behavior could account for anything. Calling the police or knocking on neighbor's doors would embarrass him if all he needed was a little fresh air. She went into the bedroom to get a sweater and sticking out from under the shoe box, not quite out of sight, was a train schedule. Though their cottage was several blocks away, they could hear the trains blaring their horns as they passed through the village. Moving at sixty miles an hour, they were fascinating for the children to watch, but frightening for Elizabeth to consider if something went terribly wrong—a collision with a stalled vehicle, a faulty track that could derail the entire chain of cars, a youthful dare to play chicken with this powerful machine, or a depressed and agitated soul wanting to find a quick and painless end to their suffering.

Elizabeth grabbed her car keys and made sure the children were asleep before she dashed out the door in search of Paul. Even before she made it to the bottom of their hill, she saw a familiar figure, wearily pulling his body up the steep incline. Paul's head was down, every step was a struggle, and he was unaware Elizabeth had pulled up beside him. She rolled down the window, convinced he could hear, and with a tearful plea yelled, "Paul! Where have you been? I've been searching for the last hour. I've been so frightened!"

Paul continued to drag himself up the hill. "I forgot to say goodbye, Elizabeth. I'm sorry. I left without saying goodbye..."

More unintelligible words spilled from Paul's mouth. Elizabeth knew she couldn't let him out of her sight, so she made a quick U-turn and they inched closer to the driveway in tandem. Her heart was racing, her only thought getting Paul to safety. A prickly chill coursed through her as his words sank in. She would ask him later what he meant, even though she already knew. Tearful, she silently mouthed towards the heavens, *Thank you.*

Rushing to open the front door, she helped Paul into the living room and threw her arms around his shaking body. He didn't return the hug, nor did he pull away. Elizabeth saw a depth of sorrow and despair deep within those beautiful blue eyes that welled with tears. "Paul, Paul, let me help you. Is this how you want your children to remember you?"

Barely audible, Paul mumbled, "No."

"Is this how you want to leave us and leave me to pick up the pieces?" Elizabeth pressed on, sad, angry, confused, and terrified. "Tell me right this second, right now, you will get back in the car with me and drive to the hospital. You need help now, not tomorrow morning, not next week, not next month. Please, Paul, please! I don't want to have to call someone to the house."

He didn't look up and she could hardly believe his response. "No. Not tonight. I'm tired. I can't go tonight."

"You will go tonight!" They had never really fought, and certainly never raised their voices to one another, but this was a fight for Paul's life, and with little concern of waking the children, Elizabeth's voice grew louder. Rex and Lily appeared in the doorway and took in the scene unfolding between their parents.

Lily, sweet Lily, ignored the argument and pressed between them. Paul bent down to give her a hug. Grasping his tear-streaked face with her velvety soft hands, Lily stroked it gently and whispered,

"Daddy, I love you." Her little arms wrapped around his neck and Paul stood up straight, clutched his little girl, and choked back tears. He gazed in Elizabeth's direction. "Let's go."

Chapter 25

"Hello, Paul. Come in." Dr. Worthington had reviewed Paul's intake report in depth. He extended his hand. Paul, reluctant at first, shook it.

"Sit down. Anywhere you're comfortable."

Paul chose a seat close to the window where the light and the sun could warm his back, as well as provide him with the ideal location to keep an eye on the door. He wasn't looking forward to individual sessions, group sessions, or any session where he would be expected to spill his guts and dredge up the awful memories he had fought so hard to suppress.

"So, how are you today? Are they treating you well?"

Paul wasn't sure how to answer. "Um… fine. Fine, I guess."

Dr. Worthington smiled and continued. "So, anything you'd like to talk about? Do you know why you're here?"

Paul felt a nervous flutter in his chest, his palms began to sweat, and he could feel beads of perspiration roll down the sides of his face. "Yes, Sir. I know. I don't think I need to be locked up though. I could have handled this on my own."

"You're not locked up, Paul. You can leave any time. All you've got to do is ask."

"Am I supposed to say something?" Paul raised his arm to his forehead and, as he wiped his brow with his shirtsleeve, a look of uncertainty swept across his face.

Dr. Worthington clicked his pen, ready to take notes. "What do you say we start with Elizabeth?"

"What about Elizabeth?" Paul felt defensive.

"Do you feel she loves you?"

"You mean after what I just tried to do, or before?'

"Either. It doesn't matter."

"I know Elizabeth has always loved me, and she still does. That part's easy. I've never figured out why. There's not a whole lot to love about me."

With his head down, pen in hand, Dr. Worthington prodded, "And you thought this would be a good way to leave her and your children? Were you always afraid you might leave like this?"

"I'm a wreck, Doc. Can I call you Doc? I'm not trying to sound disrespectful.

"That's fine. Go on."

Paul's voice was quiet. He lowered his eyes, fixated on his fingers that had begun to twitch and tremble. "I never wanted anyone to take care of me. I'm a burden."

"You don't know that. Did Elizabeth ever tell you that you were a burden?"

"Never. But it's hard to watch her and the children be so good to me after everything I've done in the past. I have blood on my hands. A lot of blood."

"Do they know what you did? In Vietnam?" Dr. Worthington continued his slow, methodical questioning as Paul shifted uncomfortably in his seat. He thought it might be a good place to stop, but decided to keep going.

Paul tapped his feet on the sterile, linoleum floor, staring down at the smooth, colorless pattern that covered the entire room. Not quite green, not yellow, not white, not brown. Colorless, antiseptic, without consequence. It was a background to everything, not important by design. He felt like the floor beneath his feet. *Why am I still here? There's no more meaning to my life than this damn floor.*

Paul wrestled with the topic of conversation. "Okay. I'll tell you what you want to hear, if it's that important to you."

Dr. Worthington showed no emotion. *No, young man, it's so important to you.*

"I never talk about it to anyone. Not even my brother-in-law, Sam. We were wounded in the same battle. Harvest Moon. December, 1965, trying to protect the Niu Loc Son Basin. No one needs to hear. No one needs to know."

"Did you see a lot of heavy fighting?"

Paul sat up straight. "Is that a watered down way of asking me if I killed a lot of people?"

Dr. Worthington shrugged. "You tell me."

"Okay. I was given permission, no actually ordered, to kill by my commanding officer, who was under orders from his commanding officer, and he was only doing his job to prepare and replace the broken equipment to get the job done. That would be us. That would be the young men barely out of high school, drafted, and reporting in record numbers to find and kill other men our very same age, who were also someone's brother, husband, or son. We were nothing more than equipment… killing machines."

"You sound disturbed, Paul." Dr. Worthington pushed back in his chair and set his pen on the table. He was a good psychiatrist, liked Paul, and wanted to do right by him.

"You're damn right I'm disturbed!" Paul jumped up from his chair and paced nervously from one corner of the room to the other. "My brain is filled with blood and body parts, explosions and scenes of medics scrambling in between bombs to save as many fallen as humanly possible. And that includes me. I was responsible for part of that carnage."

Paul struggled to control his breathing, trying not to hyperventilate and holding on by sheer will. He could feel the reverberation from his heart beating inside his chest and he stood motionless, collecting his thoughts, afraid to continue. Dr. Worthington watched with concern, his own awareness heightened by the outpouring of emotions from his patient. "Take a deep breath, Paul."

"It's hard to make love to your wife, hug your baby girl, or give your boy a high-five when these pictures consume you. I just wanted it to stop. Everyone would've been better off without me."

"You think so? Did you think about what it might have been like for your children to have a legacy of a father who took his own life? You don't think they may have carried that burden for their entire lives, knowing they were not important enough to fight for?" Dr. Worthington's eyes followed Paul, still pacing the room.

"I've treated many children of parents who have done what you tried to do, and unfortunately, they succeeded. It doesn't make any difference if their parents were in the military, drug addicts, alcoholics, or depressed. For their entire lives, these kids feel deserted. It's not a good way to leave, Paul."

With silent tears, Paul slumped back into his chair and turned to Dr. Worthington. "I just want it to go away. I want to forget. I want to take care of my family, not the other way around. I want to feel like a man. Killing other human beings does not make you feel tough, rugged, or manly."

"We talked about electric shock therapy. That's about the only way you might stand a chance of erasing these memories. You turned that option down, so we need to help you find coping mechanisms, regulate anti-depressants, continue individual therapy and group therapy sessions as an inpatient, as well as outpatient. Are you willing to put in the work?"

Paul had no alternative solution, and with a nod of his head, mumbled, "Yes." Without making eye contact with Dr. Worthington, Paul asked, "Where's the note?"

Dr. Worthington patted an innocuous-looking file, a label affixed to the middle tab that said nothing more than "O'Brien, Paul." "It's in here. You want it?"

"No. I don't want it… ever."

"Good." They stood at the same time and Dr. Worthington extended his hand, making a mental note of the strength in Paul's handshake.

Reaching for the door, Paul turned to Dr. Worthington, "You sure Elizabeth won't know anything we talked about?"

"Not unless you want to tell her."

Chapter 26

ELIZABETH STAYED CLOSE TO THE PHONE, HOPING IT would ring. The nurses at the mental health facility were kind, but strict, and informed her during Paul's admission he may not be ready for visitors for a couple of days, but that he'd be allowed to make calls from the public phone on his floor whenever he liked. As long as it didn't interfere with a therapy session or meals, Paul could call whenever he chose.

"Mom, what's for dinner?" Lily rushed past her mother as she continued to pace back and forth near the only phone in the house, an old, blue, faded wall model with a five-foot spiral cord that tangled easily and took the skill of a surgeon to untangle. Elizabeth tried substituting it once with a more modern, cordless version, easily transported throughout the house, but the batteries lost their charge too quickly if it wasn't replaced on the cradle after use and the children treated it more like a toy than the piece of equipment it was meant to be. The old phone worked better than any newer invention, and Paul especially found comfort in the familiarity, the echoes of the past, another constant in his unpredictable world.

Elizabeth hardly noticed the children the last twenty-four hours, finding it hard to concentrate on anything but the memory of the night before, still fresh and raw in her mind. She shuddered and choked back tears at the thought of how different this evening could have been for all of them if Paul had succeeded, not changed his mind in a sudden moment of clarity and reason.

Focus… focus. Rex, Lily, food, dinner. Have to make something for the kids to eat. That will take my mind off the fucking phone. Damn you, Paul! How could you be so selfish?

"Mom, did you hear me? What's for dinner?"

With her innermost thoughts interrupted once again, Elizabeth backed away from the phone. "What would you like tonight, my darling Lily?" She felt a surge of strength with the distraction. "Let's see what we have on hand. Come on, help me, we'll decide together."

While Lily peered inside the refrigerator and Elizabeth checked the cupboards, a sudden, loud pronouncement by Rex from the other room interrupted their 'what's in the house' scavenger hunt. "McDonald's. I want to go to McDonald's."

Elizabeth was startled. She wasn't even aware of Rex's whereabouts at that precise moment, but knew he would either be outside playing with GI Joe or in the living room constructing a web of buildings with his Legos. Elizabeth felt guilty for an instant. As drastic and dire as the situation was with Paul, she knew she had two precious hearts depending on her strength and resolve. The calmer she could remain, the better it would be for her babies, for their babies.

"Grand idea, Rex. What do you think, Lily?"

Rex excitedly appeared in the kitchen and waited for an answer. Elizabeth and Lily returned cans of food to the cupboard and placed the leftovers from two nights before back in the fridge. Lily's eyes widened, "Yay! McDonald's! I want to go!"

"Of course, we're all going. Thank your brother for the suggestion."

Lily rushed towards Rex and almost toppled him as she gave him a big bear hug, simultaneously pushing everyone out the door.

"I've got your keys, Mom." Rex practically threw them at Elizabeth, pleased it had been such a simple negotiation. Locking the door behind her, Elizabeth hoped she wouldn't miss a call from

Paul, and her stomach tightened with the realization he would not be joining her and the children for dinner anytime soon.

After settling into the uncomfortable, rigid seats of Rex and Lily's idea of restaurant paradise, the table top still sticky from previous little hands, Elizabeth sank back and took in the all-too-familiar scene: two Happy Meals, two small soft drinks, one fish sandwich, and a side of fries, packed neatly on the Formica tray, delivered without being asked, by Rex. Missing was the Big Mac, large Coke, and large fries. Placing the meals in front of his mother and sister, Rex muttered, "Where's Dad? When's he coming home?"

Lily was composed, serene, and matter of fact as she pried open the Happy Meal box to reveal the toy inside. She quipped, "He's at the hospital so they can fix his arm when it falls asleep, right Mom?"

Elizabeth drew a deep breath as she struggled to hold back tears. She watched her baby girl, engrossed with the molded plastic Muppet Baby—Miss Piggy, complete with her little pink car—now being pushed between the maze of drinks, fries, and burgers, on a guaranteed collision course with Rex's skate-board-riding Kermit the Frog. Elizabeth sat up straight and brushed aside a loose wisp of hair that had fallen into her daughter's eyes. "I couldn't have said it better myself, Lily. Let's eat." Rex shrugged.

◇

Elizabeth put Rex and Lily to bed before checking the answering machine. She didn't want either of her children to overhear a conversation with their father, especially Rex. She settled into a chair next to the phone, aware of the blinking light the moment they returned home. With a bit of apprehension, as well as excitement, she pressed 'play.'

"Hi, Elizabeth. This is Paul."

She thought how unnecessary it as for him to say who was calling. She knew his voice well, even though it sounded flat, unemotional, and sad. *Funny how a few words can create such distance between two people who have known each other half a lifetime.*

"Met with the doctor today… hard. I hate this, Elizabeth. I don't want to be here. I'm sorry..." Paul's voice trailed off, as though he had turned his head from the mouthpiece and was speaking into thin air. "How are Rex and Lily? Can you call me back? We can get phone calls 'til nine."

Elizabeth immediately dialed the number she had written down earlier and pinned to the kitchen wall with a thumbtack. A stranger's voice answered on the other end and she remembered it was a public telephone. Any patient was free to answer while drifting past, a weak link to their outside worlds. "May I speak with Paul O'Brien, please?"

She heard the phone drop and clatter against the wall. She hoped it meant that whoever answered would go find Paul. She waited. It seemed like forever. *How long should I listen to the silence before giving up and trying again in the morning?* Elizabeth was agitated, tired, and in no mood to be left dangling.

Finally, the muffled sound of someone picking up the receiver broke the stillness. *Don't hang up whoever you are, please don't hang up.*

"Elizabeth, you called." Paul's voice melted the tension and a grateful wave of relief washed over her.

"How did you know it was me?"

"Who else would it be? I'm so glad you called, Elizabeth. I'm so sorry for what I'm putting you and the kids through."

"Hush. You're here. You're still with us. That's all we care about."

"I can't tell you how sorry I am." Paul's voice cracked.

"Paul, it's okay. Please… get some sleep tonight and know we love you. I'll bring the kids this Sunday and I'll come visit tomorrow when they're in school. That'll give us plenty of time to talk."

"That sounds nice. I'll be here."

"See… nice attempt at humor, Paul. I know where to find you."

Paul leaned against the cold, hospital wall, and clutched the receiver like a lifeline. "Love you, Elizabeth… see you tomorrow. Kiss Lily and Rex good night for me."

"I will. Sleep well. Love you."

Paul was impatient for his first group therapy session to end. It was a relief when the hour was over and he could see Elizabeth. Although part of him was filled with dread and remorse, he felt a long-forgotten tingle of joy and anticipation, knowing she would soon be there to confirm how much she still loved him. He wanted to ask for her forgiveness, he wanted to share one candid, honest conversation, and thank her for living her life with such an undeserving soul. Dr. Worthington had made the point that Elizabeth wouldn't know anything unless he told her. Without questioning where this sudden courage was coming from, he gathered his thoughts and strength to utter them out loud, hoping words would flow effortlessly once they were in each other's presence.

Paul was sitting outside the front entrance when Elizabeth arrived. He wore a pair of green hospital pajamas, a white terry cloth robe, and the slippers without the backs that he never liked because they were hard to keep on his feet when he walked. She smiled and mentally noted to bring him some clothes when she returned for the next visit. Paul looked tired and strained, but returned the smile ever so slightly as he stood to greet her. Their silent embrace dissolved the anger and resentment that had been building in Elizabeth's mind and she gently leaned in for a kiss, soft as it was powerful, no words necessary to prove their devotion to one another and their resolve to face this battle together for a lifetime, if that's what it would take.

"Elizabeth, you look so wonderful."

"You sure about that? I'm not feeling so wonderful, but I couldn't wait to see you, Paul. My thoughts have been pretty jumbled since the other night. Do you mind if we sit on the bench in the sun spot? It's so nice to have a little sunshine follow us in January."

Wordlessly, Paul trailed Elizabeth towards the sun's warmth. Once settled, he turned to her. "I have to tell you some things. I'm sorry, I don't want to ruin our visit. I don't want to make you worry about me anymore. If I don't tell you, I'm afraid I'll never get better, I'll become a useless old fool and destroy all of you."

Elizabeth sensed the urgency, and even though she was wondering why this was the moment Paul opened up, she didn't question his intentions. "Okay. I'm good with that Paul. You can tell me anything. You always could."

"I want you to know I've had nightmares almost from the moment I got home from Vietnam."

"I know. I was there, remember? In the apartment right after Sam and I got to California?"

"I remember. You left a note under my pillow. That was the second time I fell in love with you. The first time was when I met you at the airport. Why did this damn war have to ruin everything for us, Elizabeth?" Paul let the momentum guide him to the point he was trying to make.

"It was a slaughterhouse, Elizabeth. I'll never be able to shake those visions. Whether it was the enemy or one of our own. Watching a human being take his last breath, final words hanging in midair, eyes wide with horror and pain, trying to utter goodbye to their mothers, wives, or children until their hearts stopped beating. No one but another combat veteran can understand."

Paul looked down, his heart heavy with guilt and remorse. His eyes trained on an ant struggling to carry a breadcrumb four times its size across a maze of broken concrete and fallen leaves. *You're gonna make it back home, aren't you? That's a lot of weight for one little guy to carry.* Paul saw a line of ants forming, marching towards the overburdened member of their tribe. *A family of ants, for God's sake. They're family. I'll never dismiss these small creatures ever again. How selfish could I have been?*

For a moment, Paul forgot why he was there, and he continued to stare in silence at the pint-sized drama unfolding beneath his feet. He laid his hand on the warm bench, a breath away from Elizabeth's, and waited. *She must hate me. Now she must really hate me.*

Elizabeth did the only thing she could do, determined not to cry in front of Paul. She grasped his hand in hers, squeezed every so often in a silent gesture of support, and hoped he would squeeze back. She thought if she looked at him any longer, she would be able to penetrate his skin, muscle, and bone, and actually see his heart breaking into pieces inside his chest. She felt robbed at that moment. Robbed of the present and the future, and sensed the real struggle was only beginning. No matter what kind of medication they prescribed Paul, the faceless monster that his nightmares were made of would exist in their lives, in Rex and Lily's lives, for many years to come.

"You don't have to say anymore, Paul. I can see how upsetting it is for you to talk about this out loud. I know enough. I can't say I totally understand. I don't. But we're in this together. We're family." She rested her head on his shoulder and cherished the peaceful interlude before having to rush to pick up Rex and Lily after school.

Paul abruptly changed the subject. "You let Sam know?

"I did, right away. He's as devastated as the rest of us."

"Probably thinks I'm a coward, a quitter, a weakling."

"He thinks no such thing. He offered to come out, but I asked him to wait. I'll keep him posted. It's too soon."

"At least he has some idea, maybe. Hospital in Da Nang was no picnic."

"You were there, Paul. I can only imagine."

"No, you can't. It was touch and go with your brother for days. I can't tell you how many times he said he wished the bullet had gone through his heart, instead of his hand, and he'd died on the battlefield. Once they took his hand, he didn't want to be here either."

Elizabeth shook her head and remembered how furious she was almost two decades ago that her brother deserted her family and joined the marines. Now she only felt sorrow as she recalled those dark episodes in her childhood, totally beyond her control. "I got letters and he never said anything like that to me. I thought whatever he overcame was gone forever."

"Never gone, Elizabeth, just buried. Sam's done a better job than me. He never thought about taking the chicken way out."

"Well, maybe he has, but we don't know. Let's not talk about this anymore." Elizabeth glanced at her watch. "Only thirty minutes before school's out. I don't want to be late picking up the kids. Just sit with me until I have to leave."

"I only wanted to say I'm so sorry for the other night. I couldn't leave you, Rex, Lily…" Paul squeezed Elizabeth's hand. That's all she wanted, connection, an unspoken commitment.

"Can you forgive me?"

"I already have, Paul. I already have."

Chapter 27

THAT WINTER, THE HEAVY RAINS BROUGHT A CARPET of lush grass, colorful bushes, a variety of leafing trees, and a bounty of new blooms to the garden. Along with the spring cleaning that consumed most weekends for Elizabeth and the children, came a sense of renewal and anticipation for Paul's homecoming. A fresh coat of paint in every room was soft, soothing, and relaxing. The cupboards had new hardware, and Elizabeth made new curtain valances for the living room, dining room, and kitchen. It was just enough to feel refreshed and spotless, and as much as she would have loved new carpeting and appliances, the disability payment from Paul's hospitalization was barely adequate to get by. She knew the time would come where she would have to go back to work and, although they talked about it during her daily visits, not much was decided. It was better left for another time.

She remembered the difficulty of Paul's first week in the hospital and how grateful she was for how far they had come. The children were too young to understand the underlying gravity of the situation but Lily, especially, made sure not one day went by without writing a letter, drawing a picture, or sharing a short conversation with her daddy on the phone. Rex, pragmatic and accepting, visited with his mother and sister every Saturday and Sunday afternoon. He looked forward to the indoor basketball court that was attached to the inpatient ward. Although he stayed close to his father, he was a favorite of the patients and nurses as he momentarily distracted them with a super-charged, energetic game of basketball. The activity brightened Paul's mood and, along with the proper medications, he was able to participate with his family and slowly regain his sense of humor.

It was a double-edged sword when Elizabeth visited as she could not shake the vision of the night she brought Paul to the hospital, and what their lives might be like if Paul had not changed his mind. Her weekday visits were often spent finding a sun spot in the community living room, and simply holding Paul's hand and looking at his face. *There you are,* she would think. *I see you, I see light, I see life, I see my dear, sweet Paul."* She could barely wait for the day he was well enough to join them back home, and while she saw a vast improvement within weeks, Paul's doctors felt he needed more therapy, rest, and continued monitoring of his medications.

In one therapy session, the doctor shared there were more and more Vietnam veterans with the same symptoms Paul displayed, and studies were being conducted as to the best and safest path to successful treatment. Beyond this one mention, the subject was never brought up again, and no further consideration was given to the fact he had a shared condition with an army of soldiers returning from the war. Instead, a variety of medications were used to treat Paul as an inpatient so he could be closely monitored for side effects. After two months, Paul was given a brand new anti-depressant, recently approved by the FDA. The results were astounding. Most notable of all, Paul requested a radio for his room and, once more, the music played. Music had always been the barometer for Paul's mood, and within weeks of beginning this new medication, Dr. Worthington decided Paul was ready to go home. Ready to resume his life.

"You'll need follow-up visits and close monitoring for the next twelve months, Paul. But I think you're ready. Call Elizabeth and let her know."

"Thanks, Doc. I can handle it."

Dr. Worthington extended his hand to Paul and the men shook firmly. "I haven't said anything to you before, but I need to now. Thank you for your service, Paul."

"No problem, Doc… no problem."

⊰◈⊱

The sun came out early and the day was already warming when Elizabeth and the children approached the Psychiatric Inpatient Ward that had been Paul's home for three months. She knew there might be a delay in releasing him since, as with most hospitals, timing was never exact. She brought snacks and bottles of juice, coloring books, crayons, and a deck of cards to keep Rex and Lily busy and distracted in case there was a long wait before their Paul was discharged.

Hand in hand, marching through the front doors, a glowing, happy trio rushed to the front desk. "We are here to take my Daddy home!" Barely tall enough to peek over the counter, much less see who she might be talking to, Lily felt a slight tap on her shoulder. Turning around, Paul bent over to greet her, scooping her into his arms, and making room for the whole family to encircle him.

The man that had taken leave as a damaged, hollow, bleak shell had returned to them standing straight, alive, and alert, those blue eyes once again filled with hope, joy, and contentment.

"Hey Son, would you mind asking the nurse to get my radio from the room. It's the one thing I forgot to pack."

Rex reminded him, "Dad, we already have a radio in the kitchen. Do we need more?"

"Leave it for the next man who needs music." Lily was serious as she peered intently at her Daddy's face.

"What do you think, Paul? Should we take the radio or do you want to leave it behind?" Elizabeth didn't care one way or another but was curious for Paul's response.

"Leave it. I have all the music I need right here." Lily rested her head comfortably on her daddy's shoulder, Rex flanked his left side, and Elizabeth his right as they strode outside into the bright sunshine.

"Let's go to McDonald's for lunch." Rex never missed an opportunity.

"I've been dreaming about a Big Mac for three months. You're on."

Chapter 28

AS THAT FIRST SUMMER AFTER PAUL CAME HOME FROM the hospital faded, the family took advantage of one last barbecue in the expansive back yard. Finally able to return to work, Paul worked all summer with the small staff he supervised. Most of the summer toys were back in storage and the weekend was spent gathering school supplies, plus a few pieces of new clothing for Rex and Lily. In Southern California, mothers agreed it was senseless to rush out and buy hundreds of dollars' worth of fall clothing, as September and October were some of the hottest months of the year. Even though the girls begged for new clothes and the boys convinced themselves they wanted to look like everyone else, by the end of the first week, they were back in their summer T-shirts. Expensive jackets were abandoned on campus, and bulky sweaters were folded neatly at the bottom of drawers, out of sight, until one or two rainy days in the middle of the winter months necessitated warmer clothing.

Rex and Paul had rigged a stereo system that led from the back of the house to the patio, and a stack of cassettes was kept by the back door. Though the vinyl collection lovingly maintained by Paul swallowed one whole section of the living room, he had switched to buying cassettes, as he finally came to appreciate the convenience of taking music from house to car. Their new-to-them but used minivan was equipped with a surround stereo, and speakers that could be controlled from the front and back seats. As "Can't Find My Way Home," filled in the background, Paul and Rex were deep in conversation at the grill.

Rex was almost as tall as his father, and with one more year of grade school, seemed a bit more grown up than most boys his age. Quiet, polite, and unassuming, he never had a knack for sports and didn't care to pursue most of the athletic activities offered by the school, parks and recreation, or off-campus clubs. He seemed content to warm the bench during recess as opposed to joining the fray of pre-adolescent boys, explaining that all they did was knock each other down and call each other names, or worse yet, call other people names.

"I don't need any more friends," he would tell his mother when she voiced concern about his shyness and isolation. "I can play with whoever I want, but I like listening to music on my headphones instead. Mr. Davis says it's okay as long as I put it in my backpack when we go back in the classroom." Elizabeth eventually let the matter drop and Paul convinced her there was nothing wrong with being neither a leader nor a follower, but an individual. Rex certainly was that. She was grateful for a calm, healthy husband and two happy children.

"Here, take the burgers," Paul motioned to Rex as he shut down the grill and checked twice to make sure every burner was off. "I like your idea and we can run it by your mom and Lily over dinner." With salads, drinks, chips, plates, and napkins already at the table, they strolled over with the sizzling hamburgers and buns.

"Ice cream cones for dessert," said Elizabeth, as everyone got comfortable and started to plate their favorite meal together.

"Rex and I had a thought," Paul announced, as he methodically prepared his burger, one item at a time. Mayonnaise first, but not too much. Just enough for the bread to stay soft and easy to swallow. Next one, a thin slice of tomato followed by one slice of American cheese. Only American cheese, never cheddar, or Swiss, or anything fancy.

Finally, the burger—no lettuce or avocado, only the meat, cheese, and mayo. This ritual could take fifteen minutes or more. Elizabeth and the children had long since gotten used to the diligence with which Paul did anything, the care he displayed in the simplest of tasks. More often than not, everyone else had already finished dinner before Paul tasted his first bite, but it had become a more endearing, rather than annoying, trait that everyone joked about, including Paul.

"What do you say we go to Washington DC for Thanksgiving vacation? The Vietnam Memorial is something I want to see, and Rex was asking me about how it was made, why it was made, how long it took to make. The kids are old enough, and we all have time off from school and work."

"Will we fly on an airplane?" Lily asked. She didn't know what anyone was talking about, Vietnam, a big wall, lots of names. It didn't seem like a big deal to her, but an airplane ride certainly did.

"I don't know. Do you think it is such a good idea, Paul?' Elizabeth started to worry even before the conversation began. She didn't want anything to interrupt the progress Paul had made in the last six months. She had not been privileged or included in Paul's therapy sessions, but she knew he was rung out after each one. Thankfully, they had tapered down to once a month, and he always bounced back to normal, but she sensed it was the only place Paul could unleash his demons, created in large numbers by the war in which he had served. The same war that was memorialized in the nation's capital, and surely would conjure up memories of fallen comrades and bloody battles.

"I've been thinking about it for a long time. I know it might be a difficult part of the trip, but it will only be one part of the visit. There are museums and government buildings, Lincoln Memorial, Washington Monument, and so many things to do and see. I want to go."

Sensing the burning desire in Paul, Elizabeth finally nodded in agreement and broke into a smile. They had never ventured far from home. This would be their first big family vacation, and only the second time she had been on a plane with her beloved husband. The memory of their first romantic moment, returning together from the family Thanksgiving in Boston, flashed in front of Elizabeth and she smiled. She made a mental note to get seats for the family so she and Paul would be in one row together and the children would have the two seats in front. It would be nice to fall asleep on his shoulder, high in the sky, once again. "Ice cream cones, anyone?"

Preparing ice cream cones was a favorite family event. It wasn't simply a matter of scooping ice cream into a cone. Elizabeth always bought the cones that had names stamped into them. The first time she brought that particular brand home, the children were so delighted that it became a summertime ritual and a special dessert. She knew better than to replace them with a cheaper version, or the fancy pointy sugar cones the children hated. After all, every new box presented another possibility to find a cone with one's name, and the kids loved the suspense. So far, Paul had eaten one that bore his name, and once they found one that said "Beth," and another time, "Liz," but not close enough.

The children followed their mother into the kitchen as she pulled a new box of cones from the cupboard. They were difficult to open, with no easy way to penetrate the plastic without a pair of scissors. She took a pair from the kitchen drawer and expertly cut across the top of the package. This family activity was so simple, so understated, and actually kind of silly, but everyone loved it. Gingerly pulling the first cone from the sleeve, careful not to smash the delicate confection, Elizabeth handed it to Rex. "Name, please?"

"Oh brother, 'Scott,'" he droned. 'I don't even know anyone named Scott."

"Too bad," Elizabeth smiled. "It's yours."

"Name, please?" Elizabeth echoed again as she handed the second cone to Lily.

"Francis??? Where do they get these names? They sound like Cabbage Patch Kids." Lily giggled.

As Paul brought in the last of the dirty dishes from the back yard, Elizabeth waited patiently while he set everything in the sink, one utensil, one plate, one glass at a time. Washing his hands first, slowly, and methodically going through the gestures of a routine that had become only too familiar, making everyone wait while he found a comfortable spot, Elizabeth finally shoved the box of cones in his face.

"Here Paul, just pick one. It's your turn." The whole family knew this could take some time, the effort Paul put into every last thing he did, and the pace at which he did them. He continuously interrupted himself with a joke, a question, a side story, until finally, he completed the task at hand. Even when Rex rolled his eyes or Lily tugged at his shirt motioning to hurry up, Paul took it in good humor and acknowledged them with a grin.

"Drum roll, please." This could take a while, Elizabeth knew. The children's ice cream was beginning to melt in their already-prepared cones. Paul finally reached inside the box and slowly, ever so slowly, pulled the delicate cup out of the box, being careful not to let it crumble. Holding it in one hand, covering his eyes with another, he slowly peeked through his open fingers, turned the cone around so he could see the name, and handed it immediately to Elizabeth. "I don't believe this," she squealed, "my name! An ice cream cone that says Elizabeth! Mine, all mine."

"Not so quick. I would rather immortalize this tender little morsel and put it in the freezer, and don't ever throw it away. Clear? Everyone understand? Never throw it away." Paul was emphatic, and although it was said with good humor, he sounded one-hundred-percent serious.

Elizabeth sent Lily and Rex outside to finish their ice cream cones and found a piece of Tupperware to protect the treasure Paul had uncovered. Once wrapped and stored for what she supposed was the next generation, Elizabeth finally scooped cones for herself and Paul. They joined the children on this last summer evening, and enjoyed their refreshing treat together, silently watching the sun fade away, as the promise of fall filled the air.

Chapter 29

ELIZABETH STARTLED WHEN THE ARTIFICIAL FICUS tree in the corner of the living room rustled. She inched closer, hoping it wasn't a mouse, a lizard, or some other four-legged creature that sometimes made it through the front door when it was left open too long. Glancing down, she jumped back when she saw two feet behind the large pot. Paul emerged, as if from a secret hiding place, and smiled at her.

"Damn it, Paul! How long have you been standing there? You know how much I hate it when you're so quiet and appear from out of nowhere."

"Not long. I was watching you."

"Watching me do what? Why do you do that, Paul? It makes me crazy and I keep telling you that, over and over. I don't like anyone sneaking up on me."

"Neither did I."

Elizabeth steadied herself and took a deep breath. "Did you want something?"

"I wanted to find out if you've booked our flights to DC."

Elizabeth was hesitant, "Are you sure this is a good idea, Paul? There will be some unpleasant memories and I'm not so sure it is what I would call good therapy. What if you have a flashback, or you become agitated or upset? I'm afraid it won't be the fantastic trip you're imagining, and I don't want to see you in any more pain." She laid her hand on his shoulder, "Look what just happened. You're still hiding behind bushes and making sure you're well hidden from imaginary enemies. What do you think's going to happen when you don't have the familiar surroundings of your living room?"

Paul stepped back, angered at her response. "I'm not a cripple! Everything will be okay, I promise. I want Lily and Rex to see our nation's capitol and we've never taken a vacation like this as a family. Please, don't worry about me. As a matter of fact, why don't you call Sam, and see if he, Linda, and the kids would like to join us? How many years has it been since we've seen them? They moved to Boston over three years ago. It's a drive for them, but they could easily make it in a day."

"I'll see what his work schedule's like. Should be school break from his university about that time."

"Your brother's brilliant, Elizabeth. As much as I admired him, I was always a little envious he took advantage of the GI Bill and followed his dream. Glad he isn't knocking around community colleges in Southern California anymore. Linda is married to a genuine college professor, and you're married to a Nowhere Man."

"Don't go there, Paul. Everyone has their strengths and weaknesses, and while Sam may 'think' he's superior intellectually, he can also be a real know-it-all son-of-bitch sometimes too. Linda has her hands full."

She nodded to Paul and reached for the phone. Hearing Sam on the other end, she explained what the family was planning. There wasn't a hint of hesitation from Sam when she extended the invitation.

"Get yourselves some warm jackets and boots, even if you never wear them again in sunny California. You probably don't even remember how cold it can get back East in November." No longer nervous or afraid, Elizabeth smiled when she hung up the phone.

Cruising at 36,000 feet, Elizabeth barely remembered what it was like to fly. Once they had climbed through the clouds and the '*fasten seat belt*' sign went off, the children relaxed and soon engrossed themselves in the travel games and books Elizabeth had packed for the trip. Remembering the last flight she and Paul took together, she unfastened her seat belt and leaned closer to Paul, resting her head on his shoulder. Paul returned the gesture by running his fingers across her forehead and murmuring, "Get some rest. I'll keep an eye on Rex and Lily. You are the best wife and mother. I'm only here because of you." His words sounded both melancholy and strong, making Elizabeth feel peaceful and secure.

The landing was effortless, and although a bit chilly, the sun was out and the air was crisp. Sam and Linda had already checked in and the children were wide eyed with anticipation with the idea of staying in a hotel and eating in restaurants for three whole days.

"Pancakes for breakfast, hamburgers for lunch, and pizza for dinner every day. You said it would be okay, right Mama?" Rex reminded his mother of her promise and Elizabeth wished she had never mentioned it.

"That's what I said. We're on vacation—Oh, I see Sam!" She beckoned to him from across the lobby and told Rex to grab him and let him know they were checking in.

Rex and Lily dashed together in the direction of Sam's family. Even though it had been almost three years, the cousins fell into effortless chatter and were bouncing simultaneously, excited to be spending three nights in a hotel. With his slower gait, Paul finally caught up to the group huddling in the corner, and broad smiles broke out all around. He extended his hand to Sam, followed by a brotherly hug. "How are those college freshmen treating you, old man?"

"Most are brilliant or rich or both, with a low level of maturity. Not like we were at that age."

"Yeah, learning how to shoot a moving target in the middle of raining bullets and mortar fire will do that to a kid. We grew up pretty fast. They're lucky to have someone who can set the history books straight."

Elizabeth finished at the front desk as quickly as the long line and computers would allow, and joined the group with hugs and kisses. Sam had become proficient at using a prosthetic device for his hand and no longer ashamed, scooped up his little sister in a big bear hug. "Hey, sophomore!"

Elizabeth looked at her brother cross-eyed. "Still hate that nickname," she muttered under her breath, realizing it would be hers for a lifetime.

"I probably would have stopped calling you that a long time ago if you didn't make it clear how much it irritated you—you set yourself up." With another warm hug, they laughed and turned their attention elsewhere. Linda was busy admiring Lily's long, curly hair, unlike her mother's, truly auburn. She gushed over Rex's blond good looks, until everyone was talking at once, clearly ecstatic to be together again.

"Too long, far too long," muttered Sam as they made their way to the elevators.

Paul glanced at his watch. "Almost six. Let's get ourselves settled in our rooms and see if there's a pizza place nearby."

Elizabeth agreed. "Great! See you in the lobby at six-thirty." Lily and Rex were already racing to the elevator to see who would be the first one to push the button, but they patiently held the door and waited for their father to catch up, as always.

At eight the next morning, the group met in the lobby as planned and went outside to wait for the shuttle bus. Shivering from the cold and happy to have a warm pair of boots, Rex was the first to board. He thought how glad he was he had listened to his mother when she told him no shorts, no T-shirts, no sandals, even though he had to unpack everything he had so carefully planned to bring. While it had been awhile, Elizabeth easily recalled the low temperatures in November on the East Coast, along with rain and sometimes an early snow. Though the air was still a chilly twenty-five degrees, the sun was piercing through the clouds, promising of a beautiful day.

After a stop at the Washington Monument and Lincoln Memorial, the shuttle slowly moved towards the Wall, through the Constitution Gardens, and pulled into the parking area reserved for buses and handicapped visitors. Of the children, Rex was most anxious, and he was the first off the bus as the doors opened. Elizabeth laid her hand on his shoulder. "You have to be very quiet here, Rex. This is a special place, and it means a lot to your father and uncle." Almost at that instant she said it, she knew she didn't have to. Rex was somber, attentive, and quiet, gazing towards the wall and ready to touch this hallowed ground he had only seen in pictures.

The group stayed close together and followed Sam and Paul. The children were old enough to understand the respect this monument deserved and were on their best behavior. On approach, it was hard not to stand in awe of its length and breadth, stretching well over two hundred feet, with over 58,000 names etched into the hard, cold marble. Rex inched closer to the wall and softly laid his hand on the surface, fascinated by the feel of the multitude of engraved names. He cautiously walked in a slow, measured pace, feeling the names beneath his palms and sensing an energy springing forth from the written words. Paul and Sam kept their distance, stepping back to see the entire work and the enormity of the memorial. A crowd was beginning to gather and the silence spoke volumes. Men, women, and children stood at attention, strolled past the names, held hands, wept, and remembered.

Elizabeth and Linda were nervous, staying on the sidelines at first, keeping a cautious eye on their husbands. Without words, they understood the effect on their men and watched intently. Elizabeth was praying that encountering this visual monument to the fallen wouldn't trigger an episode in Paul and readied for his reaction.

Motioning to her, Paul sensed her anxiety. He wrapped his arms around her, nuzzling her hair. "I'm okay. I was a little nervous myself, but I'm good. Don't look so worried."

At that moment, Sam caught Paul's eye and waved him over to where he was standing. He was at one end of the wall, searching through a book of endless names, in alphabetical order, each representing someone's father, son, uncle, brother—all lost in Vietnam.

"What did you find? Looking for anyone in particular?"

"I was thinking about people we knew. I wanted to take a moment to visit them, bow my head, and think about them. Damn, there are six from our battalion, but look who else I found."

Paul leaned over Sam's shoulder and peered at the name just under Sam's index finger. "No... Dr. Leonard Shapiro. Holy shit. When?"

"Says August 1, 1967."

"We hadn't even been stateside that long. Help me find his name," said Paul. "I want to pay my last respects. Sometimes it seems like a hundred years ago, and other times it feels like it was just yesterday. Do you ever think about the time we spent in the field hospital?"

"Every once in a while. I remember that really sweet nurse who helped me write the letter to Elizabeth on Christmas Eve. I wonder how many guys she saw go off the deep end."

"You mean, like me?" Paul turned to Sam and continued without a hint of apprehension. "It's okay, man. I've accepted it. We're all different. What affects one doesn't affect another. I'm glad you were able to piece your life back together, move on, get that damn history degree, and do what you had always planned to do with your life before this goddamned war interfered."

Sam looked relieved. "I didn't mean anything by what I said. Honest... sorry."

"Doesn't matter if you did or didn't. It's not a big deal. By the way, I never asked. Anything ever happen between you two? That sweet nurse? What was her name?"

"Diane. She was an excellent nurse, that's all. A beautiful, raven-haired angel with the darkest brown eyes I'd ever seen. I suppose there could've been something if we weren't in the midst of a bloody war and a stockpile of dead and wounded soldiers." Sam broke into a slight smile with the recollection of her touch; the gentle, delicate caress with which she cleaned his wound every day; the words of encouragement she murmured as she wrapped his severed limb with clean bandages, always leaving his bedside with a salute and a smile before tending to the next injured man in line.

They continued to search the wall, armed with directions written on a small piece of paper provided by a volunteer docent. The panels were arranged chronologically by date of death, small dots placed at the edge of every tenth line, making it easier to locate a particular name. It was still confusing.

Rex appeared beside them. "What are you doing?"

"We found a friend. Dr. Leonard Shapiro. Maybe you can help these two old guys. Here's the panel, row, and line where we should be able to find his name. Why can't we figure this out? It's not that hard." Exasperated, Paul handed the piece of paper with the information to his son.

"Two old guys is right. I'll find it." They let out a hearty laugh as Rex took the lead, Paul and Sam following close behind. Rex had been studying the wall like a scholar devouring a 500-year-old manuscript. He calculated the location of Dr. Shapiro's name, marched past five panels, counted the dots, up down, left, and right, and within minutes found the line with his name indelibly etched for the ages. "Here, Dad. I found him! Who was he, anyway?"

"He's the reason I was on the same plane home with your uncle. He's the reason I met your mother, and without him, you wouldn't be here."

Rex was perplexed. His father's answer didn't seem to tell him much, other than that his father and uncle knew him in Vietnam. "Well—" Rex started, but was silenced when his mother and the rest of the family approached to watch.

Paul and Sam collected themselves and with unified steps, walked towards one another, stopped, turned, and faced the spot on the wall bearing the name of Dr. Leonard Shapiro. Rex was fixated on the scene unfolding in front of him as he waited to see what the men would do next. Standing tall, shoulders tight, arms straight, flat at their sides, and fingers pointing to the ground, they simultaneously raised their arms to their brows in one crisp motion. Sam seemed unconcerned with his missing right hand, long since becoming used to the hook that replaced it. They stood motionless, holding the salute, turning to one another before releasing their hands to their sides. Rex watched breathlessly from the sidelines. He had had never been as proud of his father as he was in that moment.

Chapter 30

"Hey, Mama, what's happening?" Rex almost startled Elizabeth as she finished the morning dishes at the well-worn cast-iron sink. A high school senior now six inches taller than his mother, Rex always came into the room with the same greeting.

"What's happening, you ask? Well, I'm doing the dishes, as you can see, wishing I had a dishwasher, and getting ready to head off to work." Lingering for a moment, Elizabeth knew Rex was about to ask her something, or needed money, or wanted to go surfing instead of going to class. Just like his father, it was hard to keep Rex away from the water when the waves beckoned, even on school days. Elizabeth half expected a phone call once a week, letting her know her son had been tardy to class, and that he would need to show up to Saturday school or face a failing grade. Somehow or another, Rex always managed to make up the work, and though hardly graduating with honors, was granted admission to a state school in San Diego, with no problem staying close to home.

Most kids his age were clamoring to get away, and Elizabeth was convinced Lily would be one of those, but Rex took everything in stride and accepted life as it was thrown at him. Not the type to get excited, he nonetheless looked forward to a more adult campus and putting some distance between him and his family. He was ready. Choosing political science as a major seemed an unlikely endeavor, but Rex was never one to give anything away. An observer his whole life, he was mum, even as a child, whenever someone asked him what he wanted to be when he grew up. "It's a surprise," he would respond, and no one was more surprised than his parents when he announced his college plans. Whether or not he always knew, or it was simply a decision driven by the urgency to pick a major, his parents secretly felt one day their son would have something very significant to say.

"So you're going to be governor of California one day, right, son?"

"Something like that," Rex responded, as he segued into what he really wanted to ask his mother.

"Mama," he began again. "Last week of high school, perfect weather for the month of June. I was wondering if I could ask some friends to a party sometime next week. I promise I'll help Dad with the yard, I'll be around to clean up, and no alcohol, promise. Just want to get everyone together one more time, maybe a bon fire, chips, hot dogs, cookies, some soft drinks."

"How many?" Elizabeth actually thought it was a great idea and was already missing the activity that would be absent from the house once Rex left for school in the fall.

"Maybe around forty, mostly kids you'll know. Of course Julia, and she said she'd help with anything you needed." Julia was Rex's high school sweetheart. They had been going steady since junior year. They managed to avoid the usual pitfalls of high school romances. She was from a lovely family and had two little brothers who kept an eye on the couple when they were alone watching TV in her family den. Like Rex, she would be going to San Diego State University, and like Elizabeth had done so many years ago, she would major in education.

"I think that would be fun and I know your Dad will agree. He will need help though. His meds are having some unpleasanat side effects and he's groggy a lot. He can't seem to keep up the pace like he used to, so I'll be counting on you to help me prepare. I'm sure Lily and Julia will help me with the food."

"I'll help with everything, promise."

"I miss you already, my boy," and Elizabeth threw her arms around his waist, feeling the warmth and protection of having a man-child in the house. "Go, get to school, take your sister, and I'll see you two later tonight."

A party is just what this house needs, Elizabeth thought, as she rushed out the door for work.

⬖

Even though the forecast for the week had mentioned rain, there was nothing but sunshine on the day of the party. Rex's classmates had spent hours planning their futures, and even though they had the rest of the summer, were restless to get away and be on their own for the first time. Elizabeth was a little jealous of what lay ahead for Rex. She sometimes felt she had been robbed of a childhood, high school friends, and an easy path to college. The thought was fleeting as she reminded herself how happy she was for her son, and how proud she was of Paul and herself for being able to provide opportunities not afforded to either of them at that age. Even though the household would never be the same, and Lily was trailing very closely behind her big brother, she had reason to celebrate her son's entry into the next four years of college life.

"I need you and a few of your friends to man the barbecue, Rex." Elizabeth passed Rex a platter of hot dogs and hamburgers, while Lily and Julia were setting out the food on rented picnic tables, filling ice buckets, making lemonade, and setting chairs around a fire ring quickly constructed by Paul and Rex the day before—and sneaking a taste of the frosted cupcakes that were meant as a farewell dessert. Elizabeth had decorated them in the school colors, matching the red and gold, and crowning each with a sugar flower, made more for looking than eating. Irresistible to Lily and Rex the night before, she cautioned them not to touch. "You two are like a couple of toddlers. No sticking your fingers in the frosting!" Elizabeth smiled at the memory.

Elizabeth wanted everything to go well for her son. Paul had set up his boom box on the back porch, attached speakers to the roof, and the afternoon was warm enough to keep everyone outside.

"Bathroom breaks only," pleaded Elizabeth. The house is barely big enough for us, let alone forty teenagers."

Arriving in couples and small groups, Rex's friends made themselves at home, digging into chips and dip, filling up on hamburgers and hot dogs. Rex had transformed the lonesome, unmanicured dirt in the back portion of the yard into an instant dance floor. Weeds had been pulled, gopher holes filled, and strings of lights were creating a warm glow from one end of the yard to the other. As the sun set, the music got louder, the flames from the fire ring grew, and Elizabeth was sure the neighbors could hear the party up and down the block. You could almost touch the energy and anticipation. Her heart was full as she took a few more moments to glance around the yard before retreating inside for the rest of the evening.

Her elation was short lived. Moving towards the living room to share some quiet time with Paul, she saw her husband, head down, sobbing, waving his arms, huddled in the corner of the living room. When Elizabeth realized Paul was having another break, she hated herself for thinking more of how it was going to affect Rex and Lily in front of their friends than feeling the empathy called for at this moment. Before she could reach over to him, Rex wandered in with Julia, teasing, poking, giggling their way into the living room to ask his mother where the marshmallows were. They stopped short at the unfolding scene. Speaking with an abruptness that caught even Elizabeth off guard, Rex stopped in his tracks and shielded Julia from seeing his father.

"What the hell? Mom, do something! It's not enough we're all on pins and needles when we're alone, but I'll never hear the end of this if Dad comes out in the back yard with the claw hammer he sleeps with by his chair!"

Elizabeth motioned for them to leave. "Go back outside, Rex. I'll take care of this, and no one will ever know. Your dad and I will watch TV in the bedroom. Go back outside, and please, don't tell Lily. I have it under control." She willed herself to stay calm and prayed Paul wouldn't get any worse.

Reaching for Paul and again waving for Rex and Julia to leave, she helped him up from his crouching position in the corner.

With more fury and disgust, Rex grabbed Julia's hand and exited to the back yard to join the group of friends waiting for marshmallows to roast over the bonfire. Still angry at Paul, he turned to Julia, and whispered in her ear, "Don't you ever tell anyone about this. Do you hear?"

Confused but sympathetic, Julia nodded, and they walked hand in hand towards their friends, keeping the drama unfolding inside the house to themselves. Julia tightened her grip for wordless support and Rex calmed down, knowing inside the house, his mother had it under control.

Walking towards the bedroom together, a safe harbor for the moment, Elizabeth saw Paul clenching and unclenching his hands.

"Everyone calls me sweet. Everyone calls me sensitive. You, everyone I work with, my friends, wherever I go, people think I am sweet, or sensitive. I am neither." Although muttering under his breath, she could sense the rage behind his words and felt uneasy and sad. Paul continued to follow Elizabeth, but did not take her hand. Instead, hands still in fists, his countenance changed from his usual calm, passive demeanor to a wide-eyed, frightening, diabolical grin.

"I'm not sweet. I don't want anyone to ever call me that again, or use words like kind, peaceful, nice. I'm none of those, and I don't want anyone ever to describe me like that again!"

Breaking into a sweat, fists still twitching in rhythm, Elizabeth broke his trance, insisting, "Come on, Paul. Let the kids finish their party outside, and you and I will watch Johnny together in the bedroom."

Without a word, Paul followed Elizabeth and collapsed into bed beside her, the laughter of Johnny Carson's studio audience cutting through the tension. *Thank God for Johnny,* she thought, as she created a mental picture of their future. "We'll talk tomorrow." She touched Paul's shoulder, watched him relax, and saw his breathing return to normal. He fell into a restful sleep beside her.

Rex's departure was abrupt, unplanned, and angry when he announced he would stay with friends for the summer instead of at home before school started. No one took it well. Paul was especially devastated. In between his bouts of agitation, he tried to talk to his son and apologized for his inabilities and weaknesses, and the sorrow he had bestowed on his family.

Calmer, Rex looked at his father. "Dad..." He watched Paul shuffle into the living room and sink into is well-worn recliner. "Dad," he continued, "I want you to know I don't blame you for anything. You and mom have given me a wonderful life and opportunities neither of you ever had, but I need to start my own life. I won't be far away, and I promise to visit whenever I can come by with Julia for Sunday dinners. I promise to stay in touch. It's hard for me to watch you now because I'm about the same age you were when you went to Vietnam. I get that, I do, and in a lot of ways, I feel guilty you were there and I am here with a bright future beckoning if I buckle down and make it happen. If I can't make a success of my life and make you proud, if I can't become the son you deserve because a life no one deserved was forced on you, I would not have been worth fighting for."

Paul stood up to face his son. "I went to war so no son of mine would ever have to." With that, Paul clasped his son's hand and laying the other on his shoulder, drew him close for a hug. "You take care, Son." *We'll be here and will always have your back. Your future's waiting.*

Rex returned the hug, holding back tears, and helped his father back into his chair. Huddled by the front door, Elizabeth, and Lily watched and walked outside with Rex as he waved one last time to his father and encircled his mother and sister in a joint hug. With one last wave from the driver's seat, he backed out of the driveway, and headed down the familiar street of his childhood, on the cusp of becoming a man.

Chapter 31

"WHERE HAVE YOU BEEN?" ELIZABETH, ALMOST hysterical and running out of patience with her daughter, greeted a surprised Lily at the front door. For the third time in one week, a beleaguered Elizabeth waited up, listening the noise of a car door in the driveway and the familiar sound of the key in the door, signifying Lily's late arrival.

"Out, just out. Why do you always have to know where I am? Besides, it's summer. It's no big deal."

"It is a huge deal, Lily. It's almost one in the morning and I didn't get a phone call, a note, nothing to let me know you were all right. You can't be running around town until all hours of the morning, worrying your father and me. My hands are full as it is, my job takes up most of my day, and there's no one to help when I get home. I'm not asking you not to enjoy your summer, but I need to know you'll keep curfew and be home by midnight. If you're late one more time, we'll have to take the car away and that's not something we want to do."

"Oh, I think you would love that. Then you would know where I was every minute. You'd have someone to do the laundry, wash dishes, make dinners, take over your job in the house. Keeping me here is exactly what you want." Lily's shrill voice trailed off as she stormed through the house, retreated to her bedroom, and slammed the door behind her.

Elizabeth followed and tapped on Lily's door.

"Go away."

Elizabeth hesitated, then knocked again.

"I said go away. I don't want to talk to you right now. Leave me alone."

Elizabeth waited and hoped Lily would change her mind. Lily bounded from her bed and opened the door wide enough to see the look of heartache on her mother's face, but had no intention of permitting her inside. Her face mirrored her thoughts, with clenched jaw and narrowed eyes, and she was determined to end the dialogue.

"One more time." She wedged her foot between the narrow opening of the door and casing. "You're the reason dad is getting sicker and sicker. You're the reason our house isn't clean enough to have friends over, and you're the fucking reason why our family is so weird and crazy!"

Lily's words penetrated Elizabeth's heart like a bullet. She knew she would not win this battle with her daughter. As she turned to leave, Lily muttered under her breath, "You've made dad weak, passive, and unable to do anything for himself. I want my daddy back!"

I want my Paul back. Elizabeth stopped and turned to face her daughter. Her tone was soft and empathetic, but she struggled to maintain her composure.

"Oh, my girl. You think being loud means you're strong and being quiet makes you weak? Your father is the strongest man I know—that you will ever know—and his silence is his strength." Elizabeth, hurt, but triumphant, shut Lily's door behind her, took the half-empty carton of coffee ice cream from the freezer on the way to her room, and went to bed.

Paul had nodded off watching a late-night talk show, and the noise startled him. The doctor's prescribed medications dulled his mind and he dozed throughout the day, lethargic from the side effects. He found it harder to concentrate at work, and when he was laid off, Elizabeth was forced to find full-time employment to support the family. She hated her job. It was dull and she was underpaid, overworked, and wondered why she had exerted so much effort to obtain her teaching credential. She barely used her degree and often felt cheated out of a career because she had to keep the family afloat. Most days she could ignore her disillusionment, but tensions between her and Lily, dealing with the ever-growing state of disrepair around the house, and making every effort to keep Paul comfortable was wearing her down.

Paul puttered around the house all day, every day. With all that time on his hands, Elizabeth wondered why the lawn was never mowed, and the dishes and laundry were never done. The house was feeling smaller and tighter with the clutter that was being collected, seemingly on a daily basis. She wanted to ask Paul what he did all day while she was gone, but didn't want to put any more pressure on his already-delicate psyche. The radio played in one room while the TV battled for attention in another. It was a house in constant motion and noise, played out by characters on a screen and scripted by an invisible force of dysfunction.

"Lily home?" Paul wanted to know as soon he understood he had been awakened from sleep. "I want to see her and say good night." He shuffled through the house and knocked lightly on Lily's door. Sometimes they talked into the night, long after Elizabeth fell asleep.

"Lily, you awake? Can I come in? I need to say good night to my favorite daughter."

"Daddy, you can always come in and talk to me. And in case you haven't noticed, I'm your only daughter." That was how their conversations always started, like a secret handshake. From the very beginning, Lily had been daddy's little girl. She saw her father changing, but the one thing she could always count on was the unconditional love she sensed whenever he laid eyes on her.

Paul perked up when he heard Lily's voice. "Glad you made it home." Unlike her mother, who always questioned, worried, wondered, and tried to fix everything, Paul's expectations of people were different. He often reminded his children, "Let everyone steer their own ship, jump on board when asked, and get out of the way if they feel the need to sail solo."

Already scrunched up inside of her massive collection of soft, squishy pillows and stuffed animals that covered half the bed, Lily smiled and motioned for her father to come in. She moved over to make room for him and pulled her knees to her chin. Paul guided himself to the only available space that was left and talked about his day, the characters on TV that had become his friends, and the upcoming summer concerts at the Sports Arena.

"Been to any good concerts lately?" Paul had mastered the art of light conversation, but at the right moment, he knew how to address the real issues and concerns. He felt when someone was hurting, his own battle scars sticking to him like double-sided tape. Medications made him groggy, inactive, and overweight, but it never stopped him from being right there when someone needed him most.

Elizabeth often told her children their father was like a big heart with feet. Moving back and forth between rooms, never a harsh word or criticism for anyone. If toast was burned, meat unseasoned, or salad wilted, he would still tell her, "Best dinner ever," every time. The image of simple, pure, honest, and caring love is what carried Elizabeth through the hardest times when she saw her Paul, no longer the robust, young soldier she had met as a teenager, slip farther and farther away.

Lily saw her father nod off, fighting to keep his eyes open, and she threw her arms around him like she always did.

"Don't be so hard on your mom. She has her hands full with me, you, her job, the house. I wish I could help more. I wish I wasn't so weak."

"You're not weak, daddy. You're the strongest person I know." Lily smiled as she ushered him from her room. "Good night, Daddy. I'll see you in the morning."

Paul returned her smile. "Scrambled eggs and Wonder Bread toast for breakfast tomorrow. Glad you're home safe, sweet Lily." He closed the door behind him, worked his way to the living room and his comfortable, worn recliner. Late-night TV beckoned.

Chapter 32

"Do you think Rex and Julia will be here for Easter?" Elizabeth missed their son as much, maybe more, than Paul did, but between his studies, volunteering for a variety of social causes, and juggling a relationship with Julia, it was hard for him to make it home as often as he had promised.

"Where is that rat of a brother? He doesn't have much time for us anymore." Lily, irritated with everyone but her father, turned on her heels and rushed back to the familiar refuge of her bedroom, making sure her parents heard the tone of disappointment in her voice.

Elizabeth joined Paul in the living room where he was balancing a cup of coffee on his leg and wrestling with a tightly sealed bottle of medication. It made Elizabeth nervous to watch this ritual every morning, as Paul opened a variety of prescription pills, ranging from blood pressure medicine to anti-depressants and multi-vitamins.

"I'm wobbly today," Paul muttered as he sprung open the new bottle. Sixty more tablets waiting to be dispensed in a one-month period of time. He handed the bottle to Elizabeth without letting his coffee slip from its perch, "Could you please count me out two pills? I'm afraid I might spill them."

Elizabeth obliged, but noticed how shaky he was. "Let's make an appointment with Dr. Worthington," she suggested. "You seem to be juggling too many medications. Maybe he can cut back on the dosage. You're not eating properly or getting enough sleep, and you're staying up all night. I'm worried about you, Paul."

She watched intently as he tried to get out of the chair, but somehow couldn't find the strength to budge. Every movement was becoming an extraordinary effort. Every day, Paul took his medication, made fast friends with the characters on his favorite TV shows, waved Elizabeth off to work and Lily off to school, and waited for their return. Most days it looked like he didn't move from the chair, but if there were dishes in the sink, an empty plate on the side table, or a wet towel on the bathroom floor, Elizabeth knew he had made an attempt to eat, shower, and get dressed.

"There has to be more than this. Paul, I'm calling the doctor today to make an appointment. We'll go see him together." Paul gathered the strength to nod in agreement and glanced briefly at Elizabeth. In that one moment, when their eyes locked, Elizabeth saw a faint spark that reminded her of the man she married, her courageous, yet sensitive man, hidden behind a self-imposed mask of a beard and hair that had grown to his shoulders. In that moment she thought, *I see him. He's in there… somewhere.*

"Hi Rex, we hope you and Julia can join us Sunday for Easter dinner. We miss you, Son. Know you are busy, but want to see you. Call me as soon as you get this message. Love you." Elizabeth hung up the phone and hoped she was brief enough and to the point. Too long and she knew Rex would hit the fast-forward button or delete it without listening to the entire message. Waiting to hear back from Rex was the hard part. She was surprised to hear from him so quickly.

"Hey, Mama, what's up? Got your message in between classes."

Relieved he called back, Elizabeth rambled on about getting everyone together Easter Sunday, how she would make plenty so there would be leftovers for him and Julia, and how the weather was supposed to be absolutely perfect for enjoying the day in the back yard and spending time with each other. "Will you be able to come Sunday, around eleven?"

"Of course. Anything we can bring? Can you make strawberry shortcake for dessert?" Rex was straightforward, no long, drawn-out conversations or rhetoric. He said what needed to be said, and, unless he was unleashing an opinion on a current event or dissecting a political decision, he was all action and very few words. If he said something, he meant it. If he accepted an invitation, he would be there. If you needed his help, he would have your back. Elizabeth smiled and knew the whole mood of the house would change with Rex's visit.

"Just bring yourselves. See you Sunday."

Elizabeth tapped on Lily's door. "Come in." The tone of her voice hadn't changed. She sounded irritated and depressed.

"Wanted to let you know Rex and Julia will be joining us on Sunday for Easter dinner. Is there anything special you'd like me to make?"

Lily didn't raise her head or bother turning down the volume of the radio. "God, I can't wait to see him. It's been so depressing around here. This is good, Mama, this is really good. I don't need anything special. It makes me happy he and Julia will be here."

When Elizabeth turned and closed the door behind her. She felt that long-forgotten feeling of joy, of looking forward to something special, pleasant, and too long coming. She made her way back to the living room and touched Paul's shoulder. "Easter Sunday's all set. Rex and Julia will be here at eleven." Elizabeth beamed. Paul looked up from his chair and grinned and the pall was lifted from the room, if only for a brief moment.

Chapter 33

LILY'S JUNIOR YEAR SAW VARYING DEGREES OF FAILURES and successes. No one, including Lily, felt good about her grades as they faltered in unison with her father's declining health. She immersed herself in art and design, and her talent for both was evident, as she easily took first place in the annual school art show. She was struggling with math and science, letting her grades slip, turning in projects late or not at all, and spending less and less time with her friends. The push to make it into college was daunting, and her lack of enthusiasm disheartened her parents. No amount of encouragement seemed to change Lily's attitude or desire to get back on track. And Elizabeth was only too aware that the time she spent with Paul was time not spent with Lily.

"I have an idea, Paul. I think it would be good for Lily to have a change of scenery, I was wondering if you'd agree to send her to Massachusetts for the summer to stay with Sam and Linda."

"It sounds like a good idea, but she might accuse us of sending her away or shipping her off. Let's see what she thinks, so don't call Sam until we know how Lily feels about it. She's only been out of school a week and she may want to spend the summer at the beach with her friends." Paul was never one to make quick decisions, but this was one Elizabeth would make sure he addressed sooner than later.

"Couldn't sleep, thought about it all night." Lily was still in bed and Paul was restless at the breakfast table. He addressed Elizabeth, resuming the conversation from the previous evening. "I hate to see her go, but I'll agree if, and only if, she wants to spend the summer with her aunt, uncle, and cousins. I know my condition makes her angry, makes you angry too. I don't do this on purpose Elizabeth. I wish I could've been a better husband, father, provider—"

Elizabeth stopped him. "Don't say that! You are the best thing that has ever happened to me, and our children know how lucky they are to have you as their father. You bring the humor and music and understanding, and so much love. There's no one else in the world I would rather have for my husband or to be the father of our children. You are perfect, just the way you are. Don't ever talk like this again... please... we love you."

Paul managed to compose himself as their moody teenage daughter dragged herself to the breakfast table. "I overheard part of your conversation. You guys talking about me?"

"As a matter of fact, we were." Elizabeth motioned for Lily to take a seat and Paul pulled out the chair closest to him. It was Paul who spoke first, which was a relief to Elizabeth. Too often she was both mother and father, and a shift in Lily's summer plans as abrupt as this, might be too upsetting for everyone.

Paul chose his words carefully. "We thought you might like to get out of here for a couple months. Maybe spend the summer with your Uncle Sam and Aunt Linda before you head back to your senior year in September."

Paul didn't add another word. Instead he waited for Lily's reaction to his comment. He was good like that. He never pushed an idea on anyone. He spoke and then listened. Elizabeth had never known a grown person who was as sensitive to his surroundings or the people who shared his heart. She had never seen him raise his voice to anyone and no one ever raised their voice to him. For all his agitation, there was a calm, inner strength and peace, and he always said the right thing. Elizabeth knew he was the right one to speak to Lily, and she was grateful when he did so without having to be asked.

Lily rolled her eyes and glanced at Elizabeth. "Are you sure this has nothing to do with Dad?" She looked at her father. "Are you okay? You don't have some terrible illness, do you, and want me out of here so you don't have to tell me? Right?" Never sure, she needed to hear it from Paul. She needed to quiet her heart before she agreed to leave for the summer.

"Nope. Nothing to worry about. Just want you to have a good summer. Your mom and I'll be here cleaning up some of this mess, so when you get back, everything will be clean and buffed out."

Elizabeth kept her thoughts to herself as she listened to the conversation, but knew deep down, the house would look the same upon Lily's return. *If only,* she thought, *If only…*"

Chapter 34

"MAMA, WE'RE GOING TO BE LATE. WHAT'S TAKING Dad so long to get ready? I'm gonna miss the plane."

"You're not going to miss the plane, Lily."

"At this rate, I will. It leaves at eleven, and it's already nine thirty. What if there's traffic? On a good day, it's a thirty-minute drive, and I still have to check my bags and get my boarding pass at the counter. You know how long the lines are."

Elizabeth could see her daughter getting more and more agitated. Her bags were already in the trunk, and she sensed she was about to cry. "You're not going to miss your flight. I told your dad it leaves at eleven. It actually leaves at noon." She gave Lily a hug and hoped it would make her feel better, less nervous. Instead, Lily scowled.

"I wish you would have told me instead of making me sweat it out."

"I thought best to keep to myself so your dad would hurry up. Why don't you go see how close he is to being ready? We should get out of here soon in case there is a lot of traffic."

Lily knocked on her parent's bedroom door, somewhat annoyed. "Dad, we're ready to leave. I don't want to miss my flight. Are you almost ready?"

Paul opened the door enough to poke his head out, careful not to let Lily peer inside. He couldn't recall the exact day it happened, but at some point, he told the children they were not to go into the bedroom. Elizabeth was allowed, simply because there was no place else for her to sleep. She found it hard to enter, even though it was the bedroom she and Paul had shared for so many years. Stacks of papers and full and empty boxes concealed every wall, and mounds of clothes in every corner made it uncomfortable for her to spend any time in there. The bed was the only spot left uncluttered, and all she could do was hope sleep would come quickly every night so she wouldn't have to think about the debris that surrounded her. Paul hardly ever came to bed anymore, choosing instead to catch whatever sleep he could in his lounge chair, preferring the company of late-night TV to hers.

"Here I come, Lily. Tell your mother to get in the car. I'll be there in one more minute."

"Okay, Dad, but please hurry." The door opened, and Paul emerged with his duffle bag and cane in one hand, tennis shoes in the other. Lily wondered if they would ever leave the house.

"I'll put my shoes on in the car. Let's go."

"I'll help you, Dad," and she was careful not to tug too hard as they rushed out the door.

She was much less patient in the car. "I told you there would be traffic."

"Lily, calm down. The traffic's going the opposite direction and we're almost there. Maybe there was an accident or something."

"What time does her plane leave?" Paul asked, looking at his watch. One tennis shoe on one foot, and struggling with the other, he worked to maneuver himself between the seat and the dashboard, while still keeping his seat belt buckled. There was little room for him to manage and it was hard to watch. Lily and Elizabeth observed in silence as Paul planted his feet on the floor, shoes on each, just as they were approaching the airport parking lot.

"Noon." Checking her rear-view mirror, she could see Lily was relieved and saw the slightest of smiles emerge on her daughter's beautiful face.

The airport was bustling with summer travelers, as many leaving as arriving, and the parking lot was almost full. Elizabeth let Paul and Lily out at the curb. It seemed much easier to find a parking space on her own and run if she had to, knowing a long walk to the terminal would tire Paul before they made it to the ticket counter. Keeping everyone moving and calm was the best she could do. When she found an empty space at the farthest corner of the lot, she grabbed her keys and purse, and sprinted to meet them inside the terminal.

"I can do the rest of this myself, you know. You guys didn't have to come to the gate. You could've left me at the curb. It would've been all right." Lily muttered under her breath, "It would've been so much easier."

"Now we'll have a few minutes left to talk. I want to be there when you take off," said Paul. Lily didn't respond, but leaned over and gave her father a big hug. Elizabeth was wistful, watching the scene between father and daughter, and wished she and Lily had the same loving relationship. Her thoughts were interrupted when Lily blew her a kiss, and Elizabeth returned the gesture with a slight smile, glowing from the inside, happy to be recognized with a sign of affection from her daughter. The trio worked their way to the ticket counter, up the escalator, and to the gate. From the loudspeaker, they heard, "Attention, passengers. Flight three-twenty-one, leaving from gate fifty-four, with service from San Diego to Boston has been delayed. Your new departure time is twelve forty-five PM. We are sorry for any inconvenience."

Paul looked at his watch. It was 11:30. "I'm so glad we stayed, Lily."

"Me too. I'm glad you're both here."

Traffic was building northbound as Elizabeth managed to merge from the crowded onramp. "There must've been an accident."

"I didn't see anything on the way down, but you're probably right. Let's take the coast. I miss the beach. I'm going to miss Lily."

"I will too, but I think this trip will be good for her. She needs to take a deep breath before starting her senior year. Maybe we can do a little housekeeping while she's away. It would be a fresh start for everyone come fall."

"I'll try, Elizabeth. I don't like to see you worry. Lily's starting to worry about me too. I can feel it. I can't move fast, I can't think fast, I'm useless. Nowhere Man, that's me, just like John Lennon said… a real nowhere man.

"That's not true! That's depressing, Paul. You are not a nowhere man. Besides, Lily and I don't worry, we care."

"Same thing."

"No, it's not, at least in my book it's not the same." She was looking for the first exit that opened up. Traffic was at a standstill, so she decided no matter how many more miles she would have to drive to get back home, she would take whatever winding, surface route she could find. With the sun beating through the windshield and the air conditioning cold enough to be comfortable, it felt good to be out of the house together. It was one of the things she missed the most—simply getting out and taking in the world that revolved around them every day.

"I know you love your music, Paul, but why do you live in the lyrics and make it the most important part of your life? Everything that happens, you bring up a particular verse or song." Elizabeth hoped she wasn't bringing up a painful topic and that Paul would feel like sharing.

"Musicians are geniuses. They write about other people's problems, find the right words to make it easy for everyone to relate. Love, hate, war. It's all there in one little three-minute song. Sometimes I feel like the lyrics were written just for me. Music makes a lot of stuff go away." Paul sank back in the passenger seat, soaking up the summer sun. A contented smile swept across his face. "Keeps me sane."

"I suppose you have a better ear than most. Why didn't you ever learn to play an instrument?"

"Too much work, and no talent. I tried learning to play the guitar when I was in junior high…"

Elizabeth interrupted, surprised, "Did you, really? You never told me that."

"The subject never came up. Besides, it's kind of embarrassing to tell your wife you were a dismal failure at mastering the most basic musical instrument ever invented. I was a much better surfer." Paul's face lit up as he recalled the memories and Elizabeth relaxed as she saw the color come back to his cheeks. His eyes danced as they continued their conversation and the alternate route she had been hoping for opened up to the majestic coastline. The ocean sparkled in the midafternoon sun, with dozens of surfers in their shiny black wetsuits, bobbing up and down in the water, looking more like sea lions than a crowd of high school boys unleashed for the summer. Elizabeth was glad she and Paul worked their way down to the water from the congested freeway. It soothed Paul, just like music, and it reminded her how happy she was simply to see him smile.

"Did I ever tell you the story about when I brought my Elvis Presley record to school for show and tell?" Paul grinned as he recalled that moment etched a lifetime ago.

"Don't think I ever heard that one."

"I was nine years old, 1956, and my mother let me get Elvis's record, '*Jailhouse Rock*.' That was a bold move for a mother back in the day. She was a cool mom." Paul's face fell, but only momentarily, recalling the mother he lost too soon.

"Anyway, it was Show and Tell Day, and everyone brought dolls, trucks, family pictures. I brought my Elvis record and a little portable record player. I had the worst stomach ache just thinking about getting up in front of the class."

Elizabeth could imagine the scene with Paul's vivid storytelling, and perfect recollection. "Go on. I'm listening." Traffic slowed once again, and she didn't even care.

Paul continued, "So I got to the front of the room…"

Chapter 35

"PAUL, WE'RE GOING TO BE LATE. DO YOU NEED ANY help getting dressed?" Elizabeth, more anxious than ever, woke Paul an hour earlier than usual so there would be no chance they would be late for Lily's graduation from San Diego State University. She had made it through four years at her brother's alma mater. She was one step closer to fulfilling her dream of being an art historian. Neither Paul nor Elizabeth could understand what drew their daughter to this obscure career choice, but after months of job searching, she was hired into a coveted position as an administrative assistant for the San Diego Art Coalition in Balboa Park. An iconic and historical part of the city for almost one hundred years, there was a constant buzz of activity from school field trips, tourists, and locals, and Lily felt right at home in the midst of it all.

"I'm not slow on purpose." It was a phrase that was becoming more and more common as the days turned into weeks, folded into months, and became years in what seemed, paradoxically, like a heartbeat. The pace of the household had slowed even more since Lily left for college. Elizabeth watched Paul struggle with daily tasks, while she tried to ignore the mounds of paper, odds, and ends, nails, and screws, broken coffee mugs, and piles of clothes not touched in years, that invaded the space they shared. For every corner Elizabeth emptied, Paul filled with what she thought was more nonsense, but to Paul were necessary treasures.

Elizabeth's heart sank as she beckoned for Paul one more time, and when she got no response, knocked on the bedroom door.

"Almost done. Just trying to get my shoes on. I'll be right there."

Twenty minutes later, he appeared and closed the door behind him. She could only imagine what was on the other side, but to protect her heart, she stifled her curiosity and acquiesced to Paul's request. Whatever it was would only upset her, and she needed to maintain what little tranquility was left in the house. As soon as Lily left for college, Elizabeth moved into her bedroom, the only space amidst the clutter where she could breathe.

"You look so nice, Paul," Elizabeth was beaming. "I've always loved you in a button-down shirt and navy blue V-neck sweater. Reminds me of when we first dated. You were so cute, so handsome, and so adorable." She moved quickly towards him, and gave him a big hug, unable to get her arms completely around him, puzzled by the long beard he insisted on growing, but still knowing it was her Paul.

"You look pretty. You always look lovely, and I've always been proud to call you my wife, and the best mother Rex and Lily could ever have. You done good."

"No, we did good! The best father ever! Let's get out of here."

"One more thing. Gotta get my cane, and a bottle of water, and my duffel bag, in case I need something."

It was always one more thing. Paul packed for a two-hour event like he would be gone for a month. Elizabeth's heart ached, but she smiled as he finally made it to the car and buckled up by the time they made it to the freeway. She tried not to show her irritation. Slow, loving Paul. She knew they would need to talk, and though not happy with the decision she had made to get a little apartment, she would have to bring it up soon. She felt she was drowning and her mind was getting as muddled as the surroundings. She hoped Paul would understand. But this was a long-awaited celebration and family day, and she intended to enjoy every morsel and memory. Whatever she needed to say to Paul could wait.

Rex met them on the large football field, saving a place next to him and Julia, and broke into a large smile as they slowly approached. Elizabeth hung on to Paul's free arm, while he held his cane in the other, and they lumbered together past the rows and rows of elated parents, siblings, family, and friends of 2,000 other graduates. Rex made sure he found a shady spot, aware of his father's reaction to too much sun, one of the side effects to the one of many drugs he was taking. He was happy to see his father smiling, and got up quickly from his seat to meet them and guide them towards their places. Julia was waiting, bright, and glowing, as usual. She was centered, gracious, and caring—everything Elizabeth could ask for in a future daughter-in-law.

Although Rex continued to smile, his heart ached as his watched his parents draw closer. Paul had put on yet more weight. His hair had grown down to his shoulders and was more unruly than usual, and walking was more of an effort for him than ever before. Some of the medications puffed him up, others made him drowsy to the point of lethargy, and still others increased his appetite. It was a prescription for disaster, ill health, and poor quality of life, doled out to keep the wolf from the door—the suicidal tendencies, the depression, the memories of experiences that wounded him from the inside out forty years earlier.

"Son, Julia." Elizabeth hugged one while Paul hugged the other, and they positioned themselves into the sardine-like seating arrangement created by the growing crowd. Grasping Paul's hand, Elizabeth felt elated and glanced in his direction. She saw him, behind all that hair, the beard, a fleeting glimpse of his beautiful face and translucent blue eyes. She saw a serene countenance, and for a moment, her Paul emerged.

Everyone looked forward to the celebratory dinner she had arranged at Lily's favorite ocean-view restaurant on the coast. The evening weather promised to be clear and warm, and nothing could match a brilliant San Diego sunset. Elizabeth made sure their table would be in the front row of the restaurant, nestled up to the floor-to-ceiling plate-glass window, and in full view of the massive ocean, waves lapping a few feet away on the rocks below, front and center for the show nature would most certainly perform.

As the procession was about to begin, an out-of-breath Lily appeared, holding tight to her mortarboard so it wouldn't fly off in the breeze. Stumbling into their laps, she said as quickly as she could get the words out, "Mama, Daddy, can I bring one more person to dinner tonight? His name's Michael, he was a medic in Iraq for two years with the Marines, finished med school last year, interning at the VA in La Jolla, we've been dating for six months, and I really like him."

Lily, once a sullen teenager, was now full of energy, life, and sheer joy. Her parents nodded in delight, and she knew her mother would make sure there would be room at the table. As Lily rushed back to her place in line, she searched the crowd and gave the "thumbs up" sign to a tall, lean, bearded young man. Elizabeth figured it must be Michael.

As *Pomp and Circumstance* started, Elizabeth leaned over to Paul, "Can't wait to meet him." Paul held on tight to Elizabeth's hand. He beamed in the direction of their daughter as she marched in the distinguished procession and took her seat among the many who had accompanied her on her college journey. That evening, nature did not disappoint.

Chapter 36

"YOU'RE SO HANDSOME, SON." ELIZABETH GUSHED AS she entered the sacred domain of the groom and groomsmen. Elizabeth loved looking at her boy, her man-child as she called him. He had towered over her five-three frame since he was a sophomore in high school. Although he spent an extra year in law school, he had passed his California State bar exam on the first try and went to work immediately at a downtown law firm. Elizabeth felt the warmth of joy wash over her as she realized how focused and responsible her son had become. She and Paul often spoke of the opportunities they would afford their children, unlike the ones that were not offered to them. Rex and Lily had seized their chances at success in spite of the difficult situation at home, and neither complained about their childhood. This day would be cherished moment in the midst of the ongoing sorrow that had somehow engulfed their lives. It was a moment Elizabeth would long remember.

Rex rarely hugged his mother, but instead loved leaning on her shoulder, weighing her down with his size. When he was in grade school, he would reach up to her, stretching his arm to lay his hand on her shoulder and he never let go of this gesture, his way of showing affection to his mother. "You're way too tall to be leaning on me like that. It should be the other way around."

"You're way too healthy for that, Mama, but you know I'll be here if you ever do need someone to lean on."

Straightening his tie and cummerbund, Rex made one last goofy expression in the mirror and struck a pose. "How do I look?"

"Like my baby, like my toddler, like my teenager, like my son, all grown up. You look wonderful."

On the other side of the hotel was a suite reserved by Julia's parents, where jogging clothes, curlers, hair spray, and dirty tennis shoes were being replaced with picture perfect dresses and the stunning young women of the bridal party. The bride was being transformed by a team of expert makeup artists and hairdressers, and Lily joked with Julia as she sat on a stool beside her. They had grown close during the engagement period, and with no sisters and too many friends to choose from, Julia honored Lily by asking her to be the maid of honor. Lily was a girly girl, by all standards, and was only too happy to oblige, accepting the challenge of the engagement party, dress shopping, venue searching, and all the delicious things that are part of helping to plan a wedding.

Nine months had flown by and, overlooking the blue Pacific, a new chapter was about to unfold. Crowded with relatives, friends, and the anticipation of the impending moment, Paul and Elizabeth were escorted to their places inside the chapel and waited for the first view of the beautiful bride, about to become wife to their son and daughter-in-law to them. When the bridesmaids took their places at the altar, and the wedding march announced Julia's entrance, everyone rose to watch as she took the final steps towards her new husband. Silence filled the room as Rex took her hand in his and they recited the heartwarming words they had written for each other. It was hard not to cry, and Elizabeth couldn't help herself. She wasn't the only one.

The reception was boisterous and in full swing. "I hate to leave, but it's getting late and your father's tired. Do you mind if we take off?" Elizabeth squeezed Rex's hand then glanced over at Paul who was waiting for her to return to the table.

"I wish you could stay longer, but it's okay, Mama. Let me say goodbye to Dad."

Paul lit up when he saw Rex and Elizabeth walk towards him, and for a moment, it looked like he might have an untapped energy reserve. But he struggled to push the chair away from the table and Rex could see he had held out as long as he could.

"Great night, Son. Where's your bride? We want to say good night."

"She's over there with her parents."

He motioned for Julia to join them. She was blushing and maybe a bit tipsy. As she moved closer, Paul took her hand and bent over for a light kiss on the check. He took Elizabeth's hand. "Mrs. O'Brien, I would like you to meet Mrs. O'Brien."

"Cheesy," said Rex, but they all beamed.

Elizabeth took her sweater from the back of the chair and apologized. "Sorry we have to leave early, Julia, but us old folks are worn out. We'll catch up with everyone in the morning at breakfast."

Paul nodded in agreement, then clutched Elizabeth's arm for balance as they exited the reception hall, which was still crowded with party-goers enjoying a continuous stream of alcohol. "I'm sorry Elizabeth. I know you weren't ready to leave." She pressed her hand to his and squeezed.

The highly anticipated wedding photos finally arrived, and Rex and Julia rushed over to share them with Elizabeth, Paul, and Lily. Elizabeth was looking forward to seeing them and excited to relive the special day. Carefully turning the pages of the white leather-bound album, a special gift from Julia's parents, her heart sank.

Seeing photos of the guests; Sam, Linda, and their children; and her sisters, Laura and Tina, with their families, she saw what the years had done to her and Paul. In their 50s, they looked older than most of their friends, the strain on each of them so different, yet equally as devastating. She feigned excitement, but was disheartened as she studied the pictures of the now-blended families.

Her face looked drawn, and even though she always complained about her curly, frizzy, unruly hair, it now looked thin and lifeless. Paul, standing by her side in the photos, had a dazed look, his body pumped with one drug after another to keep him stable. No amount of visits to the VA were fixing the problem, and the answers from the overworked and understaffed medical facility were always the same. "It's the best we can do. We don't have the resources. You have to wait like everyone else. It's a long line." Elizabeth wondered if help from the VA, in the form of treatment or effort, would come in time for Paul.

The newlyweds departed, wedding treasures in hand, and Lily scooped up a few belongings she had left behind when she moved out. Everyone gone, Elizabeth knew the grim photos meant she had to find a way to bring some energy and joy back to the somber household. The small apartment she kept a block away from the house provided her sanity, and while at first Paul objected, the decision proved to be a benefit to both of them. They talked every morning, and Elizabeth could prepare them dinner in a clean kitchen, be at the house five minutes later, and share a meal with him every night after work.

"What do you say we start walking every day around the neighborhood, and take off some of this weight we've put on? The days are getting longer, the Village is a short drive away, and we can window shop, sit on a bench by the sea wall for all I care. Or we can walk in the neighborhood between the house and the apartment. What do you say, Paul?" Elizabeth was hoping he wouldn't have an excuse, knowing how he was slowing down by the minute, and never eager to make a change.

"Sounds good, Elizabeth. We'll put it on the list."

"No, not on the list, Paul. That mental list of yours to see Hawaii, start surfing again, lift weights, go to back-to-back concerts for an entire month, shed fifty pounds, clean out the debris that has piled high in the back yard. It's just a list. No more adding to 'The list.' We are absolutely planning and going to walk at least one block every day, even if I have to drag you, and we are starting right now."

"No, I promise. Tomorrow, just let me rest for today."

"Nope, we're getting in the car, driving to the Village. With that, she helped Paul from his chair. She knew he would accompany her, at least today.

"One more thing before we go. I have to get my cane and duffel bag. It has all my stuff in it."

Elizabeth had given up that fight months earlier, knowing he would need his security bag wherever they went, even if it was a block away. "Fine, no problem. I'll wait for you in the car." Emerging about thirty minutes later, Paul shuffled outside and joined Elizabeth, motioning to her he was ready at last.

"We might even catch the sunset. That would be nice."

The short walk across the street from the parking lot was a strain for Paul. Elizabeth almost wished she hadn't attempted what must seem to him a most impossible outing. But as soon as they reached a bench, overlooking the clear, blue, mesmerizing Pacific Ocean, she was glad she had insisted. Holding hands and knowing they had made it as far as they could, they sat and felt the sinking sun wrap its warmth around them. They talked in quiet tones while watching the sky turn from bright blue to yellow, to pink, and in awe, felt another day melt away into another perfect sunset. For a moment, Elizabeth laid her head on Paul's shoulder.

He stroked her hand. "Thank you, my beautiful Elizabeth. This was a good thing. We'll do it again."

Chapter 37

IT HAD BEEN TWO YEARS, AND PAUL AND ELIZABETH maintained a regular exercise program, even if on some days it wasn't more than a walk around the block. While she knew it didn't mean a cure, it was nonetheless a positive step. Their newly active life was peppered with get-togethers with old friends, occasional summer concerts in the park, and movies whenever possible. Rex and Julia, along with Lily and Michael, joined them for dinner almost every weekend at Elizabeth's apartment.

After settling themselves on the porch and looking forward to dessert, Rex asked for everyone's attention. Attempting subtlety, and trying not to give anything away, Rex started, "Mom, Dad, I have something for you." He dashed back to the car and returned with a large package wrapped in plain brown paper and set it down on the coffee table.

"Here, for you guys," as he motioned to the gift. "Go for it. I think you'll love it."

Elizabeth was shocked and curious. It was unusual for either of the children to bring gifts unless it was her birthday, Mother's Day, or Christmas. She approached the box with caution. "Please tell me there's nothing alive in there."

"Maybe, well not quite yet, sort of. Go on, open it." Rex was anxious and Julia was beaming, so a certain hint was emanating from her expression. Elizabeth thought she might know what was waiting for her and the rest of the family as she tore off the wrapping, exposing two stuffed bears. One was pink, the other blue, and each wore a T-shirt that read, *We love Grandma and Grandpa.*

Elizabeth drew her hands to her mouth and stifled a squeal, her heart melting as she realized she and Paul would be welcoming their first grandchild. She hugged Julia and cried tears of happiness. "This is so unbelievable! Is this for real? When? I don't know what to say."

Paul observed the scene and spoke up at last. "Well, all right." Always a man of few words, he smiled and stood up tall to embrace his son and daughter-in-law, with Lily and Michael waiting off to the side to do the same.

Lily feigned surprise, even though Julia had already broken her silence with her sister-in-law. Pretending to be totally shocked, she was acting like it was Christmas morning when she was five and could barely contain her delight. "When is your due date? Do you know if it's a boy or a girl?"

Julia smiled, "This could be the best or worst date. December twenty-fifth is the due date and we don't want to know the sex of the baby. That's why we got two bears. We'll have to wait and see." The bubble of happiness the news brought lasted through the evening. Exhausted by sunset, Paul and Elizabeth ushered Rex, Julia, Lily, and Michael out the door. Elizabeth couldn't help but wonder how this event would change their lives as she cleared the table, and hoped tonight Paul would stay with her a bit longer. It was their time to relish together, and he appeared to be uplifted and energized with the news.

By the time Elizabeth finished the dishes, she too was worn out from the excitement. Welcome news, yes, but she still worked forty hours a week, often with overtime hours, plus she managed Paul's health. She worried she might not have time to enjoy the baby, and would miss out on the joy of being a grandparent.

Paul had already settled into the couch, TV clicker in hand. "I know what you're thinking. You think you'll be left out of all the fun after the baby is born. I want you to have those moments, you'll be a wonderful grandmother. I promise I'll clean the house by myself, cook my own meals, make sure I have clean clothes every day. I'm tired of being your burden. I wish I were better at everything, like you. Maybe I'm amazed, Elizabeth. Remember how I told you so many years ago how that song said everything I could never say? I'm still amazed at the way you love me."

Even as Elizabeth smiled, she knew Paul's best intentions would not come to fruition, but he had a way of anchoring her heart, and even with his frailty and insecurities, had a way of making her feel safe. "That would be so helpful, Paul. But we have time to prepare. We'll just keep taking the best care of ourselves we can. There'll be a new plan that will evolve, I'm sure. For now, I want to imagine what it'll be like to have this new little person to share our world. You can stay the night if you want. If you fall asleep watching TV, that's okay. I have to get some sleep or I'll be a wreck tomorrow. Will you be all right?"

Paul's duffle bag was sitting next to the chair, filled with a week's worth of clothes, magazines, medications, and anything else he felt might be an important item to take with him when visiting a block from home. He motioned to the bag and waved Elizabeth off to catch up on her much-needed sleep. "Coffee in the morning. Sleep well." The drone of the television didn't bother Elizabeth, and sleep finally caught up with Paul, as late night TV slowly dissolved into the early morning news.

Chapter 38

CLAIRE WAS A COLICKY BABY AND HER THREE-MONTH birthday couldn't come soon enough, the age their pediatrician said she would most likely outgrow the condition. At this point, neither Julia nor Rex were enjoying any sleep, much less the rapture of having a new baby in their midst. Elizabeth helped when she could, mostly weekend mornings, so they could catch a few hours of much-needed rest. She never minded having to pace the living room for hours, waiting for little Claire to find a comfortable position to lessen the pain in her delicate little body. There were moments of relief, but never enough to quiet the household through the night and Elizabeth continued to try one trick after another to put the baby down by herself for a measurable nap whenever she had the time to help.

The sun was now a regular visitor, and the onset of an early spring brought morning light and warmth to the balcony of the couple's new townhome. With the sun soaking through Elizabeth and the baby, it became a favorite spot and seemed to lull Claire into peaceful rest, at least for an hour or so. Elizabeth found this moment of pure joy intoxicating. It renewed her sense of purpose and she wondered how the simple pleasure of sitting on a sun-soaked balcony with her brand new granddaughter could bring her heart back to the first treasured moments where it all began. From the moment she and Paul recited their vows, they shared this journey together, and they were fortunate enough to see brand new life created in this next generation. Claire stirred as Elizabeth reminisced, but settled as her grandmother moved the chair to capture the final rays of the sun before it rose higher in the sky.

True to his word, Paul started making his meals, and, with heroic effort, even managed to straighten the piles of paper strewn about the house. Old bills were neatly stacked in almost every corner, bundled in string or rubber bands with the words "Keep 4Ever" written on the top envelope of each batch. Never mind that the boxes meant to store the paperwork were still flat, and the packing tape and markers remained untouched. Knowing he might never get around to it was less important to Elizabeth than Paul's effort, and his delight in being a grandfather.

Paul managed to find room in the disorderly kitchen to prepare dinner, and, even though he had done so many times, called Elizabeth every morning to ask, "How do you cook chicken?"

She always gave the same response, "Heat the oven to three hundred and sevety-five degrees, put a little butter in one of the glass pans, not the old aluminum ones because they'll stick. Once it melts, salt and pepper the chicken, add a few pats of butter and bake for about forty-five minutes. Simple, unless you want another recipe to try."

"Nope, that's what I wanted to know. Does it matter if I defrosted it last night and forgot to put it back in the refrigerator?"

"Yes, it matters! You need to either cook it or put it back in the fridge right after it defrosts. Has it been sitting out all night?"

Elizabeth never knew for sure. Sometimes Paul wanted to get a rise out of her to bring her into his world, and still other times she would stop by after work and find the chicken long defrosted, sitting on a plate on the counter, with the oven preheated, and Paul dozing in the chair. The chicken question became a regular part of their daily banter. Whether Paul purposely forgot to put it in the oven, or was somehow unable to stay on this task, or any other, took a back seat to the joy of Claire's birth. Elizabeth kept reminding herself how these glimpses of happiness were her gift, and that watching this baby grow was the most important thing in their lives.

"Who could that be?" Julia wondered, as she groped for the phone that had somehow gotten tangled in the sheet and blanket. She had dozed off, and the muffled sound was all that was needed to jar her back to awareness. She mumbled to Rex, but there was no waking him this morning. He had taken the night shift with Claire and was dead to the world. Julia was glad Elizabeth was there to help, and it sounded like she had managed to quiet the baby for the moment. Julia reached for the phone, even though she could have let it go to voicemail. "Mmmmm… what… hello?" She didn't sound like herself since sleep deprivation had become her constant companion. She heard Lily on the other line.

"Is this a bad time?" Lily's voice was pensive, as she knew she might be intruding on what little sleep Julia was managing these past few months. Aware of Claire's restlessness, she came over to help when she had time and wanted to be there for Julia and Rex, doting on her first niece, rocking, pacing, and trying like everyone else to soothe this child into a full night's sleep.

Julia swung her legs over the bed, careful not to disturb Rex, took her robe from the foot of the bed, and moved into the living room. She saw Elizabeth and Claire on the balcony, quiet for the moment, and gave a slight wave. Elizabeth nodded and Julia poured the last cup of coffee from the pot before settling into the sofa, continuing her conversation with Lily as she got comfortable.

"No, it's okay. It was another rough night with the baby, but your mom's here now and Rex is sleeping. What's up?"

"Can Mom hear you?"

"No, she can see me, but not hear me. That's an odd question. Are you okay?"

217

"Well, yes, I'm okay, but please don't show any emotion in front of her when you hear what I'm about to tell you. I wanted to talk to you first, and then I'll talk to Mama and Daddy."

"Are you sick? Do you have cancer?" Julia was careful to turn her back to Elizabeth so she couldn't see the expression on her face.

"No, nothing like that. I'm pregnant. Michael and I found out last week, but the timing is so bad, with Claire keeping you awake all night, everyone so excited about your new baby. I didn't want to ruin anything for you guys, and the most obvious reason is that Michael and I aren't married, and I'm not sure how my parents will react."

Instantly wide awake, Julia felt a surge of excitement for her sister-in-law and what was about to be an added blessing to the family. She ducked her head quietly into the folds of her robe and, in a whispered voice, responded, "Of course, they're going to be thrilled, don't be silly! We're in the twenty-first century, and I'm sure they have long since moved past the idea that a couple needs to be married to have a baby. I'm thrilled for you both! Is Michael happy? Are you happy? That's the most important thing."

"I'm delirious. I never even thought of having children, and Michael and I have always been very careful not to get pregnant. We've never talked about starting a family, even after all these years together. But last night he proposed, so we're getting married *and* having a baby! There's just so much happening, I had to tell someone."

Standing, Julia was still talking with Lily as she joined Elizabeth on the balcony. "Lily," she started.

Elizabeth glanced up, "Oh, it's my girl. What have you two been chatting about? Is she okay?"

"Lily," Julia began again. "I think this is fantastic news, and someone else is sitting here that should hear all about it." She handed the phone to Elizabeth. Still cradling a sleeping, peaceful Claire, she carefully took it from Julia's hand.

"Hi, Lily. Is everything okay?"

"Mama, I have something to tell you and I hope you and Daddy will be okay with it. Michael asked me to marry him." She paused, waiting for her mother's response.

"Lily, that's fantastic news! Did you think I wouldn't be thrilled for you and Michael? Have you set a date?" She was struggling not to jump up and down with happiness, containing herself so she didn't wake Claire.

Hearing the tone in her mother's voice, Lily found the next part easy. "Well, we decided to have a simple wedding—immediate family and friends—in two weeks. We want to be married and settled in a new place before the baby comes." She tensed as she waited to hear what her mother was going to say next.

"Oh, my Lily, if I didn't have a sleeping baby on my lap right now, I would be shouting to the world how happy that makes me. I know your father will be over the moon, and you and Michael must stop by my apartment today if you have time. I think it would be more special if you and Michael told him together."

"We'll be there, four o'clock. That'll give you a few more hours with Rex, Julia, and the baby. Love you, Mama."

"I love you too, Lily."

❖

Paul made it down to Elizabeth's, even though it took him twenty minutes to walk the one block to her apartment. The sunshine felt good on his bones as he lumbered past familiar houses, home to families for over fifty years, like Paul and Elizabeth's. He had seen babies grow, go off to college, neighbors become grandparents, and a new generation of tricycles and super-hero toys sitting on front porches as grandchildren visited and played until the sun went down. He felt good knowing he and Elizabeth were part of the grandparent generation, and old friendships up and down the block were being renewed.

Elizabeth shared that Lily and Michael were coming over, but couldn't stay long. He also knew Elizabeth was making his favorite chicken dinner. He packed light. No sense in taking more than necessary in his duffel bag and it made the downhill walk a bit more pleasant with the more manageable load.

Paul, slightly out of breath, dropped his bag right inside the front door. "You look jumpy. Is everything okay?"

"Oh, more than okay." Elizabeth found it hard to keep secrets as important as this one, but wanted Lily to tell her father. She didn't want to ruin the surprise before the couple arrived, so changed the subject. "About to make a fresh pot of coffee."

"Good. I need some after that long walk." Paul smiled at the ridiculousness of the idea, and Elizabeth couldn't help chuckling. "Want to sit outside?" Paul set about arranging four chairs. He looked forward to the impromptu visit from his daughter and Michael.

Lily and Michael arrived as the coffee finished brewing. They planted a quick peck on her cheek as they walked past her and joined Paul on the patio. Elizabeth brought out a plate of cookies she had picked up at the little French bakery on the way home from Rex and Julia's, and set it down in the middle of the table, along with four of her best mugs and the creamer and sugar bowl she only used for special occasions. As she poured the steaming coffee into a carafe, Paul began to suspect this might be more than afternoon coffee on the patio.

"Wish it could have been fancier," she said quietly to Lily, who was bending over her father, giving him a big hug. She turned to her mother and squeezed her tightly before sitting down. Michael sat at her side, a subtle smile on his face.

"Before I tell you why we dropped by, I need to say something. I want to tell you how much you mean to me and how lucky I have been to have the best mother and father in the world. Daddy, do you know how special it is to have a parent who simply loves his children, unconditionally, no questions asked? It never made any difference if Rex and I were moody, didn't want to clean our rooms, do our homework, or broke curfew. You always listened and never yelled." Paul was embarrassed, not prepared to hear what Lily felt she had to say. He played with his coffee mug.

Lily turned to Elizabeth. "Mama, don't think I don't know how hard it has sometimes been. And no matter what, you were always there. You take care of everyone and everything, and even when the work piled up or you were worried about one thing or another, you still managed to pull us all back up, and help us make the most cherished, childhood memories." It was Elizabeth's turn to be a bit uncomfortable. She was not used to hearing these words spoken aloud.

"What I'm trying to say is I've learned patience and tolerance from you," she said, turning to her father and looking back at Elizabeth, "And resourcefulness and loyalty from you. I can't think of any better traits to pass on to my children, and I want to say thank you."

Elizabeth knew what was coming next, but still held her breath as she watched her little girl grab Michael's hand and draw him into the conversation. Lily glowed. "Mama, Daddy, Michael has asked me to marry him... and we're going to have a baby."

As she exhaled, Lily watched the expression change on her father's face. He raised his coffee cup as if to toast. "Well, all right."

Elizabeth knew it was going to be all right and let out the shout of joy she had bottled up inside. As Lily and Elizabeth talked wedding plans, Paul glanced at Michael and smiled. Paul would tell Elizabeth over dinner that Michael had asked for Lily's hand the week before and he'd been sworn to secrecy. But the baby, another grandchild, was a complete surprise. Their children having children. Paul stayed longer than expected, and as he ate chicken dinner with Elizabeth that night said, as always, "Best dinner ever."

Chapter 39

THE RINGING PHONE IN THE MIDDLE OF THE NIGHT, never expected, but always dreaded, sounded much louder than it was. Elizabeth always slept with the phone within arm's reach and fumbled to answer before the fourth, and final, ring. Her heart raced, and she braced for bad news that always seemed to accompany a late night call. "Is this Mrs. O'Brien?"

An unfamiliar voice made uneasy. Elizabeth started to tremble and could barely answer. "Yes, this is Elizabeth O'Brien. Who is this?"

"I'm calling from San Diego General Hospital. I am verifying you are the mother of Lily Cunningham." Elizabeth could barely hold onto the phone, as her hands sweat and bile rose in her throat. She felt like she was going to throw up, but managed to continue the conversation with the stranger on the other end.

"Yes, Lily's my daughter. Please, is she all right?"

"Please take a deep breath, Mrs. O'Brien. Lily, her husband Michael, and their four-year-old son, Noah, are at the hospital, and we need you and your husband to get here as quickly as possible."

Elizabeth interjected in a panic, "What? Are they okay? Are they alive? What happened?" She wanted it to be a bad dream as her mind flashed back to her fourteenth summer, the policemen in the driveway, and the unspeakable tragedy that shattered her youth and followed her like a dark shadow every day of her life. *God, don't do this to me again. I can't do this again.*

The woman gave her little information except that they had been in a car accident, Michael and Noah were being treated in the ER with minor injuries, and they were still running tests on Lily.

"You need to get to the hospital as soon as possible. The doctors will review everything when you arrive. For now, everyone's stable." The stranger's voice assured her someone would be there to answer all her questions, made sure she knew what building on the substantial hospital grounds they were being treated, and left Elizabeth shaken and numb as she hung up the phone.

Still clutching the receiver, she froze and tried to control herself as another wave of nausea swept over her. After a few deep breaths, her brain cleared a bit. She knew she had to call Paul. She couldn't take the time to think through what she was going to say or how he would react. She needed to make the call and get down to the hospital without wasting another minute. Hands shaking, she dialed, and Paul picked up the phone on the second ring.

"Hello." He neither sounded like he had been sleeping nor even surprised. "Elizabeth, I know the hospital called you. I asked them to because I knew you would know what to do."

"Paul, I want you to come with me, but you can't take all night to get ready."

"I want to go. I want to be with you."

"Can you be ready in fifteen minutes? I'll pick you up, but if you aren't ready, I'll need to go by myself."

"I can do it. I promise I'll be ready. Don't worry, Elizabeth. It'll be fine."

Grateful for the five-minute head start he had gotten by being the first one notified, Paul focused on nothing more than putting on his pants, a clean T-shirt, socks, shoes, jacket, and throwing some extra clothes into his duffel bag, along with his prescriptions and two bottles of water. When he saw the approaching headlights of

Elizabeth's car and her quick turn into the driveway, he was waiting on the porch. He grabbed his cane, walked to the passenger side of the car, poured into the seat, and buckled up.

"Told you I could do it. Be careful, Elizabeth. It's very dark. Go slow, so we get there in one piece."

Elizabeth turned to look at Paul. "What did the hospital mean: For now, everyone is stable. For now?" Her words drifted off, she didn't ask to get an answer and they found themselves gliding towards the downtown hospital on a dark, deserted freeway, unspoken words hanging in the air. She was glad Paul was with her.

Rushing to the reception desk, Paul trying to keep pace, Elizabeth asked the first person she saw where their daughter was.

It felt like hours, not seconds, before the girl looked up. "Lily Cunningham… Let me see… Oh yes, here she is. They just checked her into the ICU in the West Wing. Take those elevators on the other side of the lobby, and go to the fourth floor. The ICU will be on your right as soon as you exit."

With a hurried "Thank you," Elizabeth took Paul's hand and dragged him to the elevators, urging him to move faster, even though she knew it was difficult for him. He stood up straight and quickened his pace, focusing on the short sprint, and every bit as eager as Elizabeth to get to the fourth floor and to their daughter.

As soon as the elevator doors opened, they saw Michael and Noah in the hall. Michael was in a deep discussion with a young doctor who had been tending to Lily, and although his head was down, he wasn't crying. From afar, this seemed to be a good sign to Elizabeth, and as her imagination painted a scene, she felt a sharp tug from Paul, as if to steady her body and mind. Together they approached the trio. Noah saw them first. Rushing towards them, arm in a cast from his wrist to his elbow, he leaped into Paul's arms, almost knocking him backward.

"Grandpa, Grandpa, we were in an accident! The car who hit us was coming really fast and hit mommy's side of the car. It was so loud, and then it was quiet, and then there were ambulances, and mommy couldn't get up, and…." Paul laid a gentle hand on his grandson's shoulder and brought his shaking body close to his, allowing him to lean on his leg and guide him towards his father and the doctor.

"Shhh… it'll be okay. Take my hand, let's go talk to the doctor. Your mommy will be fine." But his heart sank and his legs almost gave way beneath him, as he braced for what he might have to hear.

Michael looked up, and it was easy to see the fear in his eyes when he stretched out his hand to greet them. Elizabeth drew him in for an extended hug and Paul did the same. Except for being shaken and scared, he appeared to be unhurt.

Dr. Brian Holcomb, who looked as though he was barely out of medical school, greeted them with a strong handshake and an air of confidence that put Elizabeth and Paul at ease. As Noah clung to his grandfather's leg, Dr. Holcomb continued his conversation with Michael and brought Paul and Elizabeth up to speed on Lily's condition.

"I was telling your son-in-law that although Lily has suffered some severe injuries and will need surgery, she's in stable condition. At first, we suspected the worst, internal bleeding, but tests ruled out any clots or damage to major organs. Both legs suffered compound fractures, but her spine is healthy and, with therapy and time, she should be able to resume her normal activities. This rehabilitation may take up to a year or two, but she is young and fit, and obviously has wonderful family support."

They breathed a collective sigh of relief, knowing that what was obviously bad, could have been so much worse. Young Dr. Holcomb lowered himself to Noah's level, and with a bedside manner that can't be taught, looked him in the eye. "Don't worry, young man. Your mother will be okay, but she's going to be staying with us for at least a week. I also want you to know before you go in and see her that some glass from the windshield also cut her face a little, so she has a few stitches and bandages and she's a little puffy. Don't be frightened. She'll be your beautiful, healthy mommy by the time she comes home."

There was a worried expression on Noah's little face, but a big smile slowly emerged, and you could see his tiny shoulders relax. Dr. Holcomb stood up, shook Noah's hand, and glanced at the adults. "I have a three-year-old at home. Lily is awake. Why don't you all go in and say hi? I'll check back in the morning and will be in charge of her recovery."

In an unusual move for surgeons and doctors, he handed Paul and Michael his card. "Call me anytime you have a question. We're going to be seeing each other quite frequently over the next year, but Lily is going to be just fine."

The fact that they were as fortunate as they were to have gotten such a caring, intuitive doctor was not lost on any of them, and Elizabeth felt, from out of nowhere, a brush of warm air as she entered into Lily's room. She thought of her beloved parents, gone so many years, and it gave her great comfort to think that maybe there had been a couple of angels in the car with her daughter that night, even if it was just her imagination. She sensed a closeness as though she had seen them yesterday, and felt somehow protected, knowing she and Paul were ready to help nurse their little girl back to health, no matter how long the journey.

Chapter 40

"WHAT DO YOU WANT FOR LUNCH TODAY, LILY?" EVEN though he was slow, Paul was eager to help. "I make a mean peanut butter and jelly or tuna sandwich, or a tuna salad, or scrambled eggs and toast. That is the extent of my ability to cook. Exciting, huh? Oh, and chicken."

"Daddy, I'm not hungry yet. It's not even lunch time. But I'll let you know when I am. She was propped up on a lounge chair, legs lifted to heart level as she was instructed and the remote within easy reach. Her father made sure the radio was tuned to a classic rock station and was careful not to bombard his daughter with too much noise.

"Either the TV or the radio, Daddy. "Not both at the same time, please. I prefer the radio. It reminds me of when I was little and I could always hear music from every room. It brings back good memories."

"Well, what do you know? I didn't know you even noticed since you and Rex were always dashing in and out, running from one spot to the next. You moved too fast for me."

"I didn't notice so much when it was playing. Mostly when it wasn't. I only remember a few times when there wasn't any music in the house, but instead of making me crazy with the constant drone of rock and roll, it made me sad when there was silence. I don't want to think about that now, Daddy. Maybe I am a little hungry. Can you make me some scrambled eggs and Wonder Bread toast?"

Paul obliged, emerging about thirty minutes later with her meal. Lily was grateful she wasn't that hungry. She knew her father moved in slow motion, and after so many years, the whole family knew to patiently wait instead of fighting it or pushing him beyond his sloth-like pace.

"Here you go, darling Lily. Did you know there's a song called 'Pictures of Lily?'" He balanced her plate of food in one hand, while he reached for the lap tray with the other. Lily didn't move, fearing he would lose his balance, sure her lunch and her father would both land on the floor.

"Yes, you told me a hundred times. By The Who. It's a pretty awesome song. I like my name. Glad you named me after your mother." Lily wondered if she looked like her, how different it would have been if she and Rex had grandparents that had been there for them like her parents were there for Claire and Noah.

"Wasn't a stretch when we were deciding what to name you." Paul's mind drifted, as he thought about the day Lily was born, so many years in the past.

"Concentrate, Daddy! Be careful!" Lily clenched her teeth, fearing the worst was about to happen. "Watch it. Here, hand me the tray." He almost dropped it, as he steadied himself and, with a sigh of relief, managed to get the plate to her lap.

"You're getting old, Daddy," Lily teased.

"I've been old for a long time. Too long." Paul shrugged his shoulders, got his plate from the kitchen, and sat down beside his daughter. By the time they finished eating, they were drowsy.

"Why don't you take a nap?" The morning activity had caught up with him and he nodded off. As familiar music filled the room from their favorite station, they fell asleep, waking only to a knock on the door that felt like it came out of nowhere.

Julia had been standing outside for more than five minutes, and, as she reached in her bag for the extra key, Paul remembered she and Claire were coming over after school to keep Lily company and let the cousins play together for the afternoon. Paul was still trying to put his body in motion. He looked up and rocked back and forth to gain momentum, "One, two, three," he stood up at last, ready to greet his daughter-in-law and granddaughter.

The older Paul got, the more he resembled Santa Claus, with a full head of thick, shoulder-length gray hair and a beard that reached to the top of his stomach. Claire and Noah boasted they knew Santa personally, and it never took long to turn the doubters into believers once they saw their grandpa. Once inside, Claire raced first to Paul and squeezed him around his legs. Paul bent down so she could stroke his beard, "Hi, Grandpa Santa," she said with a confidence of a second grader and rushed to the kitchen to find a snack.

"Keep it light." Claire rushed past her mother and made a beeline towards the cookie jar. "Your father and grandmother will be joining us for an early dinner." Claire pretended not to hear, picked up a couple of cookies, and retrieved a clean glass from the dish rack for a cold glass of milk.

Turning her attention back to Lily, and noticing how difficult it was for her to find a comfortable position, Julia added, "Are you still okay with that? If you're not doing well today, we can make it another time."

"No, I was looking forward to it. I'm beyond bored, and two months of being held captive inside these plaster casts has lost its allure. Did I tell you I have an appointment on Monday, and Dr. Holcomb is pretty confident they can be removed? I'm not looking forward to physical therapy or the sight of my legs after all this time, but anything is better than laying down all day. I feel like a prisoner in my own body,"

"Let me help you." Julia rushed to Lily's side, and propped the pillows, making sure the lounger was neither too far back, nor too far forward. Lily's hair was getting matted and looked like it needed a good wash, but Julia kept the thought to herself as she sat down next to Lily.

"I know what you're thinking. That I look pretty rough and it's been two months since I wore any makeup, but the nurse is coming tomorrow, so I'll make sure I get a shower and shampoo."

While the rest of the world moved forward just outside her front door, Lily never let on to anyone how desperate she was feeling inside, and the demoralization that accompanied the inability to do the simplest of tasks by herself, or for anyone else. Michael had been a rock, Noah thought watching cartoons with his mother was better than any video game, and Elizabeth and Julia made sure the refrigerator was stocked with easy-to-prepare meals. Paul was her daily companion and kept watch over his daughter, tending to her every need as best as he could.

I know how Daddy feels, she thought as she turned to Julia. "What's on the menu for tonight?"

"Thinking pizza, as long as everyone agrees." Julia studied Paul for an affirmative nod.

"I heard that," came a small voice from the kitchen, as Claire carefully put the cookie jar back in its place on the island, and Noah came bursting through the door.

An overloaded backpack, jacket, and lunch bag that looked like it hadn't been touched tumbled from his arms two steps into the entry. He was flushed from the day's activities. "Heard what?" He rushed into the middle of the room before he remembered his cousin and the rest of the family would be eating dinner with them. Running first to his mother, he gave her a sloppy kiss on the cheek, and spinning around to face Claire, said once more in a measured tone, "Heard what?" Ever since the accident, he felt like he had to know everything that went on in his absence, and at the beginning of Lily's recovery, spent his days in school worrying instead of paying attention in the classroom. Subsiding somewhat, he still needed to make sure everyone, not only his mother, was okay when he got home from school before he could relax.

"Silly! We're having pizza tonight. That's all. Is that okay with youuuuu?" Claire drew out the last word in mock sarcasm. The two cousins, so close in age, had a relationship more like brother and sister.

"I love pizza!" Noah nodded his approval and rushed to the cookie jar.

Elizabeth, Rex, and Michael came as early as they could, and once the food arrived, everyone relaxed. Pizza never tasted so good, life never felt so good, and miracles such as theirs didn't happen every day.

On the way home, Paul seemed particularly energized. "I feel useful. I don't like that Lily is hurting, but I feel like I have a purpose, and a reason to keep going. Is that selfish?"

Was it a rhetorical question or was he waiting for an answer? Elizabeth wasn't sure. "If that makes you selfish, then I must be selfish beyond measure. I've been keeping quiet, but seeing you guide our little girl through this painful journey, and seeing the light come back in your eyes at the same time has brought me peace and calm for the first time in decades. This ship is yours, Paul. You're a good captain."

She managed a quick kiss on his cheek as she helped him to the front door. She wished she could go inside and stay the night, curled up beside him one more time, but instead reminded herself to be happy with what they had, and got back behind the wheel to drive home.

Chapter 41

"ONE MORE VISIT TO PHYSICAL THERAPY AND I'M done." There was no hiding Lily's excitement and anticipation as she told her parents the news they had been waiting for.

"Two years, two very long years, and I can't believe it is over. Michael and I have been talking about how we should celebrate, and we thought it might be fun to take a family trip to Hawaii." She looked around her mother's small apartment, scattered with a collection of memories from her childhood, but understanding most was at the house with her father. Making her wistful and sad, she found a spot on the couch next to her father, and he pushed aside his daily magazines and newspapers to make room. She rested her hand on his, and with high hopes, asked, "Daddy, what do you think? Could you and Mama join us? It would be such a special treat."

"I'll think about it. I'm not sure I can make the plane ride, or even enjoy all the activities. I would end up staying in the hotel room all day and ruining it for everyone."

Elizabeth interjected, "I think it would be wonderful joining you. Your father and I will talk about it tonight."

Elizabeth didn't want to worry her children and ruin the celebratory mood, but after his daily visits with Lily ended, Paul had reverted back to the thick fog that surrounded his days and nights. It was taking him much longer to get ready every morning, and most days, when Elizabeth came by on her lunch hour, Paul was still in his sweat pants and T-shirt from the night before. As much as she wanted to help him shower and dress, he insisted he could do it himself and refused to ask anyone for assistance. He was brightest when surrounded by his family, and even Elizabeth was thinking how beneficial a trip like this might be for his emotional well-being.

"Always wanted to go to Hawaii." Paul became slightly more animated. "Did I ever tell you I taught guys from my squad how to surf right before we left for Vietnam? Right here in Oceanside. Did you know that, my girl?"

"I think you mentioned you taught those boys from Oklahoma and Montana to surf."

"True story." Paul's eyes brightened as he recalled the memory. "We'll try. But you and Michael, and Julia and Rex and the grandkids should plan the trip, no matter what. I think it's a solid idea."

"I have to run. I love you, Mama, I love you, Daddy." Lily hugged them and waved once more from the car.

"Be careful," Paul muttered after she had already pulled out of the driveway and headed home. He took a deep breath and lowered himself back into a comfortable position on the couch. "I can't do it. You know I can't. But why don't you take a much-needed break and join the kids."

"I wouldn't think of going anywhere without you. I would be just as happy resuming our walks at the sea wall, and having a hot coffee drink while we watch the sun go down. I've always thought we lived in paradise, and I can't imagine any place being more beautiful than our own back yard."

"Well, keep an open mind. If you want to go, that's fine with me."

"Quiet, no more discussion. I'll call Lily tomorrow and let her know the timing's not right for us, but that they should go."

Paul nodded and Elizabeth changed the subject. Paul's natural ruddy complexion had turned yellow and waxy over the last few weeks, and Elizabeth was spending too much time trying to convince

233

him to see the doctor for a full physical. The meds decreased his energy during the day, but at least there were no more night traumas and his sleep pattern had become somewhat normal. Still, she feared something was very wrong and made an appointment for Paul, whether he agreed or not.

"Paul, I made a doctor's appointment for you tomorrow at one o'clock. You don't look good." There, she said it, brutal, but honest. "I know you don't want to, but please go for me. That's all I ask. Just humor me and let me pick you up around noon. I've arranged for the afternoon off, and I'll have the rest of the day to spend with you."

Paul wasn't in the mood to argue or disagree. "Do I have a choice? I'll be ready." Already appearing tired and exhausted from his everyday routine, Paul lifted his legs onto the sofa and stretched out without removing his shoes. Tilting his head back on the firm armrest, he turned to Elizabeth, "I'm going to take a quick nap. Do you mind?"

"Never. I'll start dinner and wake you when it's ready." Tears starting to well, and a feeling of dread rolled over her like a dark shadow as she stood in the doorway and watched Paul's chest rise and fall. She memorized every hair on his head and line in his face, and studied his sleeping countenance, now peacefully at rest. "Whatever it is, I'm not ready to hear it," she thought, knowing his physical would show something irreversible and life threatening. "I'm not ready to say goodbye."

Practiced in the art of waking Paul from a sound sleep, she knew better than to approach him from behind, or get close to him until he was awake and functioning. Because he always startled easily and was constantly on high alert, the entire family knew to be cautious when rousing him. Elizabeth spoke quietly as she made her way from the kitchen to the living room. "Paul, dinner's ready." As she approached, she continued to watch his steady breathing, while trying to stir him. "Paul?"

"Mmm… what?" His eyes flashed open, and came alive, darting from one corner of the room to another. He focused on Elizabeth and realized where he was. "Did you say dinner was ready?"

Reaching out with a steady arm, Elizabeth helped him from the couch and made sure his chair was far enough away from the table so that he could settle in and adjust without falling. As painful as it was to watch, she wasn't ready to see his chair empty in her little apartment, or in the little house up the street where a lifetime of memories had been made.

"Smells wonderful, meat loaf?"

Smiling and appreciative that he still had an appetite, she patted his shoulder on the way to the stove, returning with a plate of meat loaf, steaming mashed potatoes, and fresh green beans. She already poured the tall glass of milk, and had bread and butter on the table, just in case. Elizabeth hated the white bread Paul insisted upon, but he said it was one of the fondest memories he had of his parents before his mother died. She always bought white, Wonder Bread for breakfast, lunch, and dinner, and even though he sometimes didn't touch it, he knew it was there at every meal.

Cutting his meatloaf into bite-sized pieces, Paul sat up straight. "I want you to cancel the doctor's appointment tomorrow. I know I'm sick, and at this point, it doesn't make any difference what the tests say, or how many more drugs they want to pump into me."

Elizabeth's face fell as she felt his resolve. She felt panicked at the thought of him leaving too soon. "Are you sure? Maybe it's just an infection or something. Maybe you only need a dose of antibiotics?" She felt like she was begging. "Just one, initial visit?" She didn't even want to discuss anything worse than a cold, but Paul insisted.

"I'm a tough Marine. Please let me do this by myself. I know my body and I feel it falling deeper into a state of disrepair every day. I'm like an ancient car that needs to be taken off the road."

In spite of the gravity of the conversation, they smiled at the analogy and Elizabeth knew there was nothing she could do but resign herself to whatever the near future had in store.

"One more thing, Paul. While the kids are in Hawaii, could I help you unclutter the living room and kitchen? The refrigerator needs to be cleaned, there's so much old food. And if we could put some of the papers in boxes and throw out a few things, we could have them over for Mother's Day dinner, at the house, at their home where they grew up." Paul caved, knowing how important it was to Elizabeth, and nodded his head.

"We can work all weekend and I promise I won't touch anything. I'll let you handle the living room, and I'll take care of the refrigerator if you don't mind. I can't believe some of that food is ten years old. I saw that old ice cream cone with my name on it in the back of the freezer the other day. I'm sure it's nothing but dust by now. Would you please throw that old thing out?"

"No, don't touch it Elizabeth. I'll take care of it. Let me do it."

"Okay, okay. I was only asking. I won't touch it. Just so you throw that nasty thing in the trash."

With an appetite Elizabeth hadn't seen in months, she watched Paul savor his favorite meal, Wonder Bread and all.

"Best dinner ever."

Chapter 42

"Thank you for the best Mother's Day ever, Paul." Even though it was Elizabeth's day, she went about making sure the preparations were in order. Salads chilling, a large jar of pink lemonade beckoning on the sun-soaked picnic table, plenty of plates, napkins, and hot dogs. She made a family favorite baked bean recipe at her apartment the day before, but other than that, Paul had kept his promise, and the living area of the little beach house was tidy, dusted, and warm. Absent from the freezer was the ice cream cone, along with the freezer-burned meats and vegetables.

They compromised during clean up, and while Elizabeth wanted all the yellowed papers and unopened mail tossed immediately, Paul convinced her he would sort through it one day if she would be okay with a stack of cardboard boxes in the corner.

"At least they'll be contained. I'm not trying to make you uncomfortable, Paul. But I want to have a beautiful, memorable, family dinner. And some place to sit."

In spite of his failing health, Paul managed to summon enough strength to mow the lawn, and without asking, Rex and Michael stopped by to offer their assistance in the garden. They cleared an area large enough for a few outdoor pieces of furniture and filled in enough gopher holes so the children wouldn't twist an ankle. The difference was measurable, and the mood of the house shifted from dark and foreboding to alive and welcoming. This was Elizabeth's chance to capture one more, memorable morsel of joy for Paul and the family. She didn't divulge a word, as she had promised, or speak to Rex or Lily about her suspicions. She only knew she had very little time to create one more joyful experience for Paul and their family.

"Wow! Pretty, Mama!" Lily was delighted when she arrived and could tell how hard her parents worked to make this day special. "I can see the floor, and the coffee table… and the kitchen counter!" She gave her mother an enthusiastic hug.

"I know it will revert back within a month, but today it had to be just right."

Lily went overboard when Elizabeth asked her to bring the ice cream, and had picked four flavors. "Here, let me take that from you. There's room in the freezer, now that your dad threw out all the old meat and frozen vegetables."

She had three types of ice cream cones, plus waffle bowls, and at least a dozen toppings, from coconut to chocolate syrup, whipped cream, and cherries. "I thought it would be more fun to make a sundae bar, and Noah has been begging me ever since his teacher treated the class the day before spring break. He's been so excited about putting it together, and let me know that ice cream cones are so boring."

Elizabeth chuckled, envisioning her little grandson's eyes roll, expounding on the virtues of more is much better than less, especially when it came to ice cream.

"Delightful. Sounds like you have a real party planner on your hands." Elizabeth quickly finished loading the dishwasher and gave her daughter another hug. "Happy Mother's Day, my girl."

"And Happy Mother's Day to you, Mama. It feels good to be back home. Let me put this stuff down and we can go outside with the rest of the family. Julia texted me and said they were getting off the freeway. They should be here any minute."

Michael and Paul were already engrossed in conversation, and Noah was helping himself to a glass of the sugary, pink lemonade, ice cubes already starting to melt in the afternoon sun. Paul made certain the radio was adequately filling the air with music, as he adjusted the sound level with the speakers he found in the garage. He placed them on either end of the patio, and familiar favorites brought the mood back to twenty years earlier, to summers filled with children, family, and neighbors. The air was that perfect blend of warmth and brilliance, but still being spring, it hadn't yet reached the intensity of summer, when everyone complained about how hot it was. Elizabeth thought about their luck and tried not to contemplate the future.

"Claire!" Noah raced to greet his cousin as soon as she heard their car turn in the driveway. "You should see what Mommy brought! After dinner, we're going to have a sundae bar."

"What's a sundae bar? Is it because it's Sunday? Or Mother's Day?"

"No." Noah sounded annoyed. "It's a bunch of stuff you can put on top of your ice cream and make your own sundae. It's neat. We put everything on the counter and call it a bar. Then we scoop the ice cream in bowls made of waffles and you can put anything on it you want. Like nuts, and gummy bears, fruit, candy bars, and whipped cream."

"And a cherry on top. Don't forget the cherry," Lily reminded him.

"Oh yeah, I forgot. The best part. And a cherry on top."

"Sounds gross. Can I just have an ice cream cone?"

Noah wanted to go into more detail, but Claire spied her grandfather on the patio and broke away from Noah's verbal grip.

"Grandpa Santa!" Rushing, as always, to be by his side, the greeting was returned, as Paul bent down to hug his granddaughter, and found himself being enveloped by Noah as well. One grandchild under each arm, he held them close, until they had enough.

"Go play. No one's going anywhere. We have a long, beautiful day to celebrate the mommies."

"And make ice cream sundaes," Noah commanded, as he chased Claire into the yard.

Rex and Julia appeared then, carrying a bag of toys for the children, along with coloring books, crayons, and bubbles. After Rex deposited his packages, he went back once more to the car and returned with a bottle of champagne in each hand.

"Would you see if there is room in the refrigerator for these when you go inside? We'll need them later. " He winked at Julia as she took the bottles and walked towards the house.

"Happy Mother's Day, Mom." Julia made sure to hug Elizabeth first, then Lily. Elizabeth returned the sentiment with a genuine embrace and standing back to rest her eyes on her beautiful daughter and daughter-in-law. She couldn't help but feel an overwhelming sense of love.

"Three mommies under one roof. Which by the way, begs the question, what are we doing in the kitchen? Aren't the men supposed to be waiting on us?" Julia was laughing as she found space in the over-crowded refrigerator for the champagne.

They glanced at each other, knowing that was never true, but knew that being together was the only gift they required. They joined the men on the patio and left the rest of the afternoon in their capable hands. Noah and Claire climbed on a variety of available laps throughout the day, chased each other until breathless, blew bubbles over the barbecue to see if they would fill with smoke, and danced around the gopher holes, but only if a Rolling Stones song was playing.

"Ahh," signed Paul at the sight of his grandchildren hand picking songs from the '70s. "Third generation of quality-music listeners. Makes me proud."

As the last plate was removed from the patio and everyone was about to retreat inside for ice cream, Rex summoned everyone back to the table and begged for a few more minutes. "Don't go away. I'll be right back." Within moments, he returned with the two bottles of champagne and enough plastic champagne glasses for the adults, as well as the children, which they could fill with the last drops of lemonade, now diluted to a watery, pink confection.

"If everyone would have a seat, I have an announcement to make." He uncorked the bottles and Julia helped pour everyone a glass. Elizabeth thought Lily must already know whatever Rex was about to say, and Lily thought Elizabeth probably had some inside information. Michael and Paul glanced at each other and shrugged as Rex started to speak.

"Twenty-five years ago, we took our first family vacation to Washington DC, and although I didn't know it at the time, it was a trip that would change my life. It set me on a path I never felt I planned, but was destined to take." Rex cleared his throat. "I was a bit of a screwup in high school and barely made it into college." He looked straight at his parents as they nodded in agreement. "Okay, this is serious. Let me finish." Rex began his well-rehearsed speech one more time and hoped for a more somber response.

"There was this persistent nagging that stayed with me long after we visited the Vietnam Memorial. I was raised by this man, who served our country without question." Rex raised his glass to his father, whose face turned red with embarrassment.

"While we were standing there, staring at the endless column of names that seemed to stretch for miles, I asked him why he joined the service and went to war." Paul knew what he was going to say next, and sat quietly, waiting for his son to finish.

"'I went so no son of mine would ever have to.' That's what he said, and it stuck. For years, those words haunted me, and all I wanted to do was find my way to make a difference. Not only for my father, but for all veterans from every war, in any condition, for themselves, for their families."

Elizabeth was certain Rex and Julia were going to announce they were pregnant again, but now she had no idea where this was going. Whatever Rex had been striving for, working towards, or planning for the last few years, he never let on. Everyone, including Claire and Noah, were silently waiting for Rex to finish.

"Last week, I got a call from Brigadier General Timothy Morrison, who's the head of a task force in Washington DC. He's been given the daunting assignment of working with the VA to decrease wait times, make the department more accessible to our veterans, and eliminate the red tape that has that has bogged down the system for years. He heard about the pro bono work I've been doing in San Diego for homeless veterans, and after a series of interviews, he asked me to join them as in-house attorney. I said yes. I'll start September first which means Julia, Claire, and I will be moving to DC in a few months."

Rex scanned the faces for a reaction and saw his mother choking back tears. "I remember asking you once when you were in high school what you wanted to be when you grew up and you answered with such confidence, 'It's a surprise.' Is this the surprise, Son, because it certainly is. And I couldn't be more proud of you, then, or now. Hear, Hear! Congratulations, Rex." As Elizabeth raised her glass, she felt her heart swell with pride—and sink into despair.

The mood was broken when Noah chimed in, "Can we have our ice cream sundae bar now?"

The families retreated to the house, congratulating Rex and coming to grips with the news. Paul and Elizabeth followed, closed the door to the nighttime chill, and entered the warmth of the house that still had one more celebration to enjoy.

It could be our last, Elizabeth thought, as she scooped ice cream and helped Noah lay out the bounty of toppings. *But it will be our best.*

Paul touched her hand as he brushed past her on his way to his lounge chair.

"I want a plain vanilla ice cream cone, if that's okay with you, Noah."

"Just this time Grandpa. Next time, you have to have at least one of everything, promise?"

With a thumbs up, Paul rubbed Noah's little head and wished with all his heart he knew for sure there would be a next time. Barely skipping a beat, he turned back to Noah and Claire, "How about tomorrow? I'll be ready by tomorrow." Claire just smiled as they dug into their mountain of goo, chocolate, sprinkles, marshmallows, and a cherry on top.

Chapter 43

AS THE MILD DAYS OF SPRING MOVED PAST THE coastal June gloom and sizzling days of August, Paul once again found comfort in his armor of newspapers, old magazines, and unopened mail. Ignoring the demise of everything they worked on with such diligence for Mother's Day, Elizabeth instead concentrated on Paul's quest for peace in what she feared were his final days.

Convincing Paul it was the right thing to do to at least go in for a physical exam, the tests confirmed their worst fears: stage four prostate cancer. His doctor seemed unsympathetic as he queried Paul as to why he hadn't come in sooner.

"I have my suspicion this cancer developed due to your service in Vietnam and your exposure to Agent Orange." He drilled Paul past his comfort zone. "Were you aware you could have pursued this condition through the VA and been receiving care and benefits this entire time?" He sounded almost accusatory. "The government has made great strides in reaching out to Vietnam Veterans." With that, Paul appeared to be listening but tuned out his words completely.

When the young doctor was finished with whatever he thought was important enough to impart to this battle-scarred soldier, Paul sat up straight and looked straight at him. "I appreciate your concern. Doctor, but it's fifty years too late for me and my brothers who served their time in the jungle." Grabbing Elizabeth's hand, he held on and spoke again in a low, barely audible voice, "Maybe our country has finally learned we matter. We mattered then, and we matter now. Our son, Rex, has our backs now." Elizabeth found her grip tightening as she realized Rex's departure was only weeks away.

Every morning, like clockwork, Elizabeth phoned Paul, sharing coffee from a distance. She checked in every lunch hour, restocking the refrigerator with food that had gone bad from the previous week and that Paul barely touched. She made simple dinners for them to enjoy every night, always ending with, "Best dinner ever," and a knowing smile from Paul. Few words were spoken at the end of the day when one or the other would call to say good night, but it was a comforting pattern that continued to sustain them and reassure Elizabeth that Paul had taken his medication before falling asleep. She resisted going much past the living room and had quelled her curiosity about what she might find inside Paul's bedroom, which had long since been abandoned for the purpose of sleep. It was only a matter of time before she would be forced to deal with Paul's lifelong habits of collecting, storing, and hoarding his treasures—his legacy, his gift to those he loved.

Paul had taken up the habit of seeking out a variety of mementos to touch, caress, and reminisce with. One day Elizabeth noticed his purple heart in the tattered black box, peeking out from under a few envelopes and a stack of bills.

"Remember this guy?" Paul opened the decades-old memory that contained not only the medal, but the photograph of his younger self, shirtless, propped up in his hospital bed. Elizabeth removed the purple-colored heart from the box and wondered why she had never realized how heavy it was. She was glad these hearts were given with a sense of dignity, perhaps with the knowledge it might be the only tangible keepsake for thousands of returning soldiers. She cradled the fragile black-and-white photo with care and studied the stern countenance on Paul's face, along with the somber expression of the officer bestowing the honor. It wasn't difficult to see beyond the moment at hand, captured in one brief click of a shutter, and she stiffened as she recalled the letters she received from her brother when she was only sixteen years old.

"Superman. You're a real superhero in that picture," She studied Paul's well-defined muscles, and strong, set jaw. "I knew what I was getting when I fell in love with you." With gentle hands, she returned the Purple Heart and photograph to the box, closed the lid, and laid it down with reverence beside Paul.

"Did I ever tell you why I joined the Marines instead of waiting for my draft number to be called?" Paul shifted in his chair. "I could have avoided serving altogether, as an only child and the only son, but I always thought the Marines were the toughest, grittiest, most badass branch of the service. I wanted to show my father and my friends I was every bit as rugged as any soldier, not the sensitive boy everyone assumed. I wanted to be the most competent, fearless fighter to ever serve in the US Marine Corps."

"I never knew, Paul. You never talked much about Vietnam, but I had more than an inkling of what happened over there. Sam's letters were pretty vivid. I was only sixteen and I think that's when I developed my sense of fear and constant worrying. I've never been able to shake it, never." She pulled her chair close and leaned in, "You were very badass, my Paul. And you still are."

Pulling her chair even closer, she spent the next few minutes running her fingers through the thick head of unmanageable gray hair Paul still continued to grow. As she was about to leave, Paul glanced over and said off-handedly, "Elizabeth, I think you're gorgeous."

Paul had never complimented her in such a manner, always one to show his love, as opposed to speaking it. Maybe, 'you look good,' 'you're so smart,' 'pretty dress,' 'best dinner ever,' but never 'gorgeous.' As she blew him a kiss, she tried to memorize the sound of his voice and sorrow penetrated her heart. Perhaps he was telling her, in the little time he had, some of the things he never said. Perhaps this was his way of saying goodbye, and she felt more anxiety with his comment than pleasure. She wanted to recall every expression, the timbre of his voice, the masterful way he could speak volumes using hardly any words. She needed to prepare for what she felt was close at hand.

Stalling before returning home, she found it difficult to turn on the engine to leave, and was compelled to poke her head inside the door one last time. She caught Paul off guard as she bent over his lounge chair from behind and wrapped her arms around his sagging shoulders. She was surprised at how muscular his arms still were, and she cradled him, whispering, "I love you, Paul."

"I love you too, Elizabeth." She wanted to hear it one last time, then turned to leave. "Be careful in the dark. Don't trip. I'll talk to you in the morning." Paul waved her off into the night.

Elizabeth had never cried in her sleep, but the next morning she struggled to open her eyes, stuck together and crusted over with a salty mixture of tears and makeup that she was too tired to remove the night before. Remembering her heavy heart, she brewed a strong pot of coffee and settled herself before calling Paul.

The phone never rang more than twice, as Paul always kept a full charge, and within arm's reach. On the third ring, Elizabeth's heart sank, but finally, "Hello, Elizabeth." Did Paul sound weaker or merely tired? It was hard for Elizabeth to tell, but she drew a sigh of relief when he answered.

"How are you this morning, Paul? You need to know how much I enjoy our morning coffee time. Did I ever tell you that? It brings me a sense of contentment, this ritual we have had for over forty years."

"I had a hard time making coffee this morning. I didn't have the best night."

"I have an idea. I made an extra-large pot this morning. Why don't I get dressed and I'll fill up a travel mug and come join you."

"Sure, don't rush. Talk to me while you finish your cup. Have you heard from Rex? How is the move going? Did they find a house in DC yet? Lily and Noah stopped by the other day for a visit. She's a good girl... We done good, Elizabeth... we done good," Paul said haltingly. His breathing became labored, and he was barely able to push the words past his lips.

As Paul continued to ask about Rex and Lily, his voice faded, and Elizabeth panicked. Phone in one hand, car keys in another, she continued trying to converse with Paul as she dashed out the door, not bothering to change from her pajamas, grabbing only an oversized hooded sweatshirt Paul had given her for Christmas years earlier. She fumbled with her keys trying to start the car while pressing the phone between her shoulder and ear. It didn't occur to her to turn on the speakerphone. She wasn't getting any responses from Paul as she tried without success to get him to answer. She sensed the worst as she made it to his driveway, flung open the car door, and barged through the front door of the house.

Finding Paul reclining in his lounge chair, he looked like he was taking a nap, not unlike the many other times he had dozed during the day, catching up on sleep whenever he could. Elizabeth walked slowly up to him and knew, instinctively, that this time she wouldn't be able to wake him. His face was relaxed, his eyes closed, and one limp arm lay over the side of the chair. Paul was gone.

In the heartache and shock of the moment, Elizabeth noticed something in Paul's other hand. As she moved closer to embrace the last few minutes of his warmth, she saw it was the tattered thirty-year-old Tupperware container, misshapen by the years locked inside a freezer, yet indelibly marked on Paul's heart. She knew without opening the container it was the ice cream cone. The one with her name, the one Paul promised to throw out with the trash, the one that had certainly by this time totally disintegrated, but a treasure so dear to Paul, it served as his last words to Elizabeth. Scrawled on a torn corner of yellow paper and taped to the lid were the words, "Keep 4Ever." Elizabeth felt her throat tighten and her shoulders start to shake, as she embraced him one last time, leaning her head on his shoulder. This was where she found comfort still, from the first time she rested her head on his shoulder aboard the plane from Boston forty-five years earlier, to this moment in time. Without leaving his side, Elizabeth dialed Rex, then Lily, then waited. Resting for a few more moments, she stood, and removing the Tupperware from Paul's hand, clutched it to her heart, and vowed to keep this treasured memento 4Ever.

It was 2011, and for Paul O'Brien, that was when it all ended.

Chapter 44

THE BITTER TASK OF PLANNING PAUL'S FUNERAL proved formidable for Elizabeth, but comforted by Rex and Lily, she managed to make her body move and mind function, even at a slow, sluggish pace. Her biggest concern was for her children, while they made every effort to console her. Feeling depleted of energy, she found solace in the sunshine, and settled in a garden chair, staring at the vast, unkempt yard behind the house. For now, it was the only thing she was capable of doing.

"It's going to be all right, Mama," coaxed Rex, when Elizabeth lamented she would never be the same, never work again, never smile, never be released from the feeling of the utter defeat tightening its grip around her heart. "We're here to help, and you won't be alone until we've gotten you settled back into the house."

"What about your job?"

"Morrison gave me another month, and I don't have to report until October first. Don't worry about that stuff, Mama. I have it under control." Rex offered his hand and walked with her as she willed herself to make sandwiches and a fresh pot of coffee for them. Rex couldn't help but perceive the anguish that was only his mother's to bear, the light in her eyes dim, and the spring in her step, gone overnight.

As they gathered around the dining room table, Lily attempted to bring order to the treasures and stacks of papers that surrounded them. Elizabeth was grateful for one clean surface and a sanitary place where they could sit and plan.

"This old table. I can remember sitting here in my high chair. Daddy… nothing ever changed, nothing ever got thrown out. Miss you, Daddy." Lily tilted her head upward and managed a weak smile.

Rex called to his mother over his shoulder, as he dared to peek inside his father's bedroom. "When was the last time you went in here?"

"Years. Elizabeth finished making sandwiches and poured coffee for the three of them. "I couldn't bear to look."

"Well, don't, for now." Rex closed the door and joined his mother and sister. "I'm not leaving until I've gone through every piece of paper, organized every file, and cleaned out every drawer." Rex was shaking, overcome with a wave of regret and remorse. It wasn't until that moment he realized how much he had missed.

Paul O'Brien, LCPL, U.S. Marine Corps, Vietnam, August 25, 1946 – June 1, 2011, Purple Heart. That's what the VA office suggested be written on Paul's headstone, and no one disagreed, but with one line left, Elizabeth had one more request. She suggested to the clerk, "I would like to add, *'We are all who we are because you were here.'*" It seemed appropriate to her. It was important. The clerk smiled and nodded her head.

Difficult as it was to write these words, submit the obituary, and contact family members and friends, Elizabeth gathered strength and momentum from her children and the memory of Paul's voice coaching her every step of the way. Every question she threw out to the universe she knew how Paul would answer, and without analyzing, continued to put one foot in front of the other.

Seven smart-looking young soldiers in dress blues waited, motionless, to carry out the twenty-one-gun salute. A horse-drawn caisson was at the head of the procession that formed with dozens of cars, extended family, and lifelong friends. The funeral director motioned for everyone to get into cars and Rex pulled theirs directly behind the horse-drawn buggy.

Rex was getting settled behind the wheel and Elizabeth turned to him. "Why do you think your dad's receiving the honor of a caisson? Is this normal?"

"The funeral director called me the other day and asked if we would like to use it for Dad. I didn't even check with anyone, sorry, I just said yes. I had no idea it would mean all of this." He waved to the procession that had been building behind them, as the final, solemn journey of his father was about to begin.

"It's starting." Rex saw the carriage in front of them, carrying the flag-draped coffin of his father, begin to move.

Overtaken by a bittersweet, sick feeling, finding it difficult to speak or swallow, Elizabeth fell silent as they slowly led the procession to the covered ceremony site for the service. She peered at line after line of identical headstones, exact replicas of one another, thinking how inspiring the landscape was, despite the underlying reason for its beauty.

"Almost there, Mama." Rex touched Elizabeth's hand, breaking her trance.

She uttered softly, "You deserve this, Paul."

Chapter 45

ELIZABETH VISITED PAUL MORE FREQUENTLY THAN she knew was healthy—at least three times during the week and every Sunday. Days, weeks, months were all the same, and every "first" was marked with sorrow and longing.

"It's been almost a year, Mama. Maybe you could visit dad on special occasions, like his birthday and Christmas. We know you loved him. You don't have anything to prove to us." Rex's did his best to console his mother.

"Give me a year, son. I know it sounds silly, but spending time with your dad is where I find peace, a little relief from the reality. I'm fine, honest."

Rex and Lily's concerns didn't stop Elizabeth from spending her free time at the cemetery, and she often brought a hot cup of coffee, leaned against Paul's marble headstone, and watched other visitors and caisson processions unfold in front of her. Out of place compared to the regimented color palette surrounding her, she would throw a splashy summer towel, ablaze with bright red hibiscus and golden yellow pineapples on the dirt above where Paul was resting, and depending on the day, her mood shifted from hopelessness to resigned to completely comfortable.

Paul's headstone was front and center. The road before him carried every funeral procession to the ceremony site, and his view was feet away from the somber faces of family members, friends, and beautifully adorned young military men and women in their dress blues. The same procession she had witnessed first-hand was repeated almost daily, and the number of headstones grew with every passing month. There was no way to get any closer to the road that was destined to be the last path for so many. Paul's row, which he shared with a handful of his comrades, was short compared to the rest. He and five other warriors held the front seats, while line after line of identical headstones slept silently behind them. Elizabeth often mused that if this were a concert, Paul would have the best seat in the house.

⬦

Elizabeth's behavior at the gravesite continued into the second year, and, with no end in sight to her mother's frequent visits, Lily was prompted to take a firm hand in the matter. Even though her approach was gentle, her message was not.

"Mama, you're spending more time with the dead than the living. I've always known you to be able to tackle anything, but I'm worried about you now. Maybe you should see someone, or talk about it with others who have gone through the same thing. You know Rex and I are always here for you, but we're starting to worry."

"I'm okay. Don't worry about me."

"Why are you always at the cemetery? Why don't you go out, find a friend to take to a concert, treat yourself to a glass of wine at a restaurant? Mama, you don't have to stay inside all day by yourself. We want you to be happy. Dad's been gone for more than a year."

Elizabeth reached for Lily's hand. "Sitting in the sunshine, leaning against your father's headstone, spreading a towel, and enjoying an afternoon cup of coffee like we are still together makes me forget he's not here. For a few moments it anchors my soul. I know I shouldn't be spending all my free time with your father. We'll talk later. Tonight, I'm too tired."

In the quiet of her living room once again, Elizabeth couldn't stop thinking about what Lily said. She picked up the blanket she kept draped over Paul's lounge chair, wrapped herself inside his familiar smell, and curled into a ball on the couch. *A little more time. I need a little more time before I try to socialize again. How am I supposed to do that?* Elizabeth reached for a magazine from the coffee table and hoped it would distract her from her racing thoughts. *How am I supposed to erase decades of memories? How do I move past that, Paul?*

Elizabeth wished Paul was here so she could ask him these questions. She knew he would have the solution. She plumped the pillows on the couch, too exhausted to move to the bedroom, and at the moment when wakefulness is overtaken by sleep, Paul answered, "You don't erase the old memories. You make new ones."

The restaurant was five-minutes away and Elizabeth got the last parking space available. The courtyard bar was crowded with locals and tourists alike. Some were dancing, others were talking in small groups around the fire pit. It was evident that many were single and close to Elizabeth's age, but she was only there to observe, enjoy the music, and have a glass of wine like Lily suggested. The tape in her head kept playing and she wondered why she had gone out on a Saturday night by herself. She found a chair in the corner and pulled it closer to the fire.

The more Elizabeth tried to act nonchalant, the more anxious and out of place she felt. Her hands started to sweat and she felt clammy all over. She took a deep breath and a sip of wine and told herself, *Thirty minutes. I'll stay thirty minutes, tops, then I can leave.*

She kept her head down, pretending to fish something from her purse, and when she looked up, saw a gentleman making his way through the crowd, inching towards her. He assumed the empty chair next to her was a silent invitation and casually sat down. After a few, awkward moments, he leaned in. "Hi, my name's Steven. What's yours?" He held his hand out for Elizabeth to shake. Shocked, she returned the gesture.

"My name's Elizabeth. Pleased to meet you, Steven." They sat in silence and pretended they were listening to the band. It was uncomfortable, and as quickly as he had appeared, Steven walked off to join another group.

Elizabeth focused on the guitarist, trying to look fixated and indifferent. She didn't want anyone else to notice her or attempt conversation. Her discomfort was growing by the moment and, as she finished the last of her wine, saw another man walking towards her. Brash and confident, he sat down in the chair Steven had vacated, without an introduction or any indication he might be interested in striking up a conversation. His head was in her way of seeing the band, though, so she moved her chair to one side, making an awful scraping noise on the concrete as she did. Legs crossed, purse underneath her feet, Elizabeth was taken by surprise when the man inched closer.

"I know you. I've seen you somewhere and I can't quite figure it out. Did we work together, go to school together? By the way, my name is Tyler." He extended his hand, and though she felt somewhat intimidated, Elizabeth shook it.

Tyler was quite charming and had a smile to match. His body was lean, his thick head of gray hair was neatly cropped, and he had eyes the color of the ocean. It had been a long time since Elizabeth had been in this situation, but there was something about this man that seemed oddly familiar to her too.

"Oh, you kind of caught me off guard. I'm sorry. My name's Elizabeth. My maiden name was Sutton. Could be we did go to school together? I grew up mostly in Boston but moved to Southern California my senior year. Where did you go to high school?"

She played the game with Tyler, not knowing where it was headed. Whatever he might be up to, Elizabeth started to relax. The wine appeared to be working.

"Okay, okay, I got it." Tyler was adamant. "Class of sixty-seven, Reseda Valley High School, Senior English, Mr. Williams! I was famous for being too loud and caused all sorts of grief, not only for Mr. Williams, but all my teachers. You were the quiet, studious, new girl with the thick Boston accent. You always sat in the back of the room. I knew it, I knew it! Some faces never change. Tyler Hamilton. I'm Tyler Hamilton."

Elizabeth studied his face and he continued to talk as she tried to recall her senior year in high school. Time had changed him somewhat. She wasn't even sure if her recollection was correct, but she shot back, "No way! Were you that goofy boy I met in the hall first day of class when I couldn't find Senior English?"

"And that, folks, is how I am best remembered." Tyler let out a hearty laugh. "Can I get you another glass of wine?"

"No, I'm fine, thank you. I have to drive home."

"I can't believe I ran into you like this. It's so bitchin."

"You still say bitchin? I haven't heard that in so long." Elizabeth recalled the first time she heard that word and smiled. Paul never let her forget how silly she sounded whenever she said it.

"Surfer slang. Once a surfer, always a surfer."

"You still surf? I thought we might be a little too old for those tricks."

"Never too old. I'm not as nimble as I used to be, but I still get out there in the beautiful blue when the waves aren't too big and the sun is shining. What about you? What happened to the Boston accent?"

"Oh, that was drilled out of me a long time ago. I never went back to Boston to live."

"Family, husband?"

"Widowed, two grown children and two grandchildren. You?"

"Divorced ten years ago. Three girls, in their forties already. Geesh, where did the time go?"

They talked into the night, catching up on five decades, acting like long-lost friends. When the last set ended and the seating area started to empty, Elizabeth stood up to leave.

"Would you mind if I asked for your phone number or email address? If you don't want to share with me, that's cool."

Hesitant at first, Elizabeth pulled out her business card, the one with the twelve-year-old photo, and squeezed it into Tyler's hand. He walked her to the car and gave her a spontaneous hug before he opened the door. Elizabeth instinctively pulled away, but smiled as she waved goodbye. By the time she reached her driveway, her heart was still pounding. These were feelings she hadn't experienced in years and wasn't sure if she wanted to resurrect them now or anytime in the future.

As soon as Tyler got home, he sent Elizabeth an email.

> *Hello, Elizabeth. It was great running into you tonight, and if I didn't tell you already, I thought you looked great. I was very comfortable talking to you. Maybe we could get together again. What do you think? Good night for now. Tyler Hamilton*

As soon as he pressed 'send,' he regretted it and thought it sounded like a sixth grader. Cursing the technology that made it impossible to retract words sent in haste, he fell asleep, hoping one day she might respond.

By the time Elizabeth was ready for bed, the blinking light on her phone was beckoning. It was late, and she couldn't think of a soul who would need her at this hour of the night. In the past, she would have reached for the phone immediately, knowing it was probably Paul, desperate for late-night conversation and asking her how to make chicken. Her eyes stung with the memory, but it also made her smile.

Hoping it wasn't an emergency with Lily or Rex, she pressed the middle button and saw the new email. Relieved it wasn't from either of her children, but stunned to see a message from Tyler, her heart froze. She wasn't used to the attention. Reading it and rereading it, she glanced at the time it was sent, how he signed his name and thought about what he might mean by 'comfortable.' For every reason she created to respond immediately, she came up with another, equally compelling reason for why she shouldn't. She had to decide if she should get it over with, and send a quick note, or wait for another day.

Elizabeth pulled back the covers, felt the cool, white sheets envelop her now-tired body, and placed the phone on the nightstand. She would get back to Tyler in the morning. It was the best sleep she had experienced in years.